Dark Voyage

Dark Voyage

Tales From The Dark Past Book 1

Helen Susan Swift

Contents

Chapter One

The wonder is always new that any sane man can be a sailor
Ralph Waldo Emerson

Pregnant with violence, dark with menace, the squall slid over the northern horizon like the anger of a Nordic god.

'That looks ugly,' Lauren nodded urgently toward the storm and nearly smiled at the expression on Kenny's face. 'I hope you don't get seasick!'

'Where the hell did that come from?' Kenny clutched at the side of the boat, staring at the black clouds that piled one on another in a multi-layered promise of gales and rain. He saw lightning flicker within the darkness, reflecting from the intervening sea, and he narrowed thoughtful eyes. Around them the waves rose in a sullen swell, ominously smooth, nearly oily but each one larger than its predecessor. 'It wasn't there a moment ago!'

Twenty two foot long and open save for the tiny wheelhouse in the bow, the fishing boat offered little protection against the weather. Already water was slopping inboard, splashing around their ankles in a cold foretaste of what was to come. In the past few minutes the movement increased from a slow, regular rise and fall to an irregular, plunging jerk.

'It looks like a bad one,' Lauren only had to glance at the approaching storm one more time; 'I think we'd best return.'

'You'll get no argument from me,' Kenny agreed quickly, 'and the sooner the better.' He began to pull in the fishing rods, staggering as a rogue wave broke on the stern.

Grinning briefly, Lauren took the two steps forward to the tiny wheelhouse-cum-cabin. 'The North Sea can be like that; one minute all balmy fine, the next it's a force eight and chucking it down.'

'I prefer the balmy bit,' Kenny clattered the long rods to the bottom of the boat. 'Look at that sky! It's going crazy!'

The dark band had expanded across the entire horizon, completely obscuring the secure pencil of the Bell Rock Lighthouse and blotting out anything beyond. It advanced rapidly on them, bringing unseasonably stinging hail and a wind that screamed its hate around their ears. Lauren raised her voice above the increasing wail. 'You'd best come in here, Kenny.'

He crouched in the meagre shelter of the wheelhouse as she pressed the self-starter. The engine coughed once, twice, gunned into life and then died with an apologetic grunt.

'Try again,' Kenny ordered. He glanced over his shoulder, where the darkness was already spreading, advancing visibly toward them. Sleet battered from the fibreglass body of the boat, bounced in the interior and rattled from the roof of the wheelhouse. 'Hurry up, Lauren; it's a monsoon out there!'

'It's something, anyway.' Lauren pressed the starter again, swearing frantically when the engine failed to respond. 'What the hell's wrong with this thing?'

'You're the expert,' Kenny reminded, 'you tell me!' He looked backward again, flinching as the storm clouds visibly increased in size so they rose endlessly upward, black and grey, tinged with an angry red that he had seldom seen before and with those flashes of lightning illuminating an interior that seemed more ominous with each passing minute.

Pushing past him, Lauren opened the access hatch and peered at the engine. 'I can't see anything wrong!' She shouted above the rising scream of the wind. 'Everything's connected and there's nothing broken.'

Peering helplessly over her shoulder, Kenny shrugged. 'It all looks OK to me. Try again!'

She did so, growing more frustrated with every failed attempt. 'It's no use,' she decided, 'it's buggered.' She looked at Kenny for a moment, flicking damp auburn hair from her eyes. 'We can either sit it out or call for help. They might send the Broughty Ferry lifeboat out for us.'

'Do that then,' there was genuine fear in Kenny's voice. He looked around, where the waves were now rising higher than the top of the wheelhouse, spattering spindrift and hissing as they passed. The darkness was advancing at speed, rolling over the sea, blotting out the light, pressing down upon them as if intent to thrust them into the depths of the waves. He heard thunder growling, and then it cracked like Neptune's wrath, calling the horrors of Hades onto the helpless boat. 'Jesus! What's happening here?'

'God knows; I've never seen anything like this before!' Lauren stared at the onrushing storm, wet hair clinging to her head, mouth slightly open and her eyes narrowed against the stinging sleet and spindrift. She knew that at any other time Kenny would have been distracted by the manner in which the sodden tee-shirt clung to her curves, but now the clouds mesmerised him.

'Call them, Lauren, for Christ's sake!'

'I've been sailing since I was eight,' Lauren spoke rapidly, glancing from the storm front to Kenny and back, 'and I've never called for help before. I checked that engine before we left!'

'Just call,' Kenny pleaded. 'Look at the weather and call for help!'

In the few moments since Lauren had been working on the engine, the dark clouds had closed, racing upon them with inexorable speed. The sleet and hail increased, hammering from the hull, clattering from the wheelhouse and battering into the clutching waves as if a malevolent sea god was hurling handfuls of hate.

'For God's sake,' Lauren blasphemed as she lifted the handset, 'I've never seen it get so bad so quickly!' Depressing the buttons, she looked at Kenny over her shoulder. 'Nothing's happening!' She tried again, fighting to keep the panic from her voice. 'Nothing; it's dead,' she shook her head, mouth open. 'There's nothing at all, Kenny, not even static.'

'There must be something …'

'There's nothing, I told you!' Anxiety shortened Lauren's temper so she snarled at him. 'It's dead.' Taking a deep breath, 'we'll have to try a flare.'

'You've got flares?'

There were four in the plastic screw top tub, two red handheld flares and two orange handheld smoke flares.

'They're for inshore use,' Lauren explained, so it's best to use them when we can see something definite, a ship or even the land.'

Kenny examined one. 'How do they work?'

'You wear that glove there' Lauren indicated a thick gardening glove, 'twist the top and hold it up; you have to be careful for falling bits; they'll burn your hand. The light can be seen for three miles.'

'Go on, then!' He urged her.

She fumbled the flare, nearly dropping it, but moved to the exposed stern, twisted off the cap and held it high. The light was shockingly intense, lasting for a little over half a minute, and when it died away they felt lonelier and more vulnerable than ever.

They looked at each other as Lauren hugged the remaining flares to her like a mother with a new born baby. 'Please God somebody saw it!'

'There are still three left,' Kenny pointed out.

'We'll save them in case we see another vessel.' There was no colour in her face. 'Let's get back into the wheelhouse.'

'Jesus,' Kenny stared toward the land, now invisible behind a screen of cloud and sleet. Their tiny boat was alone in a sea that heaved and boiled, shuddering under the onslaught of what was already a blizzard and promised to become much worse. 'What happens now?'

Lauren took a deep breath. 'Now we pray, Kenny' she said quietly. 'Now we pray like we've never prayed before.' Ducking out of the wheelhouse she looked around, shook her head and returned with water sluicing from her face and her hair lying in lank tendrils that dripped down her slim shoulders. 'Although I doubt even that will help.'

'I didn't know you were religious ...' but when Kenny saw the expression of naked fear on her face he knew she had passed the point of disbelief. 'Oh Jesus: is it that bad?'

She said nothing, slumping onto the single seat in front of the wheel and staring at him, so he huddled at her side. Her hand slid around his shoulder, holding tight and he slipped his fingers inside hers.

'This was meant to be a fun trip,' Lauren's voice was surprisingly calm, 'just you and me alone for a while.' She was quiet for a long minute as the wind increased in volume and the darkness closed on them. 'I'm sorry, Kenny.'

'It's hardly your fault.' Suddenly it did not matter. They were about to die out there on the sea, and all his fears and worries were irrelevant. Nothing was important save the wind and the sea and the small hand that gripped his fingers so securely. 'How long have we known each other?'

'All our lives.' Lauren's voice was small, sounding as if it came from a long distance. 'Hold me tight.'

The fishing boat was out of control, rising and swooping at the whim of waves that seemed to have no pattern, so one second they were staring over a maelstrom of screaming waves, with white froth stretching to the black clouds, the next they were deep in the chasm of the swell, facing a wall of shining green water marbled with creamy white.

'Look.' Lauren pointed as they rose again, so the wind crashed into them, whipping the words from her mouth. 'Oh dear God, would you just look at that!'

The cloud had reached them. Dark and unbelievably solid, it formed a barrier that stretched as far upward as they could see and stretched right around so they appeared to be in the vortex of a cyclone.

'What the hell is happening here? This is Scotland, not Star Trek!' Kenny felt Lauren's hand crushing his fingers as she stared around her. 'I've never seen anything like this before.'

'Nor have I.' the clouds were moving anti-clockwise in a slow, dizzying swirl that was almost hypnotic and would have been beautiful save for the utter menace they carried. 'Try the radio again.'

Lauren did so, pressing buttons and turning dials in increasing panic. 'It's not working Kenny; nothing's working! What do we do now? What the hell do we do now?'

She felt him looking at her as if he had never seen her before in his life. Five foot five and shapely, she had always been a livewire, full of energy he could only admire and zest he tried to emulate. Now she was wet, cold and frightened, with her hair plastered like a mesh across her face, her voice rising and her breathing short and shallow.

'We think,' he told her.

Lauren nodded, surprised how calm he sounded when she only wanted to scream and hide in the bottom of the boat. 'You're right. But first we should put on something warmer. Did you bring foul weather gear like I said?'

Two zipped up bags in the locker contained bright orange weatherproof clothing that they slipped on over their sodden jeans and tee-shirts. 'Our body heat will soon warm us up in these,' Lauren was calmer now, using her nautical experience.

'It suits you,' Kenny tried to grin, but even the sight of her wallowing in orange could not diminish his fear.

'And you.' He was taller than her but surprisingly vulnerable out here, where she had more knowledge and skill. 'Kenny,' reaching forward, she touched his arm, pointing urgently into the middle of the clouds, 'would you look at that?'

'What?' Kenny turned round and stared. 'What in God's name is it?'

Looming through the darkness of the storm, it towered high above the tiny fishing boat. Eighty, ninety, a hundred feet high and three times as long, it gleamed white and blue, with a dark green band where it met the leaping waves.

'It's like an iceberg,' Lauren felt her heart hammering inside her chest. 'But you don't get icebergs in the North Sea.'

'You do now,' Kenny said quietly. 'And it's coming straight for us.' He looked at her, twisting his mouth into the semblance of a smile. 'Maybe we should start to pray even harder.'

'Maybe we should.' With neither engine nor radio, Lauren could only watch as the iceberg emerged from the gloom of the clouds. She shook her head, hoping she was mistaken and it was only a trick of the light, but she knew that she was not. It closed inexorably, a mountain of ice, blue tinged and with the sea splintering along the green banded base, sending spindrift high above, to hover uncertainly before descending, joining the sleet that continued to cascade upon them.

'It's going to hit us,' Lauren heard the false calm of hysteria in her voice. She tried to smile to Kenny, 'on your first ever fishing trip too.'

Kenny pressed against the far side of the small boat as if the few feet of distance would save him. 'Maybe we can swim ashore? Or paddle? Do you have any oars?'

She shook her head, surprised that she could appear so controlled when she wanted to scream in terror. The sea was leaping, with white frothed waves lunging at the boat as if determined to capsize them and drag them under. 'We wouldn't last a minute in that, and I've never had any need for oars before.'

They could only watch as the iceberg approached, and instinct drove them together so they held hands as the monster towered above them, high as a four storey building, dangerous but strangely beautiful as the seawater poured from it like a succession of waterfalls and the darkness within became visible.

Darkness within? What darkness was within an iceberg? Lauren shook her head. This was insane!

'What the hell's that?' Kenny saw it too and pointed a quivering finger. 'There's something inside the ice.'

'Does it matter?' But despite her words, Lauren looked again. She had not been mistaken; there was something large and dark encased by the ice, and even as she watched it became more visible. 'Jesus, Kenny, it's melting. The ice is melting!'

She now saw that what she had taken to be rivulets of seawater was in reality melting ice pouring down the surface of the berg. After months or even years drifting from the Arctic pack, the iceberg was beginning to disintegrate, with great chunks cracking and falling and whole sections breaking off.

'Watch out!' Lauren pulled Kenny aside as a massive chunk split apart and toppled into the sea, throwing water high into the air and sending a massive wave toward them. 'Hold on! For God's sake, Kenny, hold on!'

Her superficial calm deserted her as the wave reached, hitting them broadside on and capsizing the light boat as if it were made of paper. Lauren heard herself scream, flailing her arms as she was tossed into water that was nearly as cold as the iceberg nearby; she had a glimpse of Kenny's face, mouth open in terror, and then she was under the surface, kicking, struggling and with the roaring of death in her ears.

Chapter Two

SEPTEMBER

Home is the sailor, home from the sea
Robert Louis Stevenson

Jesus it's cold! I'm going to die; I'm going to die right now.

'Don't panic!' Lauren strove to remember all the swimming lessons she had learned as a child, but reality in the North Sea was far different from anything imposed upon her within the safe confines of a swimming pool. She tried to scream, swallowing water by the mouthful until she heard somebody singing within her head. The sound was so sweet, so melodious that she stopped struggling to listen; the worst of her terror dissipated and she kicked feebly with her legs.

When the lights are soft and low
And the quiet shadows falling

Surfacing in an explosion of water, she shook the clinging wet hair from her face and looked around, seeing only the troubled surface of the sea, a nightmare of broken waves and blowing spindrift. She gasped, gagged and spewed out seawater.

'Kenny!'

'Here! I'm here!'

He was a few yards from her, his head bobbing in the water and one arm waving weakly. She kicked toward him, cursing the clumsy orange suit for slowing her down.

'Lauren! Look at the berg!'

In the few seconds since they were capsized, the iceberg had shrunk further, exposing the dark shape within.

'It's a ship,' Kenny's voice was husky with fear, but live with amazement. 'There's an old fashioned sailing ship inside the ice!'

Treading water desperately, Lauren nodded, 'so I see.'

With every second, great sheets of ice melted away, exposing more of the vessel within the berg. As Lauren looked, two masts were exposed, stretching toward the troubled sky. Years, perhaps centuries of enclosure in the ice had stripped the spars of everything save the bare poles, so there were no yards, no rigging or anything else to provide propulsion power. It was as if hardship had reduced the vessel to a skeleton, with all surplus flesh or fittings peeled off, leaving only basic essentials. There was a single, pencil thin smokestack between the masts, and a bowsprit thrusting delicately forward from the black, worn hull, as if the vessel was pointing a hopeless finger outward to the sea. A single small boat sat upside down on the deck.

'What in God's name ...' Kenny shook his head. 'How did that get there?'

'Who cares?' Lauren began to swim forward. 'Let's get on board!'

He glanced at her, obviously not understanding until she jabbed vigorously toward the ship. 'Come on Kenny! It's either that or we'll drown out here!'

'But it'll sink! There's no way it'll float!'

'We have no choice!' Grabbing at his arm, she pushed him in the direction of what remained of the iceberg, from which the two-masted vessel was rapidly emerging, like a butterfly from a glistening chrysalis.

They swam frantically, churning the already disturbed water, dodging the floating pieces of ice and trusting to fate or a benevolent God to help them avoid those that cascaded toward them. By the time they reached the vessel it was nearly free of ice, bucking to the rhythm of the storm but still floating, still offering a vestige of hope.

Jesus, help us here; help us survive this day!

'It's a miracle,' Lauren looked up at the black painted planking of her hull. Swimming with a powerful over arm stroke, she reached the stern, where the last remnants of ice offered a slippery foothold and access to the vessel.

'It's sinister,' Kenny dragged himself onto the ice behind her, lying gasping for air as waves smashed in white and green fury within a hand span of his face. He coughed up seawater, drawing his knees up to his chest as he began to retch uncontrollably.

Lauren was in no better shape, as her limbs began to tremble with delayed reaction. She vomited, bringing up a gush of burning fluid that racked her chest and seemed to tear her insides out.

'For God's sake!'

'We can't stay here,' Kenny drew his sodden sleeve over his face. 'At the rate the ice is melting, we'll be back in the water inside a minute.' He nodded to the ship. 'We'll have to go on board and just hope it's not rotted to hell.'

'I don't know about rotted,' Lauren tried to stand on the ice, slithered and balanced precariously, her hands wavering as she held them out to the side, 'but she's certainly been on fire; look at the taffrail.' The paint on the vessel's stern was blistered, with the wood charred in places so the name was virtually undecipherable. Lauren slowly traced the letters. '*Lady Balgay*; Dundee. I've never heard of her.'

'Nor have I,' Kenny pulled himself over the taffrail and gingerly tested the deck planking. 'It seems sound enough,' he said. 'I thought I might fall right through.' He put out a hand to help Lauren on board.

'Maybe the ice has helped preserve her,' Lauren joined him, looking around her with unconcealed interest. 'This is unbelievable; it's like a ghost ship, a Scottish *Marie Celeste*.'

'A what?' Kenny looked confused.

'*Marie Celeste*; she was found floating abandoned in mid Atlantic centuries ago and nobody knows what happened to her crew.'

'Oh aye. I remember now.' Kenny moved forward, placing every foot down with great care. 'But now we're here, what do we do?'

'We just stay put,' Lauren felt a sudden surge of confidence; she had escaped drowning, so nothing mattered as much. 'When this thing shows up on the radar, the coastguard will try to contact her, and within a week while there'll be somebody out here to ask questions.'

'As long as she stays afloat that long.'

Of course she will. Lauren did not voice the words that rose unbidden to her mind. 'We'll be fine now we're here. The squall's passing anyway.'

The wind had died to nearly nothing, and in place of the screaming gale and murderous seas, a thick mist had settled around *Lady Balgay*, clinging to the hull and dragging from the skeletal masts in tendrils of ominous grey.

'I don't like this,' Kenny glanced forward, where the mist coiled around the fittings, creating a hundred spectral shapes that moved and writhed and shifted uneasily along the deck. 'It's uncanny.'

'It's all right,' Lauren smiled to him. 'I don't know why, but I know we're safe here. I think we should explore.'

'I don't agree.' Kenny slumped against the solid wood of the mizzen mast, glancing at the binnacle. The glass was smashed and the compass needle pointed permanently south east. 'I think we should stay right here.'

Lauren shrugged; 'you do that, then. I'm going to have a look round.'

The desire was overwhelming, compelling her to investigate, forcing her to examine this vessel that had emerged from an iceberg in the middle of a North Sea squall.

I have to see more: it's safe; she's looking after me.

Who is looking after me?

Kenny sighed. 'I'll come too, then. It might be warmer than sitting here freezing my arse off.'

'And that would be a waste,' Lauren deliberately angled her eyes towards his bottom, 'it's such a nice arse, too.'

'What? Have you been taking something?'

She laughed at his embarrassment. 'Don't pretend you're shy; we know each other well enough now!'

'I think you should go first,' keeping a safe distance, Kenny followed as she explored the vessel.

Save for the charring at the stern, the deck of *Lady Balgay* was sound, although slippery after years trapped in ice. Lauren led them forward, pointing to a jagged scar under the bowsprit. 'That's interesting.' Where other visible sections of the vessel were painted black or held traces of yellow varnish, the bow was bare and raw with splintered wood weathered by years of exposure.

'These look like axe marks,' Kenny touched the bare wood. 'But why would somebody take an axe to the bow of an old sailing ship like this?'

'And then burn the stern?' Lauren grinned to him. 'It seems that we have boarded a real mystery ship.' She leaned closer, still shivering with the cold, but intrigued by *Lady Balgay* and driven by that suddenly renewed zest for life.

Perhaps it's a reaction to having survived. I don't care; I know I must see what's in this vessel.

'Who is this ship anyway, and how did she get stuck inside an iceberg? And even more importantly, how did she appear just a few miles off Scotland?' Questions raced through her mind, following one another so closely that they tripped over themselves in their rush to be answered.

'God knows.' Kenny tried to control his shivering. 'Won't there be some records on board? A log book or something?'

'Let's look,' Lauren decided for them both. 'After all, if she's survived this long, I doubt she'll sink now. And all we have to do is sit tight and wait to be rescued.'

'Let's hope it's not long,' Kenny said. 'I'm freezing.' He forced a smile and began to whistle a sad little tune.

'Where did you hear that?'

'Hear what?' Kenny stared at her.

'That tune?' It was the same tune that she had heard in the water. Frowning, she jabbed a sharp elbow into his ribs. 'Anyway, stop it. It'll bring bad luck.'

'What?' He stared at her, 'what will bring bad luck?'

'Whistling on a ship,' she smiled, slightly embarrassed. 'Or so I've heard, but I've no idea where that came from!'

Kenny looked away. 'I think we should stay on deck,' he told her. 'We don't know how safe this ship is. If it crumbles, we'll be back in the water again.'

Lauren looked over the side. The sea around *Lady Balgay* was artificially calm, as though some guardian angel had put down a blessing to protect them, or perhaps the storm was just gathering its strength for another and final assault. The cloud continued to circle, anti-clockwise and ominously dark.

'This ship saved our lives,' Lauren reminded.

'And it might take them back.' Kenny shuddered. 'It's not natural, Lauren. The iceberg should not have been here, and neither should this ship.'

He's right; I should be scared but I'm not.

'So let's make the most of it. Let's find the captain's cabin.'

That's where he will be. That's where who will be? She shook her head; what was she thinking about?

'Jesus!' Kenny stopped so suddenly that she started.

'Kenny? Don't do that to me? What's wrong?'

'Can't you see him? Can't you see somebody standing there?' Kenny stared; pointing to the mainmast, but quickly shook his head. 'No; it's just a shadow. For a second I could have sworn there was a man there.'

'Now you're being stupid. What did he look like?'

'Tall, but I could not see his face.' Kenny shrugged, dismissing the incident. 'It's just my imagination. There's no real mystery here, of course. We saw the scorch marks. This ship caught fire and the crew abandoned her.'

'Maybe you're right,' Lauren thought it best not to mention the ship's boat that lay intact and hull up on deck.

Lady Balgay was flush decked save for a small deckhouse, and while the forward hatch was covered and battened closed, the aft hatch cover opened far too easily to a short companionway leading down to the interior. Lauren looked into the depths for a moment, adjusting her eyes to the faint light that filtered from the hatch opening. The gloom should have been forbidding but she descended the oak treads with no hesitation and pulled open a door, so small that they both had to duck to enter.

'That door opened very smoothly,' Kenny pointed out wonderingly, 'There's not even a trace of rust,'

'Maybe the ice preserved it,'

'Maybe it did.'

The door led to a small passageway, cowering under low deck beams above, and with three doors, dimly seen. The first door also opened to Lauren's touch, and they peered inside. The cabin was tiny, barely more than a cupboard, but it held a single, mould riddled bunk and a sagging bookshelf complete with a row of books ruined with damp. Dim light struggled through a bolted porthole.

'Imagine a man staying in a place like this for months on end,' Kenny stepped further inside, wrinkling his nose at the stench of damp. 'Look at that, though,' raising his hand, he touched a splintered hole in the varnished wood above the door. 'I would say that was a bullet hole.'

'A bullet hole? Lauren was unimpressed as she looked closer. The hole was not large. 'Perhaps there was a mutiny.'

'God knows. Is this the captain's cabin?'

Lauren shrugged her shoulders, but somehow she knew the answer. 'No; it's not.' Leading them outside, she ignored the hatch that led to the dark bowels of the vessel and pushed open the second door. 'This looks more promising.'

She stepped forward, uncertain what she would find but sure that she was safe. She stopped dead. 'Oh my God!'

Sitting on the edge of the bed, the man was leaning forward, one hand pointing at the door, and the other resting on top of a flat, japanned tin case. Wide spaced above gaunt cheekbones on which sprouted a dark beard, his eyes stared sightlessly ahead, while the skin was taut on a fleshless face that had been dead for many decades.

'Sweet Jesus in heaven,' Kenny said softly. 'Who the hell is that?'

'It might be the captain,' Lauren stood for a minute, gazing at the corpse. That song she had heard in the sea returned, soothing sweetly around her head, strangely calming even as it augmented the atmosphere of infinite sadness in this small cabin.

It's not the captain. It's Him.

Her eyes roamed around the cabin, noting the single desk and the varnish peeling from the woodwork; instinctively she straightened the pile of papers. There was a bookshelf laden with sodden nautical volumes, a chart fixed to a small table and a bunk, neatly made except for the black mould that covered what had once been the covers. The smell of damp and decay was overpowering.

'Welcome home, Captain.' Kenny said quietly. He touched the revolver that sat on the bed, half hidden beneath a fur of red rust. 'Here's the gun. Maybe he went mad and shot the rest of the crew.'

'We'll never know by speculating,' Lauren felt a sense of infinite loss. 'Let's find the ship's papers. The log book might tell us.' She indicated the japanned case held by the dead man, 'and I think it will be in there.'

Kenny recoiled. 'You can't touch that.'

'Yes I can.' It was the first time in her life that Lauren had been in close contact with a corpse, but she felt no repugnance at all as she gently prised free the skeletal fingers. They parted easily, as if the dead man was glad to be free of the burden he had carried for so long, and she eased the case away.

'I must look in here.'

'Maybe it's full of gold.' Memories of childhood stories of treasure ships removed some of Kenny's distaste.

'Maybe it is,' Lauren encouraged his fantasy as she turned the key that protruded from the lock. It moved easily, as if it were only a few days since it had been last used, rather than scores of years. Moving back to gain more space, she opened the lid. 'No pieces of eight or doubloons,' she said quietly, 'but something far more interesting.'

Pulling out a thin pile of documents and a bound notebook, she placed them on the desk. 'These must be the captain's personal papers. There are a small sheaf of letters he must have written but been unable to post, and what looks like his journal.' She looked in the box again. 'There's no logbook though, which is disappointing.' She stared at the dead man, wondering what personal tragedy he had experienced, and how it had felt as he sat at his desk, the only man left in *Lady Balgay*, and what it had been like to die alone in an abandoned ship.

Welcome home; welcome home at last.

That music was back, syrupy smooth and insistent; the words indistinct but seeping into her mind. 'I think we should read the journal.'

'The captain may object,' Kenny did not go near the dead man.

'I don't think that's the captain.'

Why did I say that? There was no reason except a gut feeling that was so strong, enhanced with a feeling of quiet desperation she knew came from the man in the chair, that she had no doubt she was correct.

'Let's get away from here,' Kenny had retreated to the doorway. 'Get back on deck until the lifeboat comes.'

'I must read this; he wants me to.' The statement came from nowhere, but Lauren would not be denied. Although she was still dripping wet she felt no discomfort as she scraped the captain's chair back from the desk and lowered herself carefully into it.

'He wants you to?' Kenny stared at her. 'Listen to yourself, Lauren.'

'You go on deck if you like. I'm fine here.'

'With that? With him?' Kenny gestured to the dead man, who continued to point to the open door as if indicating something.

Lauren glanced over her shoulder. 'He's harmless.'

He wants me here.

Brushing fragments of white shell from the surface of the desk, she put down the journal. The leather cover was brown and shiny, as if it had just come from the shelf of a quality stationery shop. She opened it, wondering what was inside.

Chapter Three

En ma fin git mon commencement
In my end is my beginning
   Mary, Queen of Scots

My name is Iain Cosgrove, the journal began, and I shall transcribe in these pages a faithful and true account of everything that happened in our voyage from Dundee to the Greenland Sea. At present the sealing ketch *Lady Balgay* is fast to an iceberg, drifting but safe somewhere off the East Coast of Greenland and I am alone in the captain's cabin. I would wish it otherwise.

As I write this, I shall endeavour to leave nothing out and add nothing. In other words, this account will be the plain, unvarnished truth as I see it. Please remember always that I am the surgeon of this damned vessel, and have only a vague understanding of anything nautical, so if I do not write the correct terms for the various manoeuvres that we have undertaken, please forgive me.

As this journal describes my personal feelings and impressions as well as the fearful events that led to my present position, I had better begin the day before I set out to sea, the last day I was truly happy.

I do not know if this journal will ever be found, or if my fate will be forever a mystery, but I hope and pray that someday a passing ship will see the topmasts of *Lady Balgay* and rescue me from my plight. If that vessel comes too late, and I have already joined my comrades in the blessed peace of death, then I would be obliged if you, the reader, could forward this account onto my beloved sweetheart and wife, Jennifer Cosgrove, care of Balgay House, West Ferry, Dundee.

Until that day, or until the day of my release from this unremitting hell, I can give you only my love, Jennifer, and write this journal. I will begin with what transpired that beautiful afternoon of the 14th February 1914, while I was still on land and at your side.

'Iain!' I heard Jennifer's voice rise in a mixture of scandal and pleasure. 'We can't act like that here. Think of the proprieties!'

'Hang the proprieties, think of us, Mrs Cosgrove.' I kissed her again, laughing when she did not turn away. Her lips were soft and welcoming.

'Say that again,' Jennifer eased free, smiling.

'Say what again?' I enjoyed the pleasure that crossed her face.

'You know what,' Jennifer's eyes crinkled to slits of brilliant blue. 'That name.'

'Oh, that name.' I nodded. 'The Mrs Cosgrove name.'

'Yes, say it again.'

Stepping back to hold her at arm's length, I altered my tone and felt all the teasing disappear. 'I love you, Mrs Cosgrove.'

Jennifer smiled to me, her eyes brilliant, but there was just a twist of unease in the corner of her mouth. 'Now you can kiss me,' she said, 'but then we must return to the house. People will talk.'

'People will always talk about us,' I told her solemnly, 'for we are such interesting and important people.' I kissed her again, pressing luxuriously on to the softness of her lips, and held her close. I could feel the twin pressure of her breasts against my chest and thrilled to think that this was my wife, now and forever. Jennifer was mine; I gloried in the idea until a voice floated from the open French Windows a few yards behind us.

'There they are! Out in the garden! Come on in and dance, you two lovebirds. There will be time enough for that sort of thing later.'

'Will there?' Jennifer asked, and I adopted a sudden frown.

'Perhaps. If you behave yourself.'

'Well, Mr Cosgrove, I certainly don't intend to do that any longer!' Her throaty laugh tormented me with the promise of future passion until she took hold of my sleeve and I allowed her to lead me back inside the house.

Balgay House never failed to impress me. Built to the design of Jennifer's father, it had stood in Dundee's exclusive West Ferry suburb for over twenty years as a splendid example of a Jute Baron's mansion. I had been brought up in much more modest surroundings and tried to hide my amazement at the grandeur of this palace, with its huge rooms and ornate plasterwork, its acres of garden and small army of staff to attend residents and guests. As I was now married to the daughter of the house, I knew I should be treated as a member of the family, but I could sense that the servants still resented my presence; they thought me an upstart mixing with my betters.

Well, by God, I was here now and intended to make the most of it, whatever the hired help thought. If I was good enough for Jennifer, then I expected them to bow and scrape to me just as much. I shook my head; that was a complete lie; I felt nothing of the sort. My family home had run to one maid who had been as much part of the household as I was, and had considered it her right to scold me when I was a child. I would never get used to the sheer authority of the merchant class, and mostly I did not really want to.

'Come on, slowcoach!' Jennifer pulled me into what she referred to as the great hall, which had been cleared ready for the post-marriage celebrations. A dozen musicians sat in a semi-circle, working furiously on violin and piano, bass and cymbals. The music floated like audible nectar, sweetening the air and lightening the feet as Jennifer dragged me across the floor of especially imported Burmese teak. Surrounding us with aesthetic treasure, oil paintings adorned each wall, all personally selected by Sir Melville.

Moving smoothly across the floor, dinner-jacketed men waltzed with elegant ladies whose long dresses and sparkling jewellery revealed that here was the pride of Dundee society. Ship owners and merchant barons, linen manufacturers and landowners, this magnificent room contained the men who dominated the world jute trade, whose ships crossed the seas from Murmansk to Calcutta, and who enjoyed all the ease and society that hard earned wealth had brought them.

'Iain, my boy!' Sir Melville Manson eased through the dancing crowd, his long cigar held in a languid hand but his eyes shrewd, as befitted one of the richest men in Scotland. 'Welcome to the family.'

'Thank you, sir,' I accepted the outstretched hand and bowed out of habit. 'It is good to belong.'

'But you're not here for long, though. You set sail on the first tide tomorrow, I believe?' The blue eyes narrowed in a frightening reflection of his daughter. 'For the North?'

'Yes, sir.' In all the excitement of the wedding I had nearly forgotten the trials that waited. 'We must sail tomorrow, or we will be too late for the sealing.'

'I understand,' Sir Melville nodded. 'Duty must come first; even before your marriage. Life can be hard sometimes.'

'It is something that has to be done, sir. If I am to become the best doctor in Dundee, I must learn my trade, and where better than on a sealing ship? And in particular the sealing ship whose owner is my father in law.'

'Yes, but Iain,' Jennifer's voice was disapproving, 'to sail so far, so soon after the wedding and in such a small boat!'

I forced a laugh, as much for my sake as hers. '*Lady Balgay* is not such a small boat, Jennifer. She is a ketch, and Captain Milne is an experienced mariner; he will take care of me, don't you fret.'

You should not be going,'Jennifer objected. 'After all, it is not as if we need the money. Father will willingly provide for us.'

'Of that I have no doubt,' I agreed, 'but I must make my own way, you see. I do not wish to constantly hold out my hand for your father's charity.'

'It's hardly charity,' Jennifer began, but Sir Melville silenced her with a wave of his cheroot.

'I understand exactly what Iain means, Jennifer. In this world, a man is not really a man unless he can make his own way.'

I bowed my acknowledgement of Sir Melville's support. I was more than aware that the Manson family did not think me quite a good enough catch for their daughter, and there must have been fierce arguments before I was accepted into their midst. Knowing that I was of far inferior social standing to my wife made me even more determined to pay my own way without asking for financial help, and a voyage in a sealing vessel would provide valuable experience that any medical practise might welcome.

'It's still a long time away from me,' Jennifer's slight pout revealed her lack of years. She was still a few weeks short of her twentieth birthday and all the lovelier for that.

'I'm lucky to have the chance,' I told her frankly, 'considering that I have only just qualified and my sole previous voyage was on a mere yacht.'

I had fully partaken of all the joys of Edinburgh while at the university and already I missed the high jinks of student life, but Dundee was my home. It was good to be back to the forests of chimneys and the whispering, ever changing Tay. There had been Cosgroves in this city for at least three centuries, and I had every hope of continuing the line: with the co-operation of my wife, of course. She caught my sideways glance and I knew by her sudden flush that she understood exactly what I was thinking.

'Anyway,' Sir Melville added, 'there may not be many more opportunities to sail to the Arctic. The whaling business up there is long gone, and the sealing is virtually moribund. *Lady Balgay* is the last of her line.' He smiled sadly. 'We had to purchase her especially and change her name to something more suitable.' He leaned closer. 'We named her after Jennifer of course, the Lady of Balgay House.'

'Yes, sir.' Somehow it was easier knowing that I would be sailing in a ship named after my new wife. That way we could never be far apart, even if distance separated us.

'Just imagine though, Iain,' Sir Melville shook his head. 'In my youth there were fifteen, sixteen, even seventeen whaling ships, huge vessels, sailing from Dundee to chase the whales, and now there is just one small ketch hunting seals. You are part of history, sailing in the last Greenlandman.' Sir Melville smiled and for a moment his eyes darkened, as if he were reliving his own past life.

'Yes, sir,' I tried to sound dutiful but I thought then that history should be left in the past, along with all the diseases and plagues for which we had long since found a cure. Life was about progress, not reminiscing about the good old days of cholera and foul sanitation. I was so young and naive then: I had not learned how history can turn full circle to bite horrifyingly at the present. If I had known, God, if I had known, I would never have put a foot on that terrible ship.

'But you have only the one chance, Iain,' Sir Melville was still talking, 'for I have no intention of having my daughter live a solitary life. Yes, it is a man's duty to provide for his wife, but I have little time for absent husbands who spend all their life away, leaving their wives to fend for themselves at home.' His wink appeared ponderous, but there was no mistaking the sincere message behind the apparent jollity. 'One voyage to prove yourself and gain experience, and then it is a practice in town for you, my boy, dealing with old lady's fainting fits, old men's hernias and the consequences of young men's romantic misadventures.'

'Father!' Jennifer looked as scandalised as only a young newlywed bride could.

I thought it best to hide my smile. 'Indeed, sir. People will be far more likely to accept me as their doctor if they knew I had practical experience.'

'I am quite aware of that.' For a moment Sir Melville looked testy, but his paternal smile chased away the mood. 'Captain Milne is a good man, Iain. Like *Lady Balgay* he is the last of a long line of Dundee whalers. A splendid mariner, as long as you keep him away from the bottle.' He laughed. 'But that won't be a problem. I've ensured that *Lady Balgay* is a dry ship. There is no alcohol among her stores.'

'I am pleased to hear it, sir.' Growing up in Dundee, I had heard the tales of drunken Greenlandmen causing havoc among the bars of Dock Street, or under arrest in Shetland before they even entered the chilled waters of the Arctic. Their behaviour was notorious even among British seamen, a breed not renowned for sobriety and the singing of Sunday school psalms.

'So that's one less worry, eh?' Sir Melville had a long pull at his cigar. 'Now, Jennifer, I intend to rob you of your husband for five short minutes.'

'Oh father, must you?' Jennifer widened her eyes and tilted her face, but Sir Melville remained unmoved.

'Come, my boy. Five minutes.'

Shrugging my shoulders to Jennifer, I followed Sir Melville through the house to the gunroom, where, amidst racks of Purdey shotguns, boxes of cartridges and a selection of mounted antlers and other hunting trophies, a roll top desk gleamed beneath an electric globe. The room smelled of leather, tobacco and wet dog; I doubted if any woman had ever placed a dainty foot past the dark panelled door.

'This is between men,' Sir Melville said quietly, 'so not a word to Jennifer. Understand?'

'Of course, sir,' I agreed, instantly intrigued.

'Good.' Unlocking the drawer of his desk, Sir Melville produced a revolver, which he weighed in his hand for a quiet moment before breaking it open and handing it to me. 'Take this with you, in case of unforeseen eventualities. One never knows what might happen at sea.'

To say I was surprised would be to put it mildly. I took the thing and weighed it carefully; here was death packaged in functional steel. I had held a revolver before, of course, at the Officer's Training Corps at Dundee High School but I had never expected to carry one as a man. It felt cold but quite familiar and the butt fitted nicely inside my hand.

'It's a Webley Fosberry,' Sir Melville was something of an expert in firearms, having hunted all his life.

'Yes, sir.' I held the pistol before me, arm straight as I had been taught, and sighted on a pair of wildebeest antlers that hung on the far wall. It felt heavy and I could not imagine cold-bloodedly pointing it at a man and squeezing the trigger.

'It has a .45 uncoated lead bullet, so it's got tremendous stopping power; the bullet spreads on contact. If you hit your target anywhere in his body, you are almost certain to kill him. These fancy automatic weapons…' Sir Melville shook his head. 'Fine for show, but they jam at the most inconvenient moments and their light, nickel plated bullets are useless in a tight situation. The Webley will work in any conditions and will never let you down.'

'Do you think I will need it?' I listened to the musical whirr as I spun the chamber, and imagined the terrible wounds a soft lead bullet could cause to a human body. Automatically I wondered how to best treat a patient with such injuries and felt sudden repugnance; I was tempted to hand the thing back. Common sense told me that it would be unwise to alienate my father- in- law so I listened to his sage advice, nodding as if interested.

'Keep it close by you,' Sir Melville was saying. 'The rule generally is, if you do need a weapon, you will need it badly. Aim to kill, Iain, whether it is a man or a polar bear, and don't bother with this non-sensical notion of only wounding. A wounded man is quite capable of putting a bullet or a knife in you. Save your own life and worry about the consequences later.'

'Yes, sir;' I held the pistol clumsily, promising myself that it was going overboard the moment I stepped on board.

'What am I thinking of?' Sudden good humour lightened Sir Melville's eyes and a smile softened the thin mouth. 'There's Jennifer waiting anxiously for you, and on your wedding day, too. You run along now, and I will put this with your things.' Sir Melville gave an indulgent smile. 'And Iain, take care of her, will you? Tonight of all nights?'

Restraining my smile, I nodded gravely. 'I will, sir.'

Sir Melville held my eye for an awkward moment as if to confirm my sincerity. I must have impressed him for he gave a final nod. 'Fine; good; off you go then, and when you get to the Arctic, you enjoy the experience.'

Jennifer was sitting on a hard backed chair with her hands folded in her lap and her eyes focussed on the floor at her feet. She looked so demure that I was immediately suspicious, but she smiled when I entered. 'About time too, Mr Cosgrove. I suppose you have been receiving all sorts of paternalistic and manly advice?'

'Some,' I agreed, leaning forward to put my mouth near her ear. 'I've to be gentle with you tonight.'

'Well,' Jennifer gave a little humph sound that I had not heard before and put a possessive hand on my arm. 'Well, before you have any silly male notions, I will claim you for the evening. You are my husband, after all!'

As the bandmaster announced a waltz, Jennifer gave a smile of satisfaction. 'Waltzes are my favourite,' she told me, dragging me on to the floor. Moving as close as convention allowed, she whispered. 'Come on, Iain; let's show everybody what to do. I won prizes for dancing, you know.'

'I know,' I had studied the silver medals that were displayed in a glass case in the drawing room, directly beneath Sir Melville's Boer War decorations.

The other guests watched, with one or two gently clapping as she guided me through the first dance. I allowed her to lead, for I was unsure how much she knew of my time in Edinburgh when I cut an amazing dash on the floor. Jennifer was my love and my wife, but a succession of other girls had taught me a great deal about dancing; and other things. I shook away the memories; that was the *old* me.

Jennifer pressed closer so I could feel the heat of her body as the older ladies gazed fondly through their fans, recalling their own youth.

'Do come back early from Greenland,' Jennifer insisted as I took charge and whirled her round unconventionally fast. 'I do hate that you have to leave.'

'I shall return as soon as I can.' I could feel everybody watching, some critically, some with jealousy. Kate Davidson, the little blonde granddaughter of the famous whaling captain, was smiling slightly, her eyes hungry. I remembered her very well, from a time before Jennifer. Catching her eye on me, I thought I'd tease her a little and increased the pace so the musicians had to work harder and the other dancers followed.

Glancing over my shoulder, I saw Kate incline her head slightly, allowing her eyes to roam down the length of my body as we passed, and with only a slight movement out of step she contrived to brush her hip lightly against the outside of my thigh as we glided purposefully together.

That's enough of that, my girl, I decided, and leaned closer to my wife.

'You're so dashing,' Jennifer sounded slightly out of breath, but there was delight in her face. 'I must be the happiest woman in the world.'

'And I the luckiest man,' I led her in a great circle, manoeuvring our position carefully. Kate held my eye for a second, and I smiled at Jennifer. 'Kiss me,' I commanded and she looked suitably scandalised.

'Not here!'

'Why not? We're married now; it's allowed. Kiss me.'

Glancing around the crowded room, Jennifer shook her head, so I bent down and touched my lips to her blushing cheek.

'You're terrible,' Jennifer whispered.

'Much worse than you realize,' I agreed. I knew that Kate was mentally devouring me and decided to give her a proper show. 'Kiss me again,' I ordered, and abruptly stopped dancing so Jennifer gave a little gasp.

'Iain! No!'

'Oh yes.' I kissed her full on the lips, feeling the thrill of her softness beneath me as she relented. She tasted sweet. 'Isn't that better?'

I smiled directly into her eyes, seeing my image in her dilated blue pupils.

'Much,' she agreed, and then frowned. 'But why have you stopped?'

As I hesitated, open mouthed, Jennifer took the lead, placing her white-gloved hand on my cheek, opening her mouth under my own and shockingly teasing with her tongue until I pulled back.

'There now,' the saucy wench smiled directly into my eyes, 'that will help you behave for a while, Mr Iain Cosgrove, and keep Kate Davidson thinking too!' She smiled archly, eyebrows raised. 'She's right behind you, Iain, watching avidly, and I know that she still likes you.' Jennifer raised her voice just loud enough to be heard above the band and the rhythmic beat of elegant feet on the polished teak floor. 'Well, you're mine now, and she'll just have to settle for second best.'

'You little minx,' I said as my astonishment altered to pride and renewed affection chased away any lingering feelings for Kate Davidson. 'I do believe that you have me.'

'I do believe that I do,' Jennifer's smile widened into a definite grin. 'So now,' the look she threw at Kate contained a mixture of triumph and complete satisfaction, 'shall we dance again? After all we are the stars of the evening, not just hopeful, or should I say, hope*less*, admirers.'

'You are the most amazing girl,' I told her truthfully, and she shook her head.

'Woman, please, Iain. Katie Davidson is a girl, for *girls* are not married.'

She was so obviously in charge of the situation that I could not help but laugh and would have hugged her close if she had not again began to dance, forcing me to concentrate on my steps or fall in a most undignified heap in front of all the invited guests.

Jennifer felt the change in atmosphere a fraction before I did, and we both looked up as a blast of bitter air swept across the floor. She shivered and for a brief second I had a vision of the Arctic, with a flat plain of ice and a wind driving snow straight into my face. And then it was gone and instead I could see the dancers on the floor parting like the Red Sea before Moses, and Jennifer was pulling at my sleeve.

'Iain: who is that woman?'

Chapter Four

He who would keep himself busy, let him equip himself with these two; a ship and a woman. For no two things involve more business once you start to fit them out, nor are these two ever sufficiently adorned, nor is any excess of adornment enough for them.
  Titus Maccius Plautus, 254-184 BC

I knew immediately that she was not an invited guest, both by her appearance and her attitude. She had none of the wealth-fed grace of the elite, but possessed a more fundamental aura of self-awareness than I had ever seen before. The other dancers obviously knew she was an intruder and watching the expression on their faces might have been amusing if this woman had not interrupted our wedding. Some looked incredulous, others merely disapproving, but all shared disdain.

I shook my head, 'she's not from my side of the family.'

'Nor mine,' poor Jennifer sounded quite bemused.

While everybody else was in evening dress, this woman might have stepped straight from a gypsy encampment, and she possibly had. She could not have been much over five feet tall, but she seemed to dominate the dance hall, while what was visible of her hair beneath a bright handkerchief was as black as her eyes as she peered at everybody in turn. The band stopped playing, the dancers stopped dancing and the noise dropped from a cheerful, bustling hum to a silence so intense it was almost intimidating.

At last she faced me and I nearly shivered at the power behind those dark eyes.

'You'll be Iain Cosgrove,' she said quietly, and I nodded, suddenly slightly uncomfortable.

'It's you I have come for, then,' she transferred her gaze to Jennifer, 'and your bride.'

I heard Jennifer's sudden in draw of breath and squeezed her hand.

'Ah: Mrs Adams!' Sir Melville strode across the floor, hand out-stretched in welcome. 'You are as unorthodox as ever, I see.'

'Father: do you know this lady?' Trust Jennifer to keep sufficient good manners to refer to this bedraggled creature as a lady when all around her the true ladies with whisking back their skirts for fear of being contaminated by her presence. I warmed once more to my wife.

'This is Mrs Adams,' Sir Melville introduced. He raised his voice so all his guests could hear. 'We have a tradition in our family that a new bride and groom should have their fortune told: your mother and I had ours told, as did my father and my grandfather. Mrs Adams is an expert in the art.'

Jennifer looked at me and giggled as I suppressed my own smile and tried to look solemn. I had never like fairground conjuring, and to me, fortune telling was merely another obsolete superstition from a bygone age. I would play along if I had to, but I was a trained doctor, a man of science and reason.

I had not learned: yet.

'Come this way, please.' Sir Melville led us from the dance hall and upstairs to the library, with its shelves of splendid books and view over the night-dark Tay to Fife. As if by right, Mrs Adams took possession of the carved chair behind the central desk. Bright electric light shone upon her, but I do not recall seeing any shadows.

'You may leave us, Sir Melville.' That was an order, not a request. Sir Melville obeyed gracefully, leaving us alone with the gypsy woman.

Unsmiling, she beckoned Jennifer forward to the hard chair on the opposite side of the desk. 'Come here, my dear and give me your hand; we shall see what the future holds for you.'

I tried to listen but for some unaccountable reason I could not hear what was said. The two women leaned closer across the width of the desk and although the murmur of their voices was clear, the content of the conversation was not. Instead I heard the whine of wind across ice floes, the scream of a gale through rigging and a barking cry the origin of which I was uncertain but the sound of which was mournful beyond belief.

At length Jennifer stood up and withdrew, looking slightly pale. She gave me a shaky smile as I took her place at the desk.

Although I know that fortune tellers cannot see the future, and use tricks to gain the confidence of their customers, I still felt a prickle of unease as I slid onto the chair and extended my hand for the gypsy to read.

Close to, Mrs Adams did not seem intimidating in the slightest. Her face was dark through exposure to wind and sun and her clothes emanated an aroma of smoke and earth, as though she had come straight from the fields, but her eyes were unfathomable. They were deep dark pools into which I sank as she studied me.

'You are going on a long journey,' she told me what I already knew, 'and you are unhappy about leaving your bride.'

I could not disagree with that.

'I see coldness and death; I see red flowing over white,' the eyes held mine as images flitted through my mind: the vicious chill of the Arctic, blood staining the ice, men in thick furs laughing.

'I see a woman, very close to you,' I imagined Jennifer running to greet me as I stepped from the ship, her eyes bright with joy.

'I see...' Mrs Adams hesitated for a long second as my images faded. 'I see deception and fear, fire and terror; I see loneliness.'

My patience snapped then; of course there was ice and cold, death and blood, deception and loneliness; I was travelling away from my new wife to trap and kill seals in the Arctic. 'Can you tell me anything useful?'

Tightening her grip on my hand, Mrs Adams pressed a sharp-taloned finger deep into my palm, drawing a bright bead of blood. 'Beware of a silent woman,' she said and gave a little gasp, 'God save you.'

'What?' Jennifer crossed the room, her dress rustling softly, 'what does that mean? What do you mean, Mrs Adams, God save you? Will Iain come home?'

'He will come home.'

'Then that is all that matters,' Snatching my hand away, Jennifer marched away. She stopped at the door, 'are you coming, Iain?'

Of course I was coming, but my feeling of uneasiness persisted for a good half hour, until the dancing was once again in full flow and Jennifer was firm and soft in my arms.

Perhaps it was the episode with Mrs Adams, but I found myself wanting the evening to end quickly so I could claim Jennifer for myself. Inevitably the clock ticked away the minutes and the evening did draw to a close. The older guests drifted to the carriages and motor-cars that waited so patiently on the wide sweeping drive outside and the spaces on the dance floor grew larger. As the house gradually emptied Jennifer touched my arm.

'I won't be a minute,' she whispered and, lifting her skirt with her left hand, she approached the band. I watched, wondering what she was doing as she requested one final number. Of course they agreed, smiling patiently, and she returned to my side, passing through what remained of the guests.

'This one we will remember,' she whispered, 'you when you are up among the ice bergs and me when I wait alone in my bed, thinking of you.'

The reminder that I would have to leave this woman whom I felt I was just beginning to know stabbed deeply and I pulled her close. 'I wish I was not going,' I told her.

'So do I,' she whispered, pressing close, 'but let us make the most of this night while we can.'

The bandleader tapped his baton for attention, spoke a few words and the music began immediately. I recognised the song immediately, for it was one that both Jennifer and her mother sang. Annie Harrison's *In the Gloaming* had been an instant success when it was first published about thirty years ago and was still sung by sentimentally minded women. My taste ran to Gilbert and Sullivan and more robust, music hall type songs, but In the *Gloaming* had grown on me the more often I heard Jennifer sing.

As soon as the tune began, many of the remaining women looked to their husbands, hopeful of being guided to the dance floor to reawaken memories of their own youth.

'I want you to remember this evening whenever you hear this song,' Jennifer ordered, and whispered the opening verse into my ear. Her breath was soft against my neck so I could feel myself responding.

> *'In the gloaming, oh my darling,*
> *When the lights are soft and low*
> *And the quiet shadows falling*
> *Softly come and softly go.'*

'I will,' I promised, fighting the tears that threatened to un-man me and the other reactions that proved the very opposite. I knew, without any doubt, that I would never forget that song; it would be with me always, keeping me company amidst the wastes of the north. I shivered slightly, as though the Arctic wind was already biting at my face.

'Iain? Are you all right?'

'Of course I am.' I held her closer, trying to disguise my oxymoronic discomfort. 'Jennifer?'

'Yes?'

'No, nothing. It's all right.' I looked away; I could neither joke nor tease, and I wished oh-so-fervently that I was not sailing north the next morning. I closed my eyes, breathing in the scent of her perfume as I felt the yielding firmness of her waist beneath my hand. God but I wished I was returning from the north and not just setting out. Life was cruel in thus taunting me with the delights of marriage, only to pluck at my happiness and thrust it away before I had properly experienced it. I knew I was a full man, but I wanted my wife; I wanted her body and her mind, I wanted her company and the music of her voice, I wanted to watch her moving and to breathe deeply of her perfume, I wanted to be near her, not to be separated by a waste of water and months of bitter loneliness.

Perhaps it was the song, or the memory of Mrs Adams' words, but the sudden sadness was overwhelming, tinged with that haunting, unearthly moan that I had never heard before but which I knew came from the Arctic, and I shivered again.

'You're cold,' Jennifer said, already practising her wifely skills.

'No,' I denied, but I held her tighter, so she merged with my body, gasping and opening her eyes wide as she felt my reaction.

'Iain Cosgrove,' she giggled. 'I am shocked.'

After that she moved closer still, so we became a single unit on that dance floor, lost in our own world, squeezing every fraction of time from our last evening before I sailed north.

'Oh, Iain, I wish you were not going.'

'So do I,' I felt the catch in my voice and looked away, gathering my strength. We would be apart for some months and I had no desire for her to remember her husband as a man who blubbered before he sailed away.

Jennifer knew every word of the four verses of *In the Gloaming* and when the dance floor was full, with couples reflecting on their past or dreaming about their future, she breathed the final few lines, her voice soft.

> *'In the gloaming, oh my darling*
> *When the lights are soft and low*
> *Will you think of me and love me*
> *As you did once long ago?'*

'I will,' I promised, drawing strength from the depth of her love.

'Good,' she burrowed closer, and then broke away in one of the lightning changes of mood that was so typical of her. 'But that time is not yet.' Her eyes narrowed with mischief as, after a quick glance around the room, she allowed one hand to stray, rubbing my back beneath the frock coat and sliding down until a single finger touched lightly yet shockingly on my left buttock. She pressed slightly, and patted fondly.

I gasped, unable to hide my thrill of pleasure. 'Jennifer!' I knew I should be scandalised by this forward behaviour from such a well brought up creature, but, rather, I was more than pleased that she could be so familiar.

'It's all right, Iain. I am your wife,' her wide eyes teased me further as she took control of the situation. 'Is it not time that we retired?'

'Perhaps I had better announce that?'

'And have everybody looking?' Jennifer's eyes widened even further. 'My, Iain, do you really want to draw attention to yourself? Let's just slip away quietly. After all, you do have an early start in the morning.'

I think it was then that I realised exactly what I had married. Jennifer was no milk-and-water wife, no sit-in-the-corner woman who would be demure and submissive and wait for me to take charge. She was my equal and probably more than that, and I could have laughed out loud with pure joy.

I knew that Kate Davidson was watching but I was unprepared for Jennifer's sudden change of direction. Leading me by the hand, she approached the insipid blonde and smiled directly into her face.

'We're going to bed now,' my wife told her triumphantly, and made for the great double doors. Save for a gasp of astonishment and a slight lift of her hand, Kate made no comment.

'That will settle her hash,' Jennifer said with great satisfaction. 'She will not make sheep eyes at my husband again.'

I laughed; I had thought of Jennifer as my wife; now I knew I was also her husband. She would cope perfectly well when I was in the

Arctic, and she would be waiting when I returned. But other, more immediate matters demanded my attention.

It was hard to rise in the morning, to look down on the form of the woman who was now my wife in body as well as in law and know I was to leave her, but I had my duty to perform. Kissing her gently, I eased from the bed. I had spent the last restless hour pondering whether it would be best to wake Jennifer or leave without ceremony, but I eventually decided that I could not bear the pain of a lingering farewell. I dressed hurriedly, pulling on the clothes that a servant had arranged for me twelve hours previously, and slipping from the bedroom, closed the door as quietly as I could.

Even at this early hour there were servants about, heavy eyed maids who crept around the long corridors with towels and coalscuttles and chamber pots and who bobbed their respect to the young mistress's husband. I barely acknowledged them as I stumbled downstairs to share a cup of tea with the bleary-eyed butler and bite into a hunk of bread and ham. I was never a great eater in the morning, and now my nerves took control as I faced the prospect of months away from home in a hostile and utterly alien environment.

'Shall I call for the carriage, sir?' Freshly shaved and pristine as always, the butler stood at attention as he spoke.

'No,' I shook my head, 'thank you. The walk will help wake me up.' I could imagine the fuss and bustle of alerting the coachman and taking out the horses, and cringed at the impression I would make arriving at a sealing ship by coach.

'As you wish, sir.' There was no obvious emotion in the words.

After last night, I did not care what the butler thought. I was married to the best and most perfect woman in the world, and once I returned from the Arctic, my life would be full of nights such as that. Three months; four at the outside, and I would be in marital paradise.

Dundee in the dark of pre-dawn is never pretty, with streets and buildings dimly lit by flickering streetlights. The massive bulk of factories and mills dominate the town, and unseen chimneys puncture the sky while the smell of smoke is heavy amidst the lingering frost of winter. That morning was no different, but made worse by the desolation of parting; I remember that a wagon jolted over the cobblestones with fragments of raw jute floating free from its load and the carter whipping his horse in sullen bad temper.

'Get on there you lazy bitch!'

I walked quickly, listening to the echo of my footsteps against the surrounding walls. Twice I stopped, thinking that somebody was following me, and, remembering the tales I had heard of the dangers of Dundee's dockland, I wished I had slipped my revolver into my pocket rather than having it sent on ahead with my other baggage. The footsteps pattered lightly behind me and I stopped.

'Who's there?' my words sounded hollow, lost in the whispering night, and only the raucous screams of a seagull replied. I moved on, balling my hands into fists as I began to regret my decision to walk.

'Iain!' The voice was low and urgent. 'Iain!'

'Who's there?' I already knew the answer. 'Jennifer? Is that you?'

She hurried up, breathless and dishevelled, with a coat loose over her shoulders and mud spattering the bottom of her nightdress. Her hair was wild beneath the broad bonnet. 'I couldn't let you leave without saying goodbye.'

'My God!' For a moment I could only stare at her. 'Jennifer; you should not be here. It's not safe!' I reached for her, shockingly aware of her scant covering. She seemed very vulnerable amidst these predatory shadows.

'I had to come.' Jennifer raised her chin in defiance, but she could not disguise the moisture in her eyes. 'I had to say goodbye.'

'Oh Jenny!' I shook my hand and pulled her into a close hug. I had been wrong; our single night had not been enough to fully blend us together and I felt awkward, unsure what to say or do. Less restrained or more mature, Jennifer clung to me, as if by burrowing against my body she could retain me, in soul if not in body.

'Don't go,' her voice choked on the last word. 'I don't want you to go! Please don't go away from me.'

'I must,' I could feel her body warmth through the coat and closed my eyes. 'It's only for a few months.'

'Please…' Her fingers hooked into me. When she looked up, tears blurred her eyes.

'I'll come back,' I told her. 'And we can write to each other.'

'Yes,' Jennifer clung desperately to the lifeline. 'Write lots of letters; write a letter a day, so I know that you are all right.' She forced a smile. 'And write me a journal, Iain, so that when you come back we can read it together, the journal of the only time that we will ever be apart.'

'Of course I will.' Aware of the passage of time, I began to gently prise myself free. 'I must go, Jennifer, or the boat will leave without me and I'll let your father down.'

'Come back, oh come back to me.' Jennifer was crying openly now, big round tears sliding down her cheeks in a manner that made my own eyes prickle. How do women have the ability to do that to a man? What powers do they possess?

'Of course I'll come back,' I heard the gruffness in my voice as I sought to fight unaccustomed emotion. 'Come on, now.' I had no handkerchief with which to dry her face, so I used my hand, which succeeded only in further smearing her tears.

'Promise me,' her hands refused to release me. They were small but strong as they hooked into my back. 'Please please promise that you'll come back.'

I felt the change in her. She was desperate, close to breaking down as her hands seemed to dig deep into me. Holding her at arm's length, I looked directly into her eyes and injected as much sincerity as I could into my voice. 'I promise that, whatever happens in the Arctic, I will return to you, my wife.'

Jennifer nodded, her eyes liquid, searching mine, delving deep into my soul. The reminder that she was my wife had helped calm her down. 'And I will leave a candle shining in the window to guide you home. I will light it every night and count every day until we are together again.' Her teeth gleamed in a sudden small smile. 'Now that I have your word, all I need is a kiss and you may go.'

I bent down, touching my mouth to the soft lips that she offered so willingly. At that second if she had asked me to return with her I would have obeyed, and hang the consequences.

'Now go,' she stepped back bravely and pushed me gently away, 'go now, before you miss the tide.' Jennifer stood there with her hair a halo around her head and the skirts of her coat loose around her legs. 'Go!' she pointed imperiously and I turned, walking slouch shouldered as my earlier determination slipped away. I heard her singing again, the words cutting deep into what was left of my courage.

> 'In the gloaming, oh my darling
> When the lights are soft and low
> Will you think of me and love me
> As you did once long ago?'

'Of course I will,' I whispered. 'Of course I will.' The forthcoming voyage to the Arctic no longer seemed like an adventure, but an ordeal to be survived before I returned to Jennifer. When I looked back she still stood there, a lonely figure beneath the sparse streetlights, holding her coat close to her as her mouth moved with the song.

Chapter Five

VICTORIA DOCK, DUNDEE
FEBRUARY 1914

'A grey crow came and sat on our yards... which a few of the watch thought a bad omen.'
Journal of a Voyage to Baffin Bay Aboard the ship *Thomas* Commanded by Alex Cooke; John Wanless, 10th April 1833

Laden with ice, the February wind rattled the rigging of the ships that crouched miserably beside the harbour warehouses, their masts and spars stark as charity and their hulls half seen in the bleak dawn light. Intermittent sleet pattered the puddles on the quay as a train chugged past, spewing steam against the closed windows of the Seaman's Hostel and the classical authority of the Custom House.

'Who the hell's that?' A labourer paused from piling jute onto an already heavily laden cart to jerk a thumb toward me.

His colleague looked, shrugged and spat phlegm onto the ground. 'Fuck knows or cares, because I don't.' He returned to work, glowering at me as if at a mortal enemy.

When the train gave a sudden shriek of escaping steam, pigeons exploded from the Royal Arch that acted as a majestic backdrop and a reminder of the still lamented Queen Victoria. The echoes faded slowly from the dreary dockland of Dundee.

'*Lady Balgay!*' I hailed the small craft that lay forlorn between a great three master and a rust streaked coaster on whom the red ensign flapped like the duster of a Lochee housewife.

'Aye,' the reply sounded surly, as if the owner of the voice was reluctant to admit on which vessel he sailed. A tall man appeared; polishing the shine on his bald head with a filthy rag, he glowered a challenge at me. 'What do you want?'

'I'm Iain Cosgrove. I'm sailing with you this voyage.' I looked up, hoping for some encouragement or even acknowledgement before I added, 'I'm the surgeon.'

There was a few second's hesitation as the bald man voice looked me up and down, spat over the side and eventually jerked a thumb over his shoulder. 'Are you, now,' he said, and then, 'Christ help you. You'd better come on board, I suppose.'

Lady Balgay was much smaller than I had anticipated, with the vessels on either side towering over her two masts and the thin smokestack that seemed so out of place. On first sight the deck seemed dirty, littered with gear that the tattered crewmen were engaged in stowing away while a stocky, half-shaven man watched, his hands deep in his pockets and his eyes pouchy beneath a filthy cloth cap.

Another seaman, elderly, with a beard that matched the iron-grey of his eyes, was shouting obscenely and, waving his arms at a crow that perched on the deckhouse.

'Get away you dirty black bugger! I'll not have you bringing your bad luck to this ship. Fly, you evil beast!' He swore foully when the bird refused to move, and threw a short length of tarred rope. The bird rose reluctantly, black wings flapping in a weary admission of failure as it retreated to the nearby quay and stood in dejected misery with its dark eyes never leaving *Lady Balgay*.

'Bloody black bastard!' The old seaman watched the bird with a mixture of hatred and fear, until the bald headed man pushed him roughly.

'Get back to your duty, Pratt! You're not here to go bird watching!'

'But it's a crow; they're bad luck!'

'It's a bloody bird, that's all!'

I looked away, wondering what sort of life I would endure for the next few months if everybody were as surly as the bald man and this bearded crewman appeared to be.

Ignoring his swearing shipmates, the man in the cloth cap grunted and muttered something under his breath. Producing a broad-bladed knife from his pocket, he proceeded to probe the timber of the mast. He shook his head in apparent dismay at what he found.

'Excuse me,' used to the shining brass splendour of my father-in-law's steam yacht, I was not sure what to do next. 'I am looking for the master. Captain Milne?'

'Aye,' the man in the cloth cap stared at me, withdrawing the knife. 'That'll be me.' His voice was like gravel under an iron-shod wheel.

Years of training in the Officer's Training Corps had taught me to come to attention when addressing a superior, even one of such an un-prepossessing appearance as Captain Milne presented. 'Iain Cosgrove, sir, reporting for duty as surgeon.'

'So I hear.' Captain Milne looked up from beneath the peak of his cap; he appeared neither amused nor impressed. 'Surgeon eh? Well, we've not much call for a surgeon, Mister Cosgrove, so you can just turn around and piddle off back to your mummy, unless you have any other more useful skills.'

I had not expected peals of delight, but a handshake would have been acceptable. I took a deep breath. 'I am willing to do anything, sir, if required, but…'

'You're willing to do anything eh?' Captain Milne pounced on the words before they were fully free from my mouth; I wondered for what I had let myself in. 'Well, that's better. Are you sure about that, Mister Surgeon Cosgrove?'

'Well, yes, sir…' I said slowly.

'Well, you're a hostage to fortune then, but you've given your word and I'll keep you to it, by Christ. You'd better make yourself useful then, Mr Surgeon.' Captain Milne looked along the deck, shaking his head. 'You've no seagoing experience, I hear, so you'll be no bloody good up here.'

I was about to protest and explain I was a keen yachtsman who had sailed from the Tay to the Solent, but one look at Milne's bitter eyes convinced me he would not be impressed.

'*Lady Balgay* is a seagoing craft, Mr Surgeon, despite her looks. She's not your daddy's steam yacht.' Milne suddenly stopped; pointed to a boy who looked no older than fourteen and raised his voice in a ferocious bellow that scared the seagulls perched on the warehouse roofs. The crow remained, watching. 'You! Mitchell, you wee bastard! Coil that rope properly or I'll flay the skin off you! I'll have no holidays on board my ship!'

Mitchell started, gave a scared little yelp and dropped the rope on which he had been working.

Captain Milne returned his attention to me. 'Well, Mr Cosgrove, I have a job for which you are eminently suitable, as an educated man. I am a practical seaman, you see,' suddenly his tone was wheedling, his smile so insincere that I nearly laughed, 'and I am overburdened with paperwork. You have no idea how much paper is needed to sail even a small vessel like *Lady Balgay*; buckets of the bloody stuff, so I want you to take over the administration. As from right now.'

'But...' I wanted to explain that I had come on board to gain experience as a surgeon and to grow as a man. I wanted to observe the workings of the ship and deal with every possible medical and surgical contingency rather than scratch a pen across sheets of paper. Instead I found myself walking toward the cabin with my head down. I still do not know what power Milne had, but the master had already subdued me so I was acting as meekly as any schoolboy.

I will not write many details of the next few days, for in truth there was only one event worth recording, and that I will come to presently. What I will say is that it was dominated, not by seamanship and a flood of salty adventures, but by reams of paper.

Despite my stated intention to enlarge my experience as a doctor, after three days in *Lady Balgay* nearly all I had experienced was dipping a pen in an inkwell and filling in forms. By the time we rounded Rattray Head north of Aberdeen I knew all about loading documents, crew lists, custom forms, lists of stores, food, water and coals, inventories of equipment and details of pay. My medical experience had amounted to dealing with half a dozen hangovers and a brash young man named Albert Torrie who was pleased to believe he had caught a venereal disease from a Dock Street prostitute. It was hardly an auspicious start for a man who had hoped for exotic diseases and intricate surgical problems.

I started each dismal day by staring at the papers that piled on my tiny, swaying desk and wishing myself back home. If this were to be my life for the next few months, I thought I would be far better on land. I sighed often and glanced upward, where a smoking lantern circled with the motion of the ship, and I swore, dreaming of Jennifer and that single night we had spent together. What would she be doing now?

Knowing that such thoughts could only make things worse, I forced them away and admitted, however reluctantly, that working with these tedious documents had taught me much about the vessel on which I was sailing. I had learned that *Lady Balgay* was a fifty-eight ton ketch, two masted and with a crew of eleven, including myself. I knew the name and function of every one of these men, from Walter Learmonth, a veteran of over twenty Arctic voyages to George Ross the Clydeside engine-driver, who had never been north before. I knew that Robert Mitchell, the cook and steward, was only fifteen while bearded John Pratt, a fifty-nine year old able-bodied seaman, was the oldest man on board. So far, few of the crew had spoken to me, contenting themselves with a casual nod or an uncommunicative grunt. The bald man, Tom Thoms, had not uttered another word, but had a tendency to spit and grumble.

I had also learned a great deal about the stores they had, from the raisins and cheese to the truly vicious seal clubs and harpoons and from Baxter's finest quality sailcloth to the much more mysterious fibs, marline spikes and lowery tows that seemed to be indispensable to the well-being of the voyage.

However, there was one striking episode, and that had been a curious prequel to many of the events that would unfold as we journeyed north. It had been on the day we mustered in the Firth of Tay before venturing on to the northern adventure. Captain Milne, with his cloth cap pushed well back on his head and a cynical smile on his man-trap mouth, had passed round a bottle of rum and insisted that everybody take a drink.

'That's the last sensible thing anybody will taste on this voyage, boys. The owner dictates that this vessel is run on teetotal principles.' He had glowered around the hands, meeting their gaze until every man had dropped his eyes. 'But now, raise your mugs and toast the success of the voyage!'

Every man had done so, from youthful Mitchell to ancient Pratt, and they had tossed back the rum in a single swallow before lifting the mugs high. I followed the rest, coughing on the raw spirit.

'Wives and sweethearts!' Ross the engineer roared.

'Wives and sweethearts,' the others echoed, with the prostitute-hunting Albert Torrie nudging young Mitchell in a secret joke.

'May they never meet,' Learmonth the bosun supplied what I guessed was a traditional finish, and the crew gave the required laugh.

'And now we'll request luck from the figurehead!' Captain Milne ordered, and sent every man scrambling forward to touch the naked wooden buttocks of the woman who thrust out in front of *Lady Balgay*.

It had seemed strange that such a small vessel as *Lady Balgay* had a figurehead, but nobody answered my enquiry until the bosun, Walter Learmonth, usually known as Leerie, wrapped a sinewy arm around my shoulders and took me forward.

'You see, Mr Cosgrove, figureheads are important for the morale of the ship. They carry her luck, you understand.'

'Well, I do not exactly understand, Mr Learmonth.' Used to being lectured by learned doctors with a string of letters after their name, I found it hard to be educated by a weather-battered man with the accent of a Hilltown tenement, but I forced myself to listen After all, I had signed on for different experiences. 'Could you tell me more?' I tried, but failed to suppress my shiver. 'And could we find somewhere warmer? We are shockingly exposed here.'

'If you wish, doctor.' Learmonth seemed amused by my feeling the cold, but he led me into the shelter of the funnel, the warmest section of the deck. 'In a manner of speaking, a figurehead is a good luck charm. Our one, the Naked Lady, is doubly important because her udders, begging your pardon sir, her bare breasts, can calm the sea. The sea being a male, you understand.'

'I understand,' I concealed my amusement at Learmonth's attempt to civilise his language.

'As long as we keep the Naked Lady happy by painting her regularly and making sure she's in good condition, *Lady Balgay* will be a lucky ship, but if we neglect her, then anything could happen.'

'I see,' I nodded, trying not a laugh at this blatant superstition. 'But are there not practical considerations against having a figurehead in the Arctic? Will it…she…the Naked Lady… not attract ice?'

'Some seem to think so, Mr Cosgrove,' Learmonth told me seriously. 'There was a Hull whaler called *Truelove* that had her figurehead removed for that very reason, but there was also *Arctic*, a Dundee ship with a Yakkie, an Eskimo, as figurehead. Aye, *Arctic* was a good ship, a lucky ship, doctor, and I believe that was due to her Yakkie. Some say the Arctic Bar was even named after her.'

'She must have been popular then,' I agreed. I could see old Pratt moving forward now, balancing on the bowsprit with the agility of a circus performer as he leaned forward to caress the Naked Lady. The crew were cheering, calling for the next man. This bonding with a carved piece of wood was exactly the sort of experience I had hoped for, and showed just how close these seamen were to their superstitious ancestors. I decided to delve further, for I had developed an interest in psychology and these sealers, these Greenlandmen, as I had heard them called, seemed to be first class examples of the primitive.

'But why? Why do we need such a symbol?'

Learmonth shook his head. 'Well, doctor, the origins are lost in the mists of time. They say that ships once needed a human sacrifice, so they were launched across a human body, or a man was executed and his head stuck on the prow to prove the sacrifice to Neptune, but somebody fooled the sea god with a carved head and the tradition has carried on ever since.' Learmonth shrugged, 'I don't know the real reason, doctor, but I do know the captain is watching us.'

'We'd better join the others, then,' I decided, wondering at the sudden relief in Learmonth's eyes.

Young Mitchell was next to be sent forward. Slim and agile, he had walked along the bowsprit with his hands in his pockets, showing off his skill as he sought to gain the acceptance of the crew.

'Go on, Rab!' That was Albert Torrie, the muscular young fireman and would-be Casanova who was nearest to Mitchell in years.

'If you're so clever, Mitchell, then you can hop! Bloody hop!' Ross, the chief engineer, gave caustic advice in his Clydeside tongue and others had joined in so the youngster was soon bouncing on one foot along the length of the bowsprit. When a rogue wave caught *Lady Balgay* and she gave a sudden lurch, Mitchell nearly overbalanced, but he reached for the foretopmast stay, swung above the sea for an instant and returned to his position on the bowsprit, to the cheers of his audience.

When he was correctly positioned Mitchell fastened both legs around the bowsprit and swung upside down to fondle the rounded buttocks of the Naked Lady.

'That's the way, Rab,' Torrie approved, 'now give her a big smacker! Kiss her arse, man!'

Mitchell did so as the crew roared approval, and he returned with his reputation enhanced, although old John Pratt was not amused.

'Maybe that was a bit disrespectful,' he said doubtfully, 'the Naked Lady deserves better than that,' but nobody listened to him; not then. There was a time coming when they would remember Rab Mitchell's actions and shudder in horror, but that was in the unforeseen future.

'You too, doctor!'

'What?' I looked up. I had thought that my position and medical training made me immune from such horseplay, but Captain Milne was staring at me with his hypnotic green eyes. 'You're next. Up you go!'

It had been amusing watching the crew balancing on the bowsprit, but as I looked forward on that gyrating length of slithery, rounded wood I felt suddenly sick. If I slipped, it would be a short drop into the great green rollers of the Tay, but with the crew cheering me on and Captain Milne's stern eyes watching, I knew I must.

I took a step forward and stopped. I knew I did not have the skill to balance on that slender spar, so instead I took the coward's route and knelt on top, holding on with both hands as I inched forward on the tiny platform beside the figurehead.

'I want you to go all the way, Doctor.' Captain Milne's voice was as unrelenting as an Arctic storm. 'All my crew must seek their luck from the Naked Lady.'

Lady Balgay suddenly bowed her head to the waves, taking on gallons of cold water that drenched me to the skin. I yelled at the shock and some of the crew laughed as I emerged, shaking my head free of the bitter water and gasping painfully for breath. I looked up, noting who they were, for I fervently hoped they reported to me for an injection sometime soon. I vowed to use my longest and bluntest needle and it would not be their arm into which I thrust it.

That thought restored some of my courage and I inched onward, feeling my knees slide on the wet surface, and, reaching forward, I touched the smooth, white painted wood of the figurehead's backside. It felt cold, completely unlike living flesh, but the crew still cheered.

'That's the way doctor! Touch the Naked Lady for luck!'

The hands applauded as I returned, and slapped my back in somewhat forward good fellowship that completely removed my dark thoughts of only a few minutes previously. Soutar mumbled something about the success of the voyage now being assured, but then Captain Milne had shoved his cap forward on his head, tossed the empty rum bottle over the side and roared everybody back to work.

As I returned to my reams of paper, Learmonth the bosun had shaken his head. 'The young lad shouldn't have done that,' he said.

'No good will come of it. Touching Her Ladyship for luck is one thing, but kissing her is something else. Old John was right; there'll be the devil to pay for that, mark my words.'

The words had only strengthened my belief that these men were swamped by their own superstition, but I had not met her then, and I was very young and very, very ignorant.

Chapter Six

Twenty years from now you will be more disappointed by the things that you didn't do than by the ones you did so. So throw off the bowlines. Sail away from the safe harbor. Catch the trade winds in your sails. Explore. Dream. Discover.
    Mark Twain

It was a day after we passed Rattray Head that the atmosphere in *Lady Balgay* seemed to change. I was contemplating the chipped stoneware jar of wood-bodied pens, wondering which one was least likely to blot and wondering when I had last used such archaic implements when a blast of shouted words upset my fragile concentration.

'Damn and blast and bugger! Call this a seagoing vessel? She's a bloody bathtub with a figurehead, damn her to hell!'

Welcoming the interruption, I laid down the pen. After only a few days at sea I was already accustomed to the use of foul language, but it was unusual for Captain Milne to indulge quite so liberally. When the captain lowered his moral tone to even more gutter language, I used a heavy rock as a paperweight and emerged from my dingy kennel but soon wished I had not as the wind on deck nearly took my breath away.

'What's the matter, Captain? Is there anything I can do?' I prayed for something medical, something more interesting than cut fingers and head colds.

'She's sailing like a pregnant cow in a force ten gale, lopsided as a drunken Irish washerwoman.' Milne's language became more colourful as he condemned the behaviour of his vessel.

Intrigued, for anything was better than scraping a cracked pen nib across damp paper, I looked around. *Lady Balgay* seemed no worse than normal as she heeled and battered her way north with the sea churning from her forefoot and frothing in her wake. 'What's the matter, Captain Milne?'

'This damned ship of your father-in-law,' Milne glared at me as if I had personally selected, built and launched *Lady Balgay*. 'She's sailing cockeyed. She rides light on the water and every breath of air sends her skittering like a virgin in a brothel.' He looked out to sea, swearing again. 'Sail her to Greenland? This bastarding boat would wallow sailing round the Greenmarket on a wet Saturday afternoon!'

I allowed myself a tolerant smile and spoke to the captain, man to man. 'Can anything be done about her behaviour, Captain?'

Milne shrugged, glaring into my eyes as if he hated me. Putting a hand to his cap, he pulled it down so the tattered peak nearly obscured his face. 'Aye. I'll add more ballast. Weigh her down so she doesn't dance to every tune the wind plays, and when we pick up a few score tons of seal oil, we can ditch the bastarding stuff.'

'I see. That sounds simple enough.' I nodded as if I understood every word, although in truth I barely comprehended any. 'From where can we buy this ballast?'

'Buy it?' Lifting his chin, Milne looked at me as if I had uttered some foul blasphemy. 'We don't buy ballast, Mister Cosgrove.' He shook his head, obviously affronted at shore-bound ignoramuses such as me pretending to know anything. 'Buy it, by Christ! We're not all bastarding millionaires! No, we have to work for our living on this clapped out shite boat! We must *obtain* the ballast, Mr Cosgrove.'

Taking two strides toward the taffrail, Milne shook his head in disgust. 'We'll dig the bastarding stuff from a bloody shoal bank. Ten tons of shingle ought to do the trick.' He turned suddenly, his eyes hard. 'You can help with a shovel, mister. It's about time you pulled your weight, after skulking in the cabin all voyage like some bloody schoolboy, scrape-scrape-scraping away with pen-and-ink, leaving seamen to do the real work.'

Now that was manifestly unfair. I began to protest until I noticed the glint in Captain Milne's eye and quickly closed my mouth. I was unsure if he was teasing me, or preparing for an argument, but I resolved not to give him satisfaction on either account. 'I'll fetch a shovel, sir.'

'You'll fetch four bloody shovels,' Captain Milne corrected, 'you can't shift ten tons of shingle on your own. Not with your lily-white clerk's hands.' Turning abruptly, he shouted a volley of orders that saw *Lady Balgay* alter course, heading more to the west. 'Buy it by Christ! Where the fuck did we get him from?'

The wind blew chillingly from the north, flicking the top from the waves so that the sea appeared like a badly ruffled grey and white carpet, constantly in surging motion. As Captain Milne had said, *Lady Balgay* was tossing madly, one second riding high on the swell, the next crashing into a trough, with her hull shaking, rattling every loose fitting and shifting anything not lashed down around the deck. I glanced upward, where the masts gyrated against ragged grey clouds, and I fought the unaccustomed heave of my stomach. The last thing *Lady Balgay* needed was a seasick surgeon and the last thing I wanted was to further reveal my nautical ineptitude to the crew.

Soutar the helmsman swore in unconscious imitation of the captain as he stood in the stern, both hands white-knuckled on the varnished spokes of the wheel.

'Where are we?' I had to shout above the shriek of the wind through the rigging, the banging of loose gear and the constant slap of waves against the bouncing hull.

Concentrating on the binnacle in front of him, Soutar said nothing. Despite the cold, there were beads of sweat oozing from his forehead while the muscles of his forearms writhed with the effort of keeping *Lady Balgay* on the correct heading.

'That's Orkney to port,' bald headed Thoms pointed to a stern coastline of low dark cliffs, from which a regular procession of waves boomed. 'And that's the bloody Arctic up there,' he indicated northwest with a languid wave of his hand, 'where all this wind is coming from.'

'Are we going to land in Orkney?'

Thoms shook his head. 'No.' He seemed to have the knack of shouting without raising his voice, so every word was carried clearly to me. 'There's a skerry a bit offshore. The Captain is going to send us ashore in a dinghy so we can collect shingle as ballast.'

'What?' I glanced overboard. Grey waves leaped the length of the hull, smashing angrily at the timbers with their flaking green paint. *Lady Balgay* shuddered with each new assault, and I imagined rowing a small boat in such seas. 'Is that safe?'

'It's safer than sailing the bloody Greenland Sea with an improperly trimmed ketch, mister.' Captain Milne had appeared from nowhere and looked at me with unconcealed contempt. 'When you came aboard, Mr Cosgrove, you told me you were willing to do anything, didn't you?'

I nodded reluctantly, wondering what my loose mouth had condemned me to.

'Aye, well there are only two things on board a ship: duty and mutiny. All that you are ordered to do is duty. All that you refuse is mutiny.' Captain Milne leaned closer. 'Well, Mister Cosgrove; are you afraid to do your duty?'

The accusation of fear stiffened my resolve, as was no doubt intended. 'Of course not, Captain. I am only concerned for the safety of the ship.'

Milne's brief snort may have contained humour, but I could only detect derision. 'The safety of the ship is my concern you young pup. You just obey orders and we'll get along very well.'

'Yes, sir,' I thought I should say more, but Captain Milne just grunted again, jammed his cap harder on his head and stalked forward, automatically testing every line and stay that he passed.

Replacing Soutar at the wheel, old John Pratt nodded to me. 'Going for more ballast are we? About bloody time, eh?' Checking the set of the sails, he glanced to port, where the dark smear of Orkney was more distinct. What did you say this place was, Tam?'

'Gass Skerry,' Thoms told him bluntly, and Pratt started and swore foully.

'You're crazy man! Gass! We can't go there!' I could see that only his years of experience kept Pratt from releasing his hold of the varnished spokes.

'Captain's orders,' Thoms defended the obviously unpopular decision.

Pratt took a step backward, but his hands still held the spokes. 'I'll not set foot on that place,' he stated flatly. 'Does the captain not know the stories?'

'Either he doesn't know or he doesn't believe them, John,' Thoms appeared equally uncomfortable with the decision. 'But Gass does have good shingle, perfect for ballast.'

'No,' Pratt shook his head. 'I'll go to the captain and tell him. He'll listen to me, eh?'

'You'll say nothing, John,' Thoms told him, nearly smiling. 'You haven't the grit to question the captain.'

'What stories?' I asked. 'What's wrong with Gass Skerry? It is dangerous?'

Pratt looked at me, but a nudge from Thoms prevented him from speaking.

'What stories?' I repeated, but there was a yell from forward and young Mitchell scurried to me with a bleeding hand to be stitched. By the time I returned on deck Captain Milne was back in his customary position in the stern and I knew that Pratt would say nothing in front of authority.

Orkney rose before us in a display of low cliffs and recently ploughed fields. The farmhouses were lonely under a graveyard sky, but oxymoronically cosy with the drift of smoke from chimneys. A score of fishing boats clustered companionably a mile or so to the south.

'There,' Milne pointed with his chin. 'That's where you're headed, Mister Cosgrove.'

Gass Skerry was around half a mile offshore, a great curving bank of shingle and rock from which a straggle of sea birds soared. It looked innocuous enough to me, save for the breakers that crashed along the shore and the never-ending suck and surge of the sea.

'God save us all,' Thoms repeated endlessly. 'God save us all.' But when I looked at him he closed his mouth and said nothing, although his knuckles were white on *Lady Balgay's* rail.

'Captain Milne,' Pratt had been ordered to go with me, but he shook his head, staring at the skerry as he obviously gathered his courage to speak. 'We can't go there, sir. Don't you know the stories?'

'What?' Milne's face darkened. 'Are you challenging my command of this ship?'

Pratt stood with his head down and his hands twisting together in front of him. He was the most humble of mariners, always willing to obey any order, so I knew it had taken a lot for him to speak up. Captain Milne stepped to within a foot from him, nearly pressing his face against that of the old seaman.

'No, sir,' Pratt shook his head, 'but Gass Skerry...'

'You'll obey my bloody orders the instant I give them!' Captain Milne kept his voice low and those uncanny green eyes fixed on Pratt's. His hands were deep in the pockets of his tattered jacket and his chin out thrust. 'Get in that boat and do as you're told.' Although it hardly rose above a whisper there was no mistaking the authority in the captain's voice.

I could see Pratt hesitated and I could nearly read his mind as he debated whether to obey orders or remain on board. He glanced from Captain Milne to the shingle bank on which the surf bounced and echoed.

'Is there nowhere else, Captain?' There was nearly a whine in his voice.

'No.'

'Come on, John,' Thoms urged quietly. 'There's no help for it.'

'But, Captain,' Pratt gave a last despairing plea. 'You must know the stories, eh?'

'I know superstitious nonsense, Pratt!' Captain Milne looked away for a second, then adjusted his cap so it sat square on top of his head. 'Listen John, I do know the tales, but I don't believe them, and neither should you. I also know that *Lady Balgay* is riding light, so we need to trim her if we're to reach the seal fisheries, and this skerry has the finest ballast for two hundred miles.'

'Yes, Captain.' Pratt nodded. He obviously appreciated Captain Milne's tactful explanation. 'But the stories?'

'Damn and blast the stories, Pratt!' Captain's Milne's brittle patience snapped. 'Get in that bloody boat and do your duty! You too Mr Surgeon! Move!'

I nodded assent as, moaning softly, Pratt gave a last imploring glance to the captain and nodded reluctant acceptance. He fingered the scrimshaw mermaid that was suspended on a leather thong around his neck and muttered something under his breath.

Watching him closely, Captain Milne grunted but did not leave his position on the deck.

Both the small dinghy and the larger whaleboat sat bottom-up on deck, but it took only minutes for the hands to upend the dinghy and lower it over the side. While Thoms held the boat secure with a boathook, Pratt, nearly sixty but more agile than most landsmen of twenty, scrambled over the rail and took the forward oars. Mitchell followed, holding out a hand to help me. With every eye in *Lady Balgay* watching, I moved as quickly as I could to avoid becoming a figure of fun.

'Take your time, Mr Cosgrove,' Thoms advised, showing the first concern that I had experienced since coming on board. 'No sense in taking a tumble when you can take your time.'

'Mr Cosgrove,' Captain Milne leaned down from the rail, a mere three feet away, 'you take charge. Bring back as much shingle ballast as you can carry, and don't listen to Pratt's nonsense. Don't allow him to get off with anything. You understand?'

Glancing at Pratt, I could only nod, knowing that I was certainly not qualified to lead these hard-bitten men. 'Yes, captain.'

'Aye. He's a good seaman, but...' Milne did not finish the sentence. 'And mind you don't capsize the boat, you hear?'

'Yes, Captain,' I repeated.

'These boats cost money and I won't be buying another this side of the Tay, that's for certain sure.' Spitting into the sea, Milne turned away.

I had thought that *Lady Balgay* had been unsteady, but she seemed a haven of security compared to the mad gyrations of the dinghy. I gasped in sudden agitation, grabbing at the bulwark for balance and allowed Thoms to settle me on a thwart.

'All right, Doctor. Sit yourself down now.'

Taking a deep breath to steady my frayed nerves, I grasped an oar, hoping that I would not be disgraced in this simple nautical skill.

'Have you rowed before, sir?' Thoms asked, and looked relieved when I nodded false confidence. 'Then you'll be fine. Where on the shoal shall we beach?'

'Wherever is easiest, Mr Thoms.' I had long decided it would be best to treat the crew with as much respect as I could, in the somewhat forlorn hope they would do the same for me. 'I'll be guided by whatever advice you care to give.' I looked to Pratt for help, but the bearded man looked away, saying nothing. I noticed that his hands were trembling and wondered if he was genuinely nervous about landing at Gass

Skerry, or if he was still suffering withdrawal symptoms from the alcoholic excesses of shore life.

'It's a bit breezy!' I tried again as a wave exploded against the prow of the boat and sent a bucketful of spray inboard. Nobody replied, but young Robert Mitchell gave a small nod and a nervous half smile.

A pair of oystercatchers circled overhead as we approached the shoal, and a host of black-backed gulls screamed in discordant chorus around the boat. Pratt glanced up, ignoring the spindrift that spattered from the prow as he handled his oar with a casual nonchalance that did not square with his unequivocal anxiety. 'They birds are warning us about something.'

Thoms looked upward to the lowering sky. 'Maybe they're saying the weather's about to change.'

'No, it's not that, Tommy. They're warning us not to land. Should we not return to *Lady Balgay*, Dr Cosgrove?'

I hesitated, not being used to giving nautical advice. 'I'm afraid not, Mr Pratt. We must all follow the captain's orders.'

'But Dr Cosgrove…'

'Shut up, John. The doctor can't do anything about it. We'll be all right.' Thoms nodded to me. 'You just work your oar, Doctor, and leave the rest to us.'

I nodded, thankful for Thoms' intervention, and tried to concentrate on rowing. With the swell so steep, I found it hard to get the angle of the oar correct as I pulled through the water, and I was terrified that I would catch a succession of crabs that would lead to ridicule from these leather-faced men.

The gulls massed above us, beaks open, wings spread like wavering white crucifixes, their eyes unblinking, remorseless. One swooped downward, nearly catching Pratt with its talons.

'They're definitely upset,' Pratt said, resting on his oars as he ducked.

'They're only bloody birds,' Mitchell sounded scornful. 'They can't tell us anything.'

Pratt glowered at him. 'Thank you for your unwanted opinion,' he said, 'gained after days of experience.' He spat into the wind. 'You have to read the signs at sea, young Rab. Listen to the birds and the wind; understand the sky and most of all, feel the ship or you won't last very long. That's what's wrong with you youngsters nowadays with your new-fangled gramophones, steam ships and electric lights. Spoiled, that's what you are.' His glower included me, as if youth was to blame for every ill in the world.

Mitchell coloured and ducked his head, sulking in shamed silence as a single gull landed on the prow, preening its feathers as it watched the toiling men.

'Now that bastard is deciding which one of us to peck at first,' Pratt said gloomily, but nobody replied.

Gass Skerry was larger than I had thought; a great semi circle of shifting shingle and gaunt black rock all fringed by crashing surf. For a moment I was back in the university anatomy lectures, with the shovels posing as a blunt scalpel, the rock as the bones of a corpse and the shingle as the decaying flesh. The thought was unpleasant and I shook it away and concentrated on finding the best place to land. The seaward side was obviously useless, for the surf scoured savagely at the shingle and withdrew, sucking backward so violently I knew the dingy would be overturned.

'We're not landing there,' I announced and steered around the northern tip of the skerry until we could ease into the lee side. The water calmed immediately, and the boat glided in the sudden shelter. Half a mile away, the Mainland of Orkney beckoned with the farms now welcoming and the fields more familiar than the sea.

'Shall we bring her ashore here, Mr Cosgrove?' Thoms asked diplomatically and I nodded.

'It looks best to me.'

We hit the shingle with a rush, the keel digging deep into the sea-smoothed pebbles, and the men leaped out, yelling for me to join them and help drag the dinghy away from murmuring waves. Again Pratt fingered his scrimshaw mermaid.

'Don't haul the boat too far up,' Thoms warned. 'She'll be a damned sight heavier when we come to pull her off.' He looked around, his face distorted as he slithered up the sliding shingle. 'Ugly place this.'

I was more ambivalent; ugliness was in the mind, rather than in the eye of the beholder and this skerry could have been far worse. When a sudden shaft of sunlight lightened the atmosphere I found the place fascinating, a place of black rock and variegated grey and white stones set against the silver and blue backdrop of the sea. In the centre, rising high above anything else and surmounting a large cairn, a single pole nodded to the blast of the wind.

'I don't think this place is ugly at all,' I gave a tentative opinion, looking for support from Mitchell.

'It's ugly all right,' Pratt spoke first. 'It's ugly in every possible way.' He swore as he unloaded the shovels from the boat, testing them for weight and choosing the lightest before he combed his beard with stubby fingers. 'It's not a place I would have chosen for ballast, that's for certain.' He shrugged as if attempting to push the fear from his mind; it remained to haunt his eyes. 'I only hope that the story doesn't spread.'

'What story?' Mitchell asked, flinching when Pratt raised an admonitory fist.

'Never you mind, you work shy little bastard. You just get on with the shovelling.' Pratt paused, sliding his shovel just under the surface of the shingle. 'Right, we'll just throw it directly into the boat; makes it easier that way.'

About to nod agreement, I stopped. Although I was very aware of my lack of years and experience, I had no intention of allowing any mere foc'sle seaman, even one with Pratt's grey hairs, to make decisions that should belong to me. 'No,' I spoke loudly to carry my voice above the noise of the waves. 'We will fill the sacks I have brought.'

'You've brought sacks?' Pratt stared at me in disbelief, 'for bloody ballast?'

Thoms shook his head. 'The captain won't like that, Mr Cosgrove. He won't like that at all.'

'It will be easier to carry in sacks,' I explained as patiently as I could, 'and we'll dig over there,' I pointed to the cairn that rose prominently in front of us, where the seagulls voiced a rising clamour of protest.

'Not there.' Pratt's voice was high pitched and for a moment I thought he was going to run back to the boat as he glanced first at the cairn and then behind him. Instead he shook his head so violently I swear I heard his teeth rattle. 'Not ever from there.'

'It's easier,' I pointed out, reasonably I thought. 'There's less bending so it's easier for the back.'

'Jesus!' Pratt screwed up his face in disgust. 'Do you any have bloody idea what you're doing?'

'I have the idea that Captain Milne put me in command,' I reminded, lifting my shovel. 'Come along Robert; you can hold the bag for me, while Mr Thoms and Mr Pratt work together.'

Glancing toward Pratt as if for confirmation, Mitchell ducked his head and followed, clutching a small pile of sacks.

'I'm not going near that place!' Pratt shouted, 'and neither should you!'

Ignoring him, I winked at Mitchell and carried on, with my boots sliding on the shingle and the wind ruffling pleasantly through my hair.

The cairn was taller than I had expected, a full eight feet in height, with a base of large stones that tapered to a crumbling apex of small pebbles. 'I wonder what this was for,' I tried to make conversation with Mitchell. The stones shifted under my boots when I thrust my shovel into the shingle, 'maybe it is some sort of marker?'

Mitchell held open the sack. 'Maybe, sir. I don't know.' He was silent for a few moments as I filled his sack. 'It could be a sea mark, Doctor Cosgrove, something to help fishing boats find their way home.'

'You could be right, Robert. It could have been built here to mark the skerry.' I shovelled a load of small pebbles into Mitchell's sack and raised my voice against the wind. 'What do you think, Mr Thoms? What was this mound for?'

Thoms looked over. He was digging a good thirty feet away, with Pratt keeping his back turned in protest as he held open a sack. 'I'm not sure,' he said, but there was something in his voice that convinced me he was lying.

'Do you have any idea, Mr Pratt?'

'I think you'd be best to leave it well alone,' Pratt said. He turned around but did not look directly at me, or at the cairn. 'You'll not find me touching that thing, Mr Cosgrove, and if you've half the sense you should have, you'll leave it well alone. Bloody well alone.'

Just as Pratt finished complaining, I had a very unsettling experience that stayed with me for the remainder of my stay on that skerry. Perhaps it was the angle of the light, but for an instant I thought I saw a woman walking across the shingle toward me, her face shaded but sunlight silhouetting her statuesque body as through a transparent dress. I blinked and glanced away, but when I looked again she had vanished; there was nothing but the sky, the shingle and the circling, screaming seabirds.

'Did you see that?' I asked, but Pratt was still swearing foully, resolutely staring out to sea, where a mist was rising between the skerry and *Lady Balgay*.

'See what? I can see that bloody mist!'

'All right, Mr Pratt,' I decided. I was not quite sure what to make of Pratt, but that vision was a bit disturbing. I shook away the feeling and decided that either I was sleeping badly or I needed a tonic. All the same, I thought it best not to antagonise the men further. 'If you are so adamant, we'll just take the shingle from round about, rather than the cairn itself.'

'A bit further away would be better, Mr Cosgrove.' Pratt was shaking his head with surprising obstinacy. 'As far away as possible would be best of all.'

'We'll take it from here.' I made my voice as severe as possible, for I had bent far enough to this old man's superstition, and that mist was getting thicker. I had no desire to be stuck on this godforsaken island if visibility deteriorated and the tide rose. 'Come on; the captain is waiting.' I thrust in the shovel but staggered at the weight of the load. I was a doctor, not a labourer, but I must show no weakness to the men.

At least one of the men was not as naive as I had hoped. 'Dr Cosgrove,' Thoms said tactfully. 'It's not right that you should do the manual work. Best leave that to young Rab.'

About to uphold my authority by persisting with my shovelling, I noticed the expression of near terror on Pratt's face and relented. Thoms was correct: I had no need to prove anything; furthermore, my duty was to care for the mental stability of these men just as much as their physical well-being. 'If this cairn is here as a marker,' I announced grandly, 'maybe it would be best to dig elsewhere. We don't want the pole to topple for lack of support.'

I was more than curious when I saw Pratt's sudden relief.

'That's a good idea, Doctor. The shingle is better over here.' The old man guided me to his oh-so-much superior shingle, nearly dragging me away from the central mound.

'You dig, Rab, and the doctor can hold the sacks, eh?'

Seagulls circled as we worked, endlessly screaming, occasionally diving so that their dark shadow flitted briefly across the backs of the men who toiled below.

'I wish these bloody birds would go away,' Pratt glanced upward, his eyes rolling back in his head. 'I don't like their constant crying, like some damned soul calling for eternal rest.'

'They're just birds, John.' Thoms rested for a second on the handle of the shovel. 'They're nothing but bloody, useless bloody birds.'

'So why can't they go and catch some fish or something?' Pratt ducked as a gull swooped low overhead, its outspread wings nearly touching the top of his head. 'Did you see that? It tried to peck my eyes out.'

'Wish it would peck your bloody tongue out,' Thoms said. 'It might keep you quiet for a while. Moan and complain; that's all you ever do!'

I hid my grin; gratuitous insults were so normal on *Lady Balgay* that I considered them as healthy banter. I had been right to move away from the cairn for the ballast; the men were obviously more cheerful for the sake of those few yards. I did not like the look of that mist though, hazing the sea and creeping slowly toward us. I wondered if the woman had disappeared into it and grunted at my own imagination. Obviously, I told myself, I had spent too much time in Pratt's company.

Light rain was falling as we dragged the boat back into the water before loading the sacks. Despite the late-winter chill we were all sweating, although the men were used to working every bit as hard on board *Lady Balgay*.

'Ballast, by Christ! I'll ballast Captain bloody Milne, given the chance.' Thoms hauled another sack onto the dinghy, swearing mightily as Pratt mumbled under his breath and fingered his scrimshaw mermaid. Only Mitchell said nothing, but I think that he was more overawed by the older men than anything else. When all the sacks were on the boat, I nodded to Thoms.

'That's the last now, Mr Thoms. We'll be back on board soon.'

Thoms spat into the sea. 'Aye. So what? We're just exchanging one type of work for another. Why did I not choose to work in a mill?'

'They wouldn't bloody have a bald old bugger like you, that's why.' Pratt glowered at him. 'Come on Tommy, let's get away from here.'

Chapter Seven

NORTH SEA
FEBRUARY 1914

He that will not sail until all dangers are over will never put to sea
Thomas Fuller

As Thoms had predicted, Captain Milne snarled at us for the time we had taken, and for loading sacks rather than just shovelling the shingle directly into the boat. 'Bloody longshore amateurs,' he spat over the side and thrust his cap forward over his eyes before jerking his thumb at Learmonth the bosun. 'Leerie, take two men and the whaler; bring me another load.'

'Aye, sir,' Learmonth nodded to Donaldson and Mackie, two men so inseparable they could almost have been brothers. 'You two are with me.'

'We shouldn't have taken it,' Pratt was still unhappy as he dragged the first sack on board Lady Balgay. When he released it the shingle slithered onto the deck and lay damp and glistening under the cold sun. 'Not from there.'

'Will you keep your mouth shut?' Captain Milne snarled at him. 'You'll unsettle the men with your nonsense. Now, give a hand here.'

'They deserve to know,' Pratt backed off from the next sack, his hands held in front of him, palm upward, 'and I'm not touching that. Not ever. It should not be on the ship.' He faced the captain. 'It's still not too late, Captain. But we can't just throw the damned stuff overboard. We'll have to replace it exactly where we got it.'

'Why?' I had wanted to ask that question ever since I first heard Pratt complain, but now I could not contain myself. 'What is the story of Gass Skerry, Mr Pratt?' and Pratt's eyes brightened at the chance to unburden himself.

'It's old…' he began, but Captain Milne stepped in front of him, rocking back on his heels so he was within an inch of the taller man and with his stare stabbing into Pratt's eyes.

'You're a superstitious old bugger, Pratt, and I warn you to keep your nonsense to yourself.'

'The lads ought to know,' Pratt insisted, until Captain Milne leaned closer, forcing Pratt to retreat until his back was hard against the mainmast. The captain dropped his voice to a menacing hiss.

'If you repeat one word of your fairy tales, Pratt, I'll personally gut you, and throw the remains to the fish. You know that I mean exactly what I say, don't you?'

There was a moment's silence as Pratt licked his lips. He looked from me to Captain Milne and back.

'Don't you, Pratt?' Captain Milne balled his fists. His eyes were cloudy green.

'Yes, Captain.' Pratt nodded, his head moving in a succession of rapid, uncoordinated jerks. Sweat was running from his forehead.

'All right. Here's to help you remember.' Without any seeming effort, Milne landed a succession of swinging punches into Pratt's stomach, so the older seamen doubled up, gasping with pain. As he slid down the mast, Milne stepped back, aimed and landed a vicious kick into his ribs, following up by pressing the sole of his boot on Pratt's throat.

'You won't forget, will you, Pratt?'

'For God's sake...' I stepped forward to stop the violence, but Learmonth grabbed my shoulder.

'Best not interfere, Mr Cosgrove.'

'He'll kill him...' I began.

'No.' Learmonth shook his head. 'Think where we are, Mr Cosgrove, and what our situation is. There's no King's Regulations here, and no policeman at the corner of the street if things go wrong. There's only the captain's authority, or anarchy. Duty or mutiny, remember? Is there any other way Captain Milne can exercise his will?'

I restrained myself, looking around; this was not the hushed halls of Edinburgh University, nor even the policed streets of Dundee. Bleak grey waves rose on three sides, hissing as the wind whipped off the tops, tumbling in on themselves and gathering strength for a renewed assault on *Lady Balgay*. On the fourth side, Gass Skerry brooded under its booming surf, a trap to mariners and a vicious full stop to hundreds of miles of ocean. Anarchy out here would mean a horrible death of broken men and splintered wood. If the captain's authority was overturned, there was nothing to replace it. However brutal Learmonth's advice was, he was probably correct; primitive places required primitive action.

Captain Milne stepped back, breathing easily. 'Are there any questions, Pratt?'

'No, sir.' Pratt looked up, his eyes wild and both hands at his throat.

'Good. That's settled then. Now, empty the damned sacks into the holds, and carefully, in case the stuff tears a hole in my ship!'

'Yes, Captain.' Pratt nodded weakly. I lent him my arm to help him struggle upright.

'Get it done now!' Captain Milne's sudden bellow echoed around the ship.

Knocking back the battens that secured the hatch cover, Thoms and Pratt stared into the hollow blackness of the hold as the wafting air brought a stench of dampness. Dragging the first sack across the deck, Thom upended it so the shingle roared onto the bare planks ten feet below, spreading out in a grey and white mass, half seen in the dark.

The second sack load followed, and the third, each one over a hundredweight, each one helping the trim of *Lady Balgay*, but each one adding to Pratt's patent misery.

'Speed that up, damn you!' Captain Milne's roar shook the halliards. 'Here's the bosun nearly finished and you're still emptying sacks! I want to catch this wind while we can!'

It took the rest of that day to load the ballast, and I was utterly exhausted when at last I withdrew to my bunk. I waited for a few moments for Pratt to come to have his injuries attended, but he seemed to accept them as part of shipboard life and did not complain.

'He'll be all right,' Learmonth told me, unconcerned. 'He's been at sea a long time. Let it pass now.'

About to protest, I realised that nobody else had even mentioned the incident and gave a reluctant nod. It was obvious that I had a lot to learn about working with seamen.

In such a small craft, living accommodation was scarce, so I shared a cabin with Learmonth the bosun, who also doubled as mate. Little more than a cubbyhole, six feet long by five broad, the cabin had less than five feet of headroom except under the deck light, which allowed an extra four inches. I am a whisper less than five feet ten so I had to move in a half crouch at all times or risk concussion from frequent collision with the deck beams above. As the bunk and the desk occupied nearly all the room, Learmonth and I took it in turns to sleep, sharing the watch keeping duties. Already after only a week at sea, the bedding was damp and the cabin stank of wet clothes, wet boots and wet socks.

To be honest, I was relieved that Pratt had not turned up, for I was in no fit state to attend a patient. I groaned, massaging my aching muscles, and collapsed on to the bunk without removing my boots or clothes. This was not how I had imagined life as a surgeon aboard a sealing vessel, but all the same, I knew I was lucky, for the rest of the crew crowded into the forecastle, or foc'sle as they pronounced it. This was a cabin that was only twice the size of mine but which held eight men. I tried not to imagine the squalor in which the crew lived as I closed my eyes. Instead I saw shovels hacking into piles of shingle, a grey sea that stretched forever and, shadowy at the periphery of my vision, the shape of an approaching woman. I knew I was not yet dreaming, but the figure was neither real nor unreal, an ephemeral creature whose origins I could not fathom.

The fear was immediate and unreasonable, yet tinged with some sensual fascination that was nearly as powerful. I knew without question that she was the woman from the skerry, and I tried to shout out even as I watched those wide hips swaying tantalisingly and her head held quizzically to one side.

'Who are you?' My voice was little more than a whisper in the void as she approached, walking with a well-defined roll. 'What do you want?'

Although she came closer I could not make out her face. It was if she was veiled, hiding her identity from me even as she offered me the pleasures of her body. I called out again.

'Jennifer? Is that you?' I reached out for her yearningly, but then somebody took hold of my shoulder and shook savagely.

'Your watch!' Captain Milne stood over me, smiling sourly as water dripped slowly from his cap to form a small puddle on the single blanket. 'Just keep the same course and call me if anything untoward happens.' He nodded, eyes grave. 'Don't try anything on your own, Mr Cosgrove.'

The woman had vanished and chill reality blasted in from the open door of the cabin. 'Is that the time already?' I staggered up and swore loudly as I banged my head on the solid deck beams above.

'That's the time.'

Captain Milne stepped aside as the bosun took my place on the bunk, folded his arms behind his head and closed his eyes. 'I'll see you at dawn, Mr Surgeon.'

The sea seemed to be particularly malicious that night, tossing *Lady Balgay* in a series of lumbering jolts that sent me staggering from the cabin to the stern. Momentarily hunching in the imaginary shelter of the smokestack, I wished fervently that I was home in Dundee with my wife. That glimpse of the veiled woman in my dream had brought everything hauntingly back, and if I inhaled deeply I could imagine Jennifer's perfume, rather than the tar, soot and damp canvas smell of the ketch.

God but I missed her; her touch, her voice, her scent, her presence, her humour and that low, throaty chuckle the meaning of which I was just beginning to understand.

I listened to the moan of the wind through the rigging and the constant slap of waves against the hull, fought the churning sickness in my stomach and waited in passive misery for my watch to pass. I had expected that life at sea would be hard work, but had hoped for a tinge of romance, instead there was nothing but the constant tedium of paperwork combined with sheer muscle ripping labour. At best I was a petty clerk; at worst an itinerant, undervalued labourer.

Why in God's name had I ever come out here?

As a rogue wave baptised my watch with a cold bathful of the North Atlantic, I lurched and swore, using words that would never have entered my head a few days before. At that time I did not realise how much I was changing, but now, looking back, I can see how *Lady Balgay* was altering me in subtle, ugly steps so I was descending the long ladder from gentleman to what I am today. She was the catalyst, that terrible, tantalising, terrifying siren from the skerry. God help us all.

I approached the helmsman as he stood watching the stars above and the compass in the binnacle.

'Your watch, Dr Cosgrove?'

'It is;' I recognised Soutar, one of the steadiest men aboard.

'Aye,' Soutar nodded. 'You'll be all right.' There was a moment's pause as he made a minute adjustment to his course. 'I don't think it's right for a doctor to be doing the manual tasks.' He hesitated for a second and shrugged, shifting a quid of tobacco from one side of his mouth to the other. 'Still, I expect the captain knows best.' He allowed me to place a hand on the spokes of the wheel. 'Can you feel the way she handles now? She's deeper in the water, so she's got more of a bite. That's what this new ballast has done for her.'

'She was too light before,' I reminded, still half asleep.

'That's for certain sure,' Soutar nodded his head but did not meet my eye as he repeated, 'I expect the captain knows best. That's why he's the captain.'

I could tell he was unhappy and decided to probe a little. 'What do you think of that affair with Pratt?' I could trust Soutar to steer a straight course even while he spoke.

He shrugged. 'Pratt shouldn't have argued with the captain. Everybody knows that you don't disagree with Captain Milne.' He checked the stars again and spat a long stream of brown tobacco juice into the wind.

'Is the captain that dangerous?' I asked.

'He's not a man you want to cross.' Soutar said solemnly. 'He's a fine seaman though; none better. If anybody can find seals, Captain Milne can. That's why he's the last surviving sealing captain in Dundee. He always brings the ship home, and he always finds the seal fish.'

When Soutar ducked his head to the binnacle, a gust of chill wind sent stinging spindrift across the taffrail to splash on to my back. I shivered, very aware of the huge expanse of sea all around.

'I am glad about that,' I tried to smile, which is not easy when one is wet and cold. 'I made a promise to my wife that I would come home safe.'

The wind had increased even since I had come on deck, and now a squall struck us, howling through the rigging like a tormented soul. Soutar placed his feet even more firmly on the deck and tightened his grip on the wheel. His knuckles shone white against the varnished wood.

'Well, you're in good hands, Mr Cosgrove, as long as you do what you're told.' He looked upward and all around. 'I wouldn't like to be John Pratt though. Not now.'

'Why is that?' I waited until Soutar relaxed a little, although his eyes were never still as they checked the stars, the rigging and the compass in a ceaseless circle of movement. However calm he appeared, Soutar was aware of everything that was happening in the ship and within the radius of his vision. 'Why would you not like to be Mr Pratt?'

Soutar shook his head, frowning. 'Captain Milne won't forget John stood up to him, that's why. He's not finished with old John yet. Not ever on this voyage.' He glanced at me again. 'Don't argue with Captain Milne, Mr Cosgrove,' he repeated once more. 'Not if you value your health.'

I nodded, reliving again the sudden violence of Milne's attack on Pratt, and the manner in which the old seaman had accepted the blows without retaliating. It was more surprising because Pratt was taller by at least four inches and must have accumulated a vast amount of brawling experience throughout his life. 'I'll remember that,' I said.

Soutar shifted his tobacco and squirted another stream over the side. 'Best to, Mr Cosgrove.' He was silent for a long moment but when he spoke, his voice was low, as if he was scared of being overheard on that wind-tormented deck in the wastes of the northern Atlantic.

'We should be glad that Captain Milne is in charge, Mr Cosgrove, for some of the boys are unhappy to sail on a ship with nothing to drink; and there was that crow on the deckhouse just before we sailed...' he shook his head again. 'And then that nonsense over the ballast. I only hope that this is a short voyage.'

I looked at him, shaking my head. I knew that seamen used to be superstitious, but surely not in this twentieth century? Perhaps there were still some old salts such as John Pratt, but he was a product of an earlier age, a nineteenth century seaman nearing the end of his time at sea. 'I am sure that we'll be all right.'

Soutar adjusted the wheel slightly as the wind altered. 'I've been at sea for upwards of twenty years, Mister Cosgrove, and I've seen many bad things, but I've never been on a dry ship and...' he looked astern, where our wake was white and straight across the dark sea. 'I'll be glad to get back to the Tay, Doctor, and that's all that I'm saying.'

In the overcast, gusty night there was no need to hide my smile, but I was a surgeon, trained to obey the laws of science, and then I had no place for fantasy, superstition or luck, good or bad. 'Well, Mr Soutar, let's hope that you are wrong and we enjoy an uneventful voyage.'

Soutar eyed me for only a second before transferring his attention to the ship. 'Aye, Mr Cosgrove, we can only hope.' He was silent for a while, and then glanced to starboard. 'Sweet God in heaven, Mr Cosgrove! Look at that!'

A subtle shaft of moonlight had penetrated the clouds to gleam on the white sails of another ship.

'Where the hell did she come from? And she's making straight for us!'

Chapter Eight

ATLANTIC OCEAN

MARCH 1914

29 August 1874 This morning before breakfast I went away with the second mate, bear shooting; we shot three... we were away from the ship forty minutes only.

Thomas T Macklin, *Journal of a Voyage to Davis Strait aboard SS Narwhal 1874*

'Sweet Christ and all his angels!' Soutar could only stare at the gleaming pyramid of canvas that had appeared out of nowhere and was now thrusting silently toward us. 'It's a ghost ship, that's what it is!'

For a moment I felt the small hairs at the back of my neck prickle, but I shook away the irrational fear. 'It's only another ship,' I tried to appear calm. 'Alter course and we'll avoid her. Anyway, the *Flying Dutchman's* off the Cape of Good Hope, not in the North Atlantic.'

'There's more than one ghost ship on the sea!' There was panic in Soutar's voice. Dropping the wheel, he backed away, 'Johnnie Pratt was right!'

Grabbing for the madly spinning spokes, I heard the rustle of the sails as they spilled wind and *Lady Balgay* veered to port. I swore foully when the ketch dipped her head and water surged over the prow and washed ankle deep and bitter cold over the deck.

'What the hell's happening out there?' Captain Milne thrust out of the deckhouse with his braces flapping around his waist but the cloth cap firm on his head. 'You! Mr soft-hands-surgeon! I should have known! I said to keep the same course and call me if anything happened and you've done neither, mister. We're three points to port and there's a damned great three-master bearing so close to us I can smell the cheese on their square-headed Dutchy breath!'

Roughly shoving me aside, Captain Milne took control of the wheel.

I glanced at Soutar, who seemed to have recovered some of his equanimity. 'There's a sailing ship approaching, Captain. We altered course to be safe.' I was aware of Soutar's grateful nod.

'Aye. I noticed, but I ordered you to keep the same course.' Captain Milne stared at the distant sail and grunted, straightening his cap. 'You may have been a bit premature in your alteration, Mr Cosgrove, but I see what you mean. She doesn't seem to be inclined to move, does she?' He spat expertly overboard. 'Bloody square headed non-seamen!'

'That's what Mr Soutar thought,' I refused to condemn a man for being afraid.

'Is that right, Soutar?' Milne glared at the helmsman.

'Yes, sir. That's what Mr Cosgrove and I thought,' Soutar did not mention that the approaching ship might be spectral.

'You should have taken the wheel, Soutar, rather than leave it with the good doctor.' Captain Milne smoothed his hands over the rim of the wheel. 'But let's have a look at this bugger. I don't like strange sails that bear down on us like that.' He glanced at Soutar. 'Did you not see her coming?'

'One minute the sea was clear and the next she was right on us, Captain.' Soutar hesitated a second, glanced at me and said. 'There must be a fog bank out there. We can't see it in the dark, and she's not wearing any lights.'

'I can't smell any bloody fog: you were sleeping, Soutar.' Captain Milne's quick glare could have melted lead, but he spat overboard and concentrated on his duty. He stared at the oncoming ship for a second, and then spun the wheel, allowing the spokes to whirl past his hand before catching them. *Lady Balgay* altered course and again spray and spindrift rose high, gleamed for a second in the light of a myriad stars, and spattered on to the deck.

'Would we not be best avoiding her completely?' I tried to redeem myself with helpful advice.

'Would you not be better keeping your prattling mouth shut and letting me run my own ship?' Captain Milne responded.

Remembering the example of Pratt, I glanced at Soutar and said nothing.

'Aye, she's Dutch, right enough,' Milne said a few minutes later. 'Or maybe German; she has some weird rig though. Old fashioned as buggery. She might be some Baltic trader with a cargo of flax.'

The vessel was much larger than *Lady Balgay*; a square rigged three-master with a figurehead of Neptune pointing a trident and black paint peeling from her hull. Only when we were five cables lengths apart did the strange vessel's lookout appear to notice them and a surprised hail sounded across the water.

'About time you woke up you dozy Dutch bugger,' Milne roared into a speaking trumpet. 'You've been bearing down on us for half the night, driving about the Atlantic with no blasted lights! Are you all blind or just bloody stupid?'

The reply was incomprehensible, but seemed to satisfy Milne, who called out the hands and, in a display of seamanship all the more impressive for the casual manner in which it was carried out, eased *Lady Balgay* round in a course parallel to that of the larger vessel.

'What are we doing, skipper?' Learmonth, the bosun had staggered from the foc'sle. He had sailed with Captain Milne before and held a privileged position in *Lady Balgay*.

'Going alongside, Leerie.' Milne told him. 'Or do you like sailing in a dry ship?'

'There will be the devil to pay if the owner hears,' Learmonth warned, grinning. He wiped his sleeve across his mouth. 'She's Prussian, isn't she? She'll have schnapps then, or gin.'

Milne shrugged. 'By the time the owner hears it won't matter, will it? This is my last voyage; I'm going to buy myself a nice wee cottage somewhere a long, long way from the sea, put my feet on the fireplace and tend my garden. So what can the owner do, even if he does find out?'

'Well, I won't tell him,' Learmonth's grin widened. 'He and I don't often drink in the same pub.'

I glanced from Captain Milne to the bosun and back, unsure what was best to do. I remembered Sir Melville mentioning that Milne enjoyed his drink rather too much, but I had also heard the crew grumbling about sailing in a dry ship. I had a choice: either I could say nothing and trust to the captain's professionalism, or I could interfere and try to pull rank through my relationship with the owner.

There was still a long voyage ahead of us, and, call me coward if you will, but the thought of being probably the most unpopular man in a small vessel in the Arctic was not pleasant. I looked around the men who had clustered on deck to watch the strange ship. News had spread that the captain intended purchasing bottles of what they termed 'something sensible', and they watched expectantly. I had already learned that seamen had a very hard life with meagre wages, disgusting conditions and always the risk of death or injury. I knew that their home life was little better as they existed in tiny one-roomed houses in the poorer parts of Dundee or some other coastal town and a drunken binge was their only escape from the constant misery of existence.

The faces were intent, eyes bright as they watched the nearby ship. These men were hardened by experience, leathered by maritime storms, inured to privation. Did I have the right to deprive them of nearly their only pleasure? Legally I probably had, as I was the owner's son-in-law, but I was not in command of the ship. Morally? I dismissed the entire idea as absurd. Captain Milne would not listen to me anyway, and if I did try to interfere, I would only create bad blood that would auger ill for the remainder of this voyage.

I tried to imagine the reaction if I ordered them not to buy alcohol. A ship was not a safe place for an unpopular man, for accidents could be arranged and there would be no witnesses. There was only one decision that I could sensibly make, so I decided to put a smile on my face and do so with good grace.

'Captain Milne!' I pressed through the crowd to come close.

Milne looked at me, his face closed with suspicion. 'What is it, Mister Surgeon?'

I felt the sudden tension of the crew as they wondered what I was about to say. 'Captain Milne, I was thinking; would you consider it an imposition if I helped pay for the drink? Rather than the sum coming out of the ship's funds, I mean?'

'Good God!' For a terrifying second I thought that Milne was about to strike me for some impropriety, but instead he grabbed my upper arms in a grip like a gorilla. 'You are a gentleman after all!' The captain raised his voice. 'Did you hear that lads? Doctor Cosgrove has offered to buy us all a drink, and that's something his father-in-law has never done in the last twenty years!'

The cheer that followed raised my spirits and I admit I enjoyed the sudden feeling of good fellowship. Even Pratt allowed his frown to relax for an instant, while Soutar beamed his approval.

It was certainly a surreal picture, two ships rolling side by side under the flitting stars, with the waves splintering in silver white surges under their prows and both crews lining their respective rails, exchanging raucous insults and cheerful greetings as the masters shouted across the dark water.

The strange vessel proved to be a German vessel, *Fortuna Gretel* from the Prussian port of Greifswald, and she was a willing trading party. Her captain was a jovial barrel of a man who wore clothes as old fashioned as his ship but provided an entire cask of Geneva gin as well as a dozen bottles of good West Indian rum in exchange for some of my supply of guineas.

'I'll look after these,' Captain Milne said, his eyes hungry as he grabbed eight of the bottles, 'in case some of you boys try to drink it at one session.' I thought I saw genuine pleasure in the grin he directed at me. 'This is our share, Dr Cosgrove.'

I nodded obligingly but I wondered if I should attempt to wrest control of the rum from the captain. Sanity told me that I could not out-fight Milne, and after hearing Soutar's stories, I doubted I had the moral courage to out argue him. 'We'll drink them together, Captain, over the course of the voyage.'

'And a much more pleasant voyage it will be now, Iain, my boy!' Captain Milne took me in a crushing bear hug so I wondered if I had been adopted as the ship's pet, and what would have happened if I had tried to prevent any alcohol being bought.

I did not know if my decision had prevented or caused trouble and that question haunted me as *Lady Balgay* thrashed her way north. My apparent generosity had definitely made me a more popular man, and the helmsman even trained me in the basics of steering, provided the wind was dead astern and steady and the sea was as calm as it ever was in these latitudes.

'Just do as I say,' Soutar advised, 'and you will be fine.'

Sir Melville had never allowed me to steer his yacht, so I was very nervous as I grasped the varnished wood, but I admit that I came to enjoy standing at the helm, feeling the throb of the vessel through the spokes as I learned to meet each advancing wave and watch for wind and drift. With her ballast providing new stability, *Lady Balgay* handled well, rising to the swell, hovering for an instant and swooping down, with all fifty-eight tons of her handling as easily as any yacht.

'Can you feel her?' Soutar sucked at an empty pipe, his face conveying only pleasure as he taught his new apprentice. 'The helmsman is the first to feel the mood of the ship. You can feel when she is happy; that's when he wants to sail forward, when she is a joy to steer.'

'I can feel her,' I confirmed, for it was true. It felt as if *Lady Balgay* was a live thing, rather than a machine of wood and metal and canvas.

'Yet she's still not quite right, is she?' Soutar said, suddenly sober. 'She wants to sail, but she knows that something is wrong and I'm damned if I know what.'

For a moment I was tempted to mention's Pratt's distress, but I changed my mind before allowing that particular superstition out of the bag. I kicked myself mentally, wondering if I was somehow affected by the uneasy atmosphere that had pervaded this boat, which was insane. I was a doctor, for God's sake, trained to work with hard facts and logic, not vague fears and superstition. I thought of Jennifer waiting for me in the magnificence of Balgay House and shook away the old seaman's fears. In a few months I would be home, and I vowed never to leave Jennifer again, never again to venture north in the power of irrational megalomaniacs such as Captain Milne and these seamen with their hints and stories and ancient superstitions.

Turning away, I listened to *Lady Balgay's* voice. She sang to the caress of the wind through her rigging and hummed with the vibration of the mainmast and mizzen, while the bowsprit and that intriguing figurehead of a naked woman thrust forward, quivering like a pointer dog as she hunted for her best route through the sea. I looked forward and smiled at those plump wooden buttocks that were so unlike Jennifer's slim figure but so like those of that other woman.

That other woman?

What other woman?

The image came unbidden into my mind. She was smaller than Jennifer, dark haired and moved with an awareness of her body that was more sensual than anything I ever previously imagined. Instinctively I knew she had been with me since our visit to Gass Skerry, hovering at the fringes of my mind, waiting for me to summon her out. But who was she? I knew she was not Jennifer, so she could only be some ethereal fantasy brought forth by my nocturnal longings.

I needed to find out, and as I concentrated my mind she returned, stepping easily toward the forefront of my consciousness with swivelling hips and shapely breasts.

'No!' I shook my head, rejecting the image I had willingly conjured up.

'Mr Cosgrove?' Soutar sounded concerned. 'Are you all right?'

'Oh yes,' I forced a grin; Soutar would never understand. 'I was miles away there.'

'Were you in Dundee perhaps?' Soutar's eyes softened, 'with a certain young lady?'

'Something like that,' I admitted, and Soutar chuckled.

'Well, Mr Cosgrove, this voyage won't last forever and then you'll be back with her, and things will be all the sweeter for the absence.'

I nodded. 'Of course they will. You're right, Mr Soutar.' When I looked forward again the image was gone and the figurehead was of plain wood, white painted but without any movement other than that occasioned by the sea.

I continued my scrutiny of the ketch. I could see the masts quiver under the pressure of the sails, the ropes and spars and pulleys all working together, a miracle of ingenuity, a picture of man's skill in bringing together a disparate mass of wood and pitch and hemp and canvas and iron to create such a wonder as this seagoing vessel. I saw the slender funnel and realised we had not yet used the engine, but we had the power of steam ready to aid us and all the engineering skills of our man from the Clyde.

I laughed as my mood abruptly changed; I knew the image was from my own imagination: my life contained no woman apart from Jennifer and until this moment I had my priorities all wrong. I had to tell Sir Melville that work was not about amassing wealth, it was about steering a fifty-eight ton ketch in the North Atlantic, it was about watching the great waves rise and break and ease away, it was about listening to the lonely scream of the seagull and enjoying the caress of the wind. There was always the wind; day or night, it dominated our thoughts and actions; too much and we were in discomfort; too little and we might wallow between the great green troughs; just enough and everybody's spirits soared.

I laughed with the sheer joy of controlling this beautiful creation, and I did not mind that there came an echoing laugh from somewhere just outside my awareness. For once that woman was no threat but a partner and I allowed her a share in my pleasure.

I did not know, yet, just how dangerous she was.

'Stop daydreaming, you idle bugger, and keep a straight course!' Captain Milne broke into my reverie and although his voice was harsh, the set of his cloth cap at the back of his head was a sure sign that he was in a good mood.

'Aye, Captain.' I made the miniscule correction necessary and returned Milne's nod.

'You might even make a seaman someday, Mr Surgeon,' Captain Milne gave grudging approval. 'But only with a hell of a lot of work and far more concentration.' He glanced at the western sky, from which the sun was sinking. We seemed to be sailing into clouds of tawny copper, centred by a sad orb of gold. 'Winds getting up,' Milne said, oblivious to the beauty. 'Not to worry, we'll be at the ice soon, and then we can make some more money for your father-in-law.'

I nodded, captivated by the unexpected, nearly melancholy loveliness as I listened to the growing whine of the wind. 'This is a good life, Captain. Indeed, I can't think of a better.'

I was surprised at the bitterness in Milne's stare. 'It's a life, Mr Surgeon, like any other. Your father-in-law's money allows you to choose how you live your life; others do not have that extravagance. For us, the sea is a necessity, not a luxury.'

The change of mood was so sudden that I could not even protest, but the words remained to hurt me when my watch ended. I had never thought of myself as privileged, indeed, like many in my position I regarded the working class as something separate, people who lived parallel lives in a different existence, yet in sharing this small ketch I had discovered that they were in many ways no different.

We all had aspirations, only the degree altered; I wanted a career and a comfortable life, they sought a few hours alcoholic escape from the bitter poverty they had long realised would dominate their lives.

I smiled as the realisation hit; maybe that was why Sir Melville had agreed that I should sail on *Lady Balgay*: not to enhance my medical experience but to increase my knowledge of people.

I stretched out on my bunk, pressing my feet against the dark-stained planking that marked the edge of my tiny cabin. Well, I had learned. I had seen the men working hard and swearing hard. I had seen them dripping wet under the lash of an Atlantic gale, and singing around the table as the rum bit home. I had heard the superstitious and the blasphemous, the godly and the sincere; I had witnessed something of the appalling violence of the seamen's existence, and I guessed that if I had been born in their underprivileged circumstances, I would re-act in just the same way. Now that I had gained that insight into our similarities, I was sure I was ready to return to my wife.

It was Jennifer that I thought of when I stood on deck or worked in the cabin, but my dreams were haunted by images of that female I had never met, the dark eyed, dark headed and utterly voluptuous woman who drifted toward me on a silken crimson sea. I could not help myself from reaching for her, wondering who she was as I accepted the truth she had shared my life for some days now, subtly and slowly altering from a shifting, wraithlike figure to somebody more substantial.

When had I first seen her? Had it really been on Gass Skerry, or had she been with me for longer? Indeed, had she always been there, an image of feminine temptation, the lust of which our schoolmasters had warned us and at which we had scoffed or surreptitiously enjoyed. I was not sure, but now she was approaching closer, tossing her fine dark hair. For a moment I imagined that it was Kate Davidson, but the colouring and curves were wrong, and then the woman opened her mouth in a loving kiss that turned into a scream of rage as Captain Milne's roar shattered the mirage.

'All hands! Come on, lads, there's work to be done!'

'Jesus!' The iced blast of the Arctic replaced the promise of sensuality and female caress.

Chapter Nine

"The sea, this truth must be confessed, has no generosity. No display of manly qualities, courage, hardihood, endurance, faithfulness, has ever been known to touch its irresponsible consciousness of power."
Joseph Conrad

The closest iceberg was small, about twenty feet long, and floated sullenly on an oily sea. There was an ugly dark green band just above the waterline, and groups of what appeared to be pebbles above that. Behind the first berg were others, of all shapes and sizes, from floes no larger than *Lady Balgay's* dinghy to giants that would dwarf Dundee Law.

'Fenders lads, in case they get too close.' Captain Milne sounded very casual as he gave orders that steered *Lady Balgay* through the bergs, with the crew shoving at any that came too close.

'Are these the first icebergs you have seen?' Soutar noticed how I was staring.

'Yes, they are.' I confirmed.

'There will be plenty more,' Soutar said. 'Some are small and some massive, but all dangerous to the ship. What you see above the water is nothing to the ice beneath, so we have to be careful.'

'Can't we sail around them?' I asked.

'We'll meet hundreds more Doctor, and we can't avoid them all. The captain will keep his distance when he can, and move in if there's fishing.'

'Fishing?' I wondered.

'Seal fishing,' Soutar told me flatly. 'We'll start to get prepared very shortly now, you mark my words.'

Soutar was correct. The next morning Captain Milne ordered the sealing clubs to be taken from storage and the boats overhauled, with harpoons, rifles and stores checked. I had expected the clubs to be simple lengths of heavy wood, but instead they were five feet long, with an ugly spike at the back, more like a mediaeval mace or a pickaxe than a club. I lifted the nearest, marvelling at the weight.

'This is an evil thing.'

'So is an angry bladdernose seal,' Pratt told me quietly. 'They've got a mouthful of teeth that would put a tiger to shame, and the largest could crush you to death simply by looking at you.' He brooded quietly for a moment, obviously reliving past experiences. 'If an adult bull seal attacks you, Mr Cosgrove, particularly a bladdernose, then you'll want as much protection as you can get, and you'll think that club is far too puny by half.' He gave a sudden grin that took ten years off his age. 'There's no need to worry though, we shoot the dangerous ones long before they get too close.'

I held the weapon, feeling the weight in my hands and trying to imagine swinging it against an animal. I thought of the sensation and the look in the seal's eyes, and knew I could never do it. I could never deliberately kill a living thing.

'Put that pick down, Doctor, and help me check here!' Captain Milne was watching. 'Make sure there are sufficient lowery tows, won't you? And each man needs a skinning knife.'

The lowery tows were lengths of rope for dragging sealskins over the ice, essential, functional and as romantic as a drunken kiss. The knives were coldly practical, heavy and broad bladed in a simple wooden sheath. I shivered; I had dedicated my life to healing, not destruction and I realized again that I did not belong here, so far north with a crew of hard-bitten Greenlandmen.

'In the gloaming, oh my darling
When the lights are soft and low
Will you think of me and love me
As you did once long ago?'

The words crept into my mind with such subtlety that I did not realise I was singing them until I saw Soutar watching. They belonged to Jennifer, a warm dance hall in West Ferry and soft tenderness, not to this place of icebergs and clubs and brutal slaughter.

But who was that woman at the back of my mind? The dark haired, curvaceous female who eased back into my consciousness was certainly not Jennifer as she slowly allowed her clothes to ease from her body until she stood entirely naked in my imagination. She came closer, emerging from the darkness to stand clear on deck, vibrant in her invitation, extending her arms toward me as she glided closer. I could not see her face, but knew she was enticingly beautiful, but repugnant in some hideous way that had nothing to do with her physicality.

She was nearly within touching distance, sliding on that crimson silk that was not a fabric at all, but came from somewhere else, somewhere outside my imagination.

'No,' I said quietly, and the woman, the product of some youthful fantasy or a distorted memory of my wedding night, faded slightly.

'No!' I said the word with more emphasis and the woman slithered back, to hover beside the mizzenmast, now partially veiled by some semi-transparent gauze.

'No!'

'No, Mr Cosgrove?' Soutar looked at me as if I was insane. 'I didn't say anything.'

'No?' I shook away the vision. 'Of course not. I'm sorry, Mr Soutar. I must have been imagining things.'

'Aye.' Soutar gave an understanding grin. 'It's not surprising that you imagine things, with this being your first time up here. Many seamen actually see things, Mr Cosgrove, mermaids or mirages or suchlike, particularly in the long night watches. But don't you worry; you'll learn to ignore your imaginings.'

'I'm not concerned about that,' I was very aware of the tune that continued to play through my head and wished I had never decided to go on this voyage. When this gloom was upon me I thought I had gained nothing at all from the enforced absence from Jennifer.

The shadow behind the mizzenmast was motionless but I knew she was there, waiting for me to relax my concentration before she appeared, tempting me with the allure of unadorned femininity that belonged only partially to my wife. I knew I must fight the image; I must fight to retain the morality Jennifer deserved and my upbringing as a British gentleman required. I had not fully recognised this aspect of my character before, but the lonely voyage had obviously awakened dormant desires that only a true marriage would cure. Closing my eyes, I fled below to find solace in the medical journals I had brought with me and the comforting bite of a deep glass of rum.

I did not want to sleep that night because I knew she would still be there, waiting, her presence a temptation that would menace the decorum of any gentleman, but yet I knew I wanted her caress and the pleasure of her imaginary company. Oh God help me, if only she had remained in my imagination!

'All hands on deck. Prepare for a stormy time!'

Captain Milne's bellow had almost been a relief, dragging me from the torments of disturbed sleep, but when I stepped on deck I could not resist my gasp. Where a few days ago there had been a scattering of icebergs on an otherwise normal sea, now *Lady Balgay* was approaching what seemed like a never-ending plateau of ice. If I looked north or west or east, all I could see was white desolation, mile after mile of featureless wilderness, scoured by a low but penetrating wind that simultaneously brought forth tears and froze them to my cheeks.

'Where are we?'

'At the ice,' Soutar was at the helm, remorselessly chewing tobacco but with his eyes busy, watching everything at once. 'This is what it's all about, Iain my boy... I mean, Dr Cosgrove, ice and snow and bitter cold. We'll be at the seals soon, you mark my words.'

'I knew there was ice,' I said, 'but not like this!'

'Ice comes in a thousand different shapes,' Soutar told me, and returned all his attention to the wheel. *Lady Balgay* was making slow progress, gliding a cables' length from the edge of the ice plateau with her bow barely making a ripple in the water and the Naked Lady under her bowsprit pointing the way forward. Birds flocked around us, clamouring for food.

'Bloody birds,' Thom grunted. 'They'll die before they get anything from this starvation ship. Bloody sawdust and rancid spittle, that's what we're fed on here. God save us if we're nipped in the ice.'

'There's no God out here,' Pratt said slowly. 'We discarded him back on Gass Skerry.' Ignoring Thoms' glower he nodded to me. 'Good morning Doctor; best put your furs on, or you'll bloody freeze.'

I was already aware of the frost forming around my lips and the warning numbness in my fingers. Returning below, I hauled on what Jennifer had called my cold weather gear before returning on deck to stare at my surroundings. The ice stretched into the void that was the horizon, awesome in its infinity, but without a whisper of wind to ruffle the limp sails so only the engine pushed *Lady Balgay* onward, the steady putt-putt and trail of greasy smoke reassuringly civilised amidst the rawness of the Arctic wilderness.

'That's better, doctor.' Thoms grinned to me through the fringe of his fur hood. He gestured to the north. 'Do you like it? This is where we earn our money. This is the land of the seal fish.'

'You won't need your surgery here, doc; not for the seals anyway.' Mackie had been quiet most of the voyage, but he seemed lively enough now as he tested the swing of a sealing club. The weapon hissed as it passed through the air a few inches from my head. 'We'll massacre the buggers!'

'That's what we'll do, Macks!' Like Mackie, Donaldson was in his early thirties, both men of middle height and with nothing distinctive in feature or speech. 'Crash! And there's another dead seal. Batter! And one more for the flensing knife!'

'That's the way, Billy! Smash the bastards! Break their skulls!' Mackay gave a high pitched laugh as he swung again, so both men stood on deck, swinging their clubs and grinning with pleasure at the prospect of the forthcoming butchery.

Captain Milne was half way up the mast, his cloth cap finally discarded in these frighteningly low temperatures and a fur cap with spaniel-like earflaps covering his head. He extended a battered brass telescope to its full extent as he examined the ice ahead. 'Can you hear them?'

I shook my head, and Pratt and Thoms looked at each other. 'Not yet Captain,' Thoms said. 'We can't hear them yet.'

'You bloody will. Can't you smell them?'

I took a deep breath. There was nothing in the wind but salt air and the curiously damp smell of sea ice, unlike anything I had smelled before.

'I can't smell them yet, Captain,' Thoms repeated. 'Where are they?'

'Not far ahead. Follow the ice, Soutar, and watch for the seal fishes.'

'Yes, Captain.' Soutar did not seem surprised at this addition to his responsibilities as *Lady Balgay* cruised slowly onward, nosing aside tiny floes and with her wash bouncing off the ice plateau as the hands clustered on deck, waiting for their captain to find the seals. Astern, our smoke left a sooty smudge on the once-pristine ice.

For a moment I envisaged Ross the chief engineer caring for his machinery as Torrie the fireman shovelled coal into the furnace. They were the unseen and often unappreciated men who made the difference between a vessel at the mercy of the weather and one capable of independent motion; the engine room was the beating heart of the ship, as Captain Milne was the brain and the seamen were the muscles and sinews. And me? What part did I play? For most of this voyage I had been little more than an appendage, a useless observer shuffling documents that few would ever read.

'Mitchell!' Captain Milne hardly raised his voice but the youngster looked up, all youth and eagerness. 'Get to the masthead! See if you can see anything!'

Without taking breath, Mitchell ran aloft, using the backstay for balance and then shinning up the mast until he reached the very tip, where he clung unconcerned by the height as he scanned the ice.

'That lad's like a bloody monkey,' Thoms said sourly. 'He should be a fairground acrobat, not a sailor.' He looked up, grudging admiration in his eyes.

'Sing out when you see them, Mitchell!' Milne ordered, and altered his position slightly to look ahead.

'I hear them Captain,' Pratt said, eager to please despite the still healing bruises on his face. 'You were right!'

'Of course I was bloody right!' Captain Milne showed no pleasure in Pratt's praise.

'Aye, Captain,' Pratt said. 'They're maybe three miles ahead.' He looked aloft, where Milne was scanning the ice with his telescope. 'Only you could hear them at that distance, Captain.'

'Hear what? What can you hear?' I asked. I strained as best I could, but heard only the ever present creaking of *Lady Balgay*, the faint growl of the engine, the cold clink of ice and the sound of the waves slapping at the hull.

'I can hear the seals, Mr Cosgrove. Can't you hear the bloody seals? They're as plain as the tits on a Dock Street whore!' Captain Milne glared at me, his eyes as poisonous as ever. 'Now close your mouth and open your ears, Mr Surgeon!' Looking away, he spat overboard in obvious disgust. 'God save us from amateur sailors.' Shaking his head, he scampered up the ratlines for a better look.

As we cruised just off the edge of the ice, I watched the tiny waves wash against the shelf, and the occasional floe break free to be sucked under the iron-shod forefoot and destroyed by the churning screw. Eider duck hopped along the silver white plateau, perched on infrequent hummocks or flew alongside, to dive and swim as travelling companions to the Greenlandmen. I looked in vain for a feature on which to focus but mostly this ice was flat, empty and featureless as it stretched forever into the vast vacuum of the north.

Then she was there again; that enigmatic woman was watching me, her smile enticing even though her features were unclear as she emerged from the shadows. She drifted closer, brushing unfelt and unseen against Learmonth's hand as she approached, her face still nebulous but her shape as distinct as a classical goddess and as disturbing as un-confessed sin. I shook my head; she could not be real, I knew she must be merely a personification of womanhood that desire had called from my subconscious. I had to school myself to ignore her; I must maintain my concentration, apply myself to my work here and remember that Jennifer was waiting.

Jennifer was real. Jennifer was my wife. This creature was unreal; this creature was a manifestation of my desire, a warped fantasy that natural marriage would cure.

'There! We have them!' Snapping shut his telescope, Milne slid down the ratlines as if he were a youth of twenty rather than a man who would never see his fifties again. 'There is an entire shoal of seals, ripe for the capture!' He raised his voice. 'We'll have the sails down, Bosun, for all the bloody good they are in this calm, and tell Ross to stop the engine.' Captain Milne glowered around the deck, his flash of good humour quickly replaced by his customary distrust of everything and everybody. 'We'll make fast to the ice, Learmonth, and see how good this crew really is.' He raised his voice only slightly. 'Ice anchor on each bow, lads, and make sure the cables are stout and secure.'

The crew chattered contentedly amongst themselves as they obeyed. Knowing I was as useless on deck as I was below, I leaned back, my professional interest roused by the attitude of men immediately prior to a hunt; they were relaxed, cheerful with the prospect of adding to their wages, but only Mackie and Donaldson seemed in any way animated. With the captain watching everything through suspicious eyes, Learmonth spoke into the voice pipe that led to the engine room, giving quiet orders that brought *Lady Balgay* to a stop. She sat there, rocking very gently with her masts swaying in unison against the unending ice.

'It's different from Dundee, eh Doctor?' Learmonth was a middle-sized, stocky man with a down turned mouth but intelligent eyes. Producing a squashed packet of Woodbine cigarettes from his pocket, he thrust one between his lips and offered me another.

'No, thank you,' I refused and turned slightly away, trying to ignore the woman who stood in profile, half hidden by the mainmast, just as a sudden gust of wind came from the south, slamming *Lady Balgay* against her cable. 'Blast!' I staggered and grasped the rail for balance.

Cursing more forcibly, Learmonth put his left hand backward, onto the winch. He yelled sharply and loudly, and looked down, swearing in a long repetitive monotone. At first I could see nothing but the blood that oozed onto the deck, but I quickly realized that the sudden tightening of the cable chains had moved the cogwheel of the winch, trapping Learmonth's hand.

'Leerie!' I stepped closer, but Soutar was there first.

'What the hell happened?'

'My hand's caught in the winch!' Learmonth swore again as *Lady Balgay* moved and the teeth of the cogwheel chewed into his palm, gnawing at the flesh.

'You stupid bugger!' Pushing me out of the way, Soutar took over. 'Reverse the winch! Free Leerie's hand!'

I heard a definite crunch of bone as the cogwheel relaxed its grip, agonisingly dragging the metal teeth clear of Learmonth's palm. 'That's a bit of a mess,' Soutar stared at the blooded ribbons of flesh that hung down from the injured hand. 'Thank God we've got a real doctor on board. Get below and let Doctor Cosgrove sort you out.'

Perversely pleased that there had been an accident so I could show my skills, I took charge, leading the bosun down to our cabin as the remainder of the crew got on with the much more important task of hunting for seals.

Lack of space in the tiny room had forced me to stow my medical chest under the shared bunk while the half dozen medical volumes that were all I could take were squeezed onto a makeshift bookshelf against the bulkhead.

'You just make yourself comfortable,' I ordered in my professionally cheerfully tone as I pored over the contents of the chest, wondering which was best. 'There are all sorts of useful things in here.' I looked up, 'we'll have you right in a jiffy, Mr Learmonth.'

The laughter was sudden and disturbing as it echoed sardonically through the cabin. I looked up, shaken. That was not Leerie; I knew that other woman was waiting in a dark recess of my mind, but this concrete and useful work made it easier to ignore her.

'Are you all right, Doctor?' Learmonth asked. 'You looked all queer there for a moment.'

'Me? You're the patient, Mr Learmonth.' I calmed my nerves by examined the wound for longer than was necessary. Ignoring Learmonth's instinctive flinch of pain, I felt for broken bones. 'There: you have a broken finger and a nasty gash. We'll clean up the mess, splint the bone and then we'll soon have you stitched up all nice and pretty, and with a handsome scar to show your wife.'

'My wife left me three years ago,' Learmonth's eyes were like hot coals. 'She ran off with a riveter from the shipyard. It's not easy for a woman when her man's away all the time.'

'I'm sorry,' I looked up quickly, cursing my wayward tongue. 'I didn't know.'

'Well you should have damned well asked,' Learmonth snarled. 'Now get on with your job so I can get back to mine!' He opened his hand, staring without expression as I set the bone and swabbed the wound. He showed no more emotion as I threaded a needle with catgut and prepared to stitch.

'Now you hold still, Mr Learmonth, and we'll have you right.'

'Get a bloody move on, man and don't prattle so much!'

After years of working at sea, Learmonth's skin was so tough it resisted the push of the needle so I had to work the point through the mangled flesh. Bright blood dripped onto the cabin deck, joining the thousand stains that were already there, but Learmonth did not flinch, merely watching to ensure I made a seamanlike job of his hand.

'That will scar nicely,' I stepped back, holding my head to one side as I examined his handiwork. 'It will be sore for a couple of days, and you can't use the finger anyway, so you have a fine excuse not to do any work,' my satisfied grin quickly faded as the bosun looked up.

'I'll be working in five minutes if you get a bloody move on.' Learmonth's voice was sour as week old milk.

'I'm surprised that such a thing happened to such an experienced man as you are.' I decided to ignore Leerie's caustic remarks. Pain can have such an effect.

'It's not surprising it happened on this ship of the damned.' Learmonth spoke so matter- of- factly that at first I thought I had not heard properly and asked him to repeat his words.

'I said it was not surprising,' Learmonth explained. 'Some of the men believe this ship is damned, Dr Cosgrove. You must know that by now as much as we all do.'

'Well, let's hope that they are wrong,' I heard the unease in my own laughter but quickly dismissed the idea as another example of seaman's superstition. I wrapped a clean linen bandage around Learmonth's hand. 'How does that feel?'

'It's all right,' the bosun gave grudging praise, which I realised was all that he was capable of.

'You can get back to work now, if you must,' I said. 'But try to keep your hand dry.' I smiled at the ironic look that Learmonth gave me. We both knew it was impossible to keep dry on a small ketch tossing and bobbing in the Arctic, so the bandage would be a sodden mess within five minutes. Short of ordering Learmonth not to work at all, there was nothing more that I could do. 'Come and see me tomorrow.'

'We're in the same cabin, Doctor. Of course I'll see you tomorrow!'

Chapter Ten

GREENLAND SEA
MARCH 1914

It is by no means enough that an officer of the navy should be a capable mariner... He should be as well a gentleman of liberal education, refined manners, punctilious courtesy, and the nicest sense of personal honor. He should be the soul of tact, patience, justice, firmness, and charity.'
John Paul Jones 1775

Returning to deck, I looked again at the surroundings, already hating the bright starkness of the terrain; this would be a terrible place to die, I thought, and wondered what morbid fantasy had brought that into my head. The old time whaler men had spoken of beauty up here, the romance of the wilderness with nights that never grew dim and the spectacular aurora borealis, dazzling colouring and intricate patterns of ice, but today I could see none of that. Instead everything was white and grey, with danger lurking at every corner and cold so intense that every tormenting breath augmented the beard of ice around my mouth.

Pratt looked up and sniffed the air. 'There's a wee breath of wind, lads, but it's coming from the north. Can't you smell the seals?'

Thoms nodded, and Mackie laughed, swinging his club against an imaginary object. 'I can smell them, Johnny boy!'

Captain Milne grunted. 'You'll be among them soon enough, Mackie. Bosun! You look after the ship. 'Mitchell, stay with him, and Ross, you attend the engines. I want everybody else ashore; everybody! That includes you, Torrie, and you, Doctor. Take seal clubs and rifles, boys; Pratt, you carry the lowery tows and let's get to the fishing!'

Unsure what to expect and unable to help, I could only watch as the crew bustled around. The seal clubs with their vicious spikes were wielded and displayed, together with half a dozen rifles of various makes from the truly terrible Martini Henry to the more modern Lee-Enfield and an assortment of ropes and lines.

'Remember the food and water, boys, in case we get separated!' Captain Milne gave his orders in a tone much more cheerful than that he normally employed. 'And I want every man to touch the Lady for luck before we go.' He stood sentinel to ensure that everybody going on to the ice scrambled forward to fondle the figurehead. I had to go too, of course, inching slowly forward and fumbling my hands over the smooth wood as I thought of the terrible woman of my dreams and felt the sickness deep in my stomach. The captain was last, balancing on the bowsprit and cupping a wooden buttock in each gloved hand. He gave a final affectionate pat. 'There we go now.'

All padded up and looking more like bears than men, we stepped on to the booms that had been hung protectively over side and jumped the two feet to the ice. I could feel the tense excitement underlying the men's normal air of competence, and I knew they were looking forward to the coming slaughter; they were professional hunters, perfectly at home in this harsh environment of snow and ice.

Thoms winked at me. 'Just leave the killing to us, Doctor, and you enjoy the scenery.'

My smile was forced; I could sense that woman again, a shadowy figure lurking at the fringe of the hunters. She did not look at me but slithered around the bodies of men, as if searching, and then she smoothed a wanton hand over Pratt's face. I am sure I heard a low, taunting laugh, but it might have been the moan of wind across the ice. Shivering, I looked again but there was no woman at all, only the bulky-clothed Greenlandmen lumbering into the waste. Pratt was speaking with Thoms, hefting a seal club with casual unconcern, Captain Milne was in front and the rest hunched against the cold and moved forward, step by slow step.

To these men, hunting in the high latitudes was normal; this was how they made their living, paid their bills, and supported their wives and families. I shook my head; I had been wrong. However much I had enjoyed steering *Lady Balgay*, I could never become accustomed to this life.

Nor could I become inured to the environment. There was no landscape in this stretch of the Greenland Sea, no scenery, nothing on which to focus the imagination; nothing but the ice stretching in a monotonous plateau to the far horizon, white and featureless and ugly under bulging grey clouds. Only *Lady Balgay* broke the dreariness, with a thin wisp of smoke from her funnel and her sails neatly furled on slender spars. At that moment I thought she looked beautiful, for she was their only link with civilisation and with Jennifer.

'Have you been on a seal hunt before?' Donaldson hefted the only harpoon on board and looked directly at me. Normally a morose man who communicated in single syllables, today his eyes were glowing with some inner fire as he prepared to fish the seals.

I shook my head. 'No.'

'Well, it's a bloody business, Mr Cosgrove, and people are often squeamish the first time, but it's necessary.' He hefted the harpoon. 'If you want to stay behind...'

'He's a doctor,' Thoms pointed out. 'Of course he'll be all right. He's used to blood and gore and guts. It's his job. Look at the way he patched up the bosun's hand.' Thoms lightened his voice in what might have been an attempt to flatter me. "Ho hum, it's just a wee cut, and I'll soon have you stitched up, my boy".'He grinned. 'This will be nothing to you, Doctor. This will be nothing at all. Just avoid the great bulls and you'll be fine, eh?'

As they slithered and slid north, I became aware of the noise. At first I thought a trick of the wind caused that persistent moaning, but as we continued, the sound increased, altering its tone but always present until it seemed as if we were advancing into bedlam, a cacophony of moans and yells and screams that stretched in an unbroken arc before me.

'What's that?'

'That, Mr Cosgrove, is what you could not hear from *Lady Balgay.*' Captain Milne seemed quite pleased to explain. He lowered the Lee-Enfield rifle that was balanced on his shoulder and clicked the magazine into place. 'That is the sound of profit for the owners and wages for us men who have to work for our living. That, Mr Cosgrove, is the sound of seal-fish.' He gestured ahead, 'and there we have the shoal.'

I stopped in disbelief as I realised what I was seeing. It was my first sight of the sheer scale of this enterprise and it sucked the breath from my body. I had expected perhaps fifty or a hundred seals, something similar to the numbers that rested on the sandbanks off Tentsmuir at the entrance to the Firth of Tay, but here the seals were numbered in the thousands and tens of thousands. They lay on the ice in a seething mass of animals, from the massively old to the newly born; males, females and pups all together, crying and moaning in a sound fit only for the deepest pits of hell, or the shaded borders of a madman's mind.

'I've never seen the like. There must be acres and acres of them.'

'Aye, but such a sight is very rare, Mr Cosgrove.' Thoms balanced his club across his shoulder. 'Only Captain Milne can find them. My father was a sealing man, and he told me of shoals twice, three times, ten times this size. He had tales of shoals of seals so vast that two or three ships could work the same one, but never be in sight of each other. Imagine, mile after square mile of seal fish, just waiting to be captured.' He shook his head. 'I just don't know what's happened to them.'

Captain Milne shook his head. 'I don't know and I don't care, Thoms, but all that matters is that we have found our seals, so let's get busy, eh?'

'That's not all! Look over there!' Charles Mackie sounded like a schoolboy as he pointed. 'There's a bear!'

'You're right, Macks!' Donaldson lifted his club and waved it threateningly. 'Come here, Bruin! See what I have for you! Come over here!'

I followed the direction of their pointing fingers and nodded. The bear was on all fours but when it caught the scent of Man it rose to its back legs. Nine feet high, it raised its forepaws in the air before falling back down and approaching at a lumbering walk, and it was a sight so menacing that I felt any courage I had drain through my boots into the ice. An animal safely confined in a zoo is a pitiable sight, a creature as bereft of its natural vitality as a patient in a hospital, but the same animal loose in its own wilderness is a different proposition; wild savage, dangerous; frightening. I could hear the sullen pad of its paws and imagined the great claws slashing me to gobbets of bloody flesh.

'They say that the Polar Bear is one of the few animals that hunts a man by choice,' Pratt murmured, and I wondered where such an obviously undereducated man collected such a snippet of information, but the reactions of the other Greenlandmen were more expected.

'It's going to attack us!' Mackie yelled, but there was no fear in his voice. 'Give me a rifle!' Snatching a Martini Henry from the nearest man, he depressed the under lever and slid a cartridge into the open breech. Raising the lever back into place he aimed quickly. 'I'll take a trophy home with me!'

'He's after the seals,' Soutar said quietly, 'he's not interested in us.' But Mackie was not listening.

There was an outburst of giggling from Donaldson, who held his club as if it were a talisman, but the other hunters only watched as Mackie fired.

The shot was shockingly loud, an obscenity amidst the seal sounds in that vast expanse of nothing. When the gust of greasy white smoke cleared, I could see that the bear had been struck in the shoulder. The animal stopped, shook his head and bit frantically at the wound before turning away and heading toward the seals that were its natural prey.

'Leave it now,' Soutar advised. 'We're after seals.'

'I want a trophy. I want its head for my wall!' Mackie worked the lever again, thrusting another cartridge into the breach. He knelt on the ice and took careful aim, as Donaldson pointed excitedly.

'There are more, Macks; there's a female and cubs.'

Mackie's second shot hit the bear high in the left hind leg and it staggered and roared, turning around to bite at the wound.

'Good shot, Macks! Shoot again! Put one right up its arse!' Donaldson was giggling in his excitement.

'Watch this, Billy!' Standing, Mackie leaned forward and jerked the trigger. The shot missed completely.

'You stupid bugger! Give it to me! Let me try!' Donaldson grabbed at the rifle, but Mackie wrestled it free.

'No! It's my bear!'

The other men were watching, some silent, others encouraging Mackie or jeering as he failed to kill the bear.

'His wife will get you!' Donaldson was laughing as the female bear came closer, sniffing the air. She raised her head in the air and looked directly at Mackie. 'Look! Here she comes!'

'Come on, you big white bugger! Come this way!' Working the bolt like a machine, Mackie fired again, putting two more shots into the male bear, each one causing it to stagger, while bright blood stained the off-white fur. He swore as he realised his package of cartridges was empty and fumbled for another, tearing at the stiff paper with clumsy, gloved fingers.

'Jesus!' I saw the sweat suddenly start from Mackie's face as the female bear began to move purposefully toward him. Great pieces of loose ice flew from her paws as she advanced, head held low. 'Christ help me!'

'Oh for God's sake!' Lifting his more modern Lee-Enfield, Captain Milne took aim and fired a single shot that crashed into the female's skull. The great bear jerked, hesitated and fell, slithering forward so her head was within a few feet of Mackie. 'Now finish off the male, Mackie, and we can capture some seals. Shoot it between the eyes.'

Sliding in one of the huge Martini cartridges, Mackie worked the lever, took careful aim and fired, but when the bear kept moving; again Captain Milne killed it with a single shot. 'You'd better deal with the cubs,' he said quietly, 'if you want your trophy.'

Laughing now that the danger was past, Mackie ran past the dead female and shot each cub in the body, watching as they squealed and writhed on the ice. 'I want to keep the heads,' he said, as he watched them die. Lifting the club, he crashed it down on the nearest animal's chest. 'There! That's for you!' He raised it again, grunting with each blow until the cubs lay in a mess of mangled bloody fur. When Mackie looked up there were blood spots on his face. His eyes danced with excitement.

'You can behead them in your own time,' Captain Milne told him. 'We're here for the sealing.'

'What do we do now?' I had been a sickened spectator but the other hunters did not seem concerned at the slaughter of the family of bears. Only Soutar looked annoyed, but I suspected it was more at the waste than the cruelty.

'We capture seals,' Soutar said sourly. 'Watch and learn.'

Levelling his rifle, Captain Milne aimed at a mother seal the size of a young cow and fired, blasting a hole in her head from five feet range. The seal jerked backward and slithered down in a bloody heap. Moving forward, Mackie smashed his club on the skull of both dog-sized pup, killing them instantly. The other men were equally busy, moving from seal to seal with quick murder, shooting the males or large females and clubbing the pups in a display of controlled slaughter that was appallingly fascinating in its ruthlessness.

'Come on Doc! This is why we're here.' Already spattered with blood, Thoms dispatched a brace of pups with two deft blows and moved on to a young female, who stared at him through huge brown eyes but made no attempt to leave the pups that suckled her.

Although I had never hunted myself, I had no objection to others shooting grouse in the Glens of Angus or wild fowl by the Tay, but this was murder. This utterly unconcerned slaughter of squealing animals turned my stomach.

'If the weather was better we would wait a few days,' Donaldson explained, casually thrusting his harpoon into a large male and twisting to enlarge the wound. 'That way the pups would have finished suckling and they would have more blubber on them, but there's a blow on the way.'

'Is there?' Hiding the nausea that threatened to overcome me, I looked at the sky. The drab, featureless grey reached without a break from horizon to horizon. There was no indication of wind or storm. 'How can you tell?'

'The captain said so,' Donaldson said, ripping out his harpoon with as much emotion as if he were shifting a forkful of hay. The seal squealed, its mouth wide open.

'I see.' I watched the seal writhe in its death agony. I was surrounded by similar scenes as the crew of *Lady Balgay* earned their wages, shooting and clubbing and butchering the helpless animals. The ice began to change colour from white to watery red as the blood spread all around.

'Over here!' That was Thoms' voice. 'This one is fighting back!'

The large male was rearing up, slashing at Thoms with teeth far larger than I had expected.

'It's a bladdernose,' Soutar said calmly. He balanced his club across his shoulder and watched for a moment. 'Vicious buggers them. If they get a hold of you they'd rip your arm off, if you're lucky.' He raised his voice. 'Just shoot the bastard!'

Nodding, Thoms reached back to exchange his dripping club for the Martini-Henry, but as he did so Captain Milne arrived with his Lee-Enfield under one arm and a bloody club in his left hand.

'No. We've wasted enough money on bullets killing these bears. What will the owners say when they hear about all this expenditure?

It's only a seal.' Pulling his fur cap forward so the peak extended level with his nose, he glowered around the circle of panting hunters.

'Pratt. You always have too much to say for yourself. Go and kill that bugger. Show us all how it's done.'

The order was so casual that I thought the captain was joking, until I saw the expressionless green eyes and sensed Pratt's dismay. Suddenly I remembered Soutar's words:

'Captain Milne won't forget John stood up to him, that's why. He's not finished with old John yet. Not ever on this voyage.'

Chapter Eleven

GREENLAND SEA
MARCH 1914

There are three sorts of people; those who are alive, those who are dead, and those who are at sea.
Attributed to Acharsis, 6th Century BC

Was this order the captain's retaliation for John Pratt's earlier opposition? Was Captain Milne proving his authority by sending Pratt forward to kill a bladdernose seal with only a club? It was unbelievable, and yet, the men were in a semi- circle, watching, waiting to see what would happen. They expected Pratt to obey.

When the seal reared up, I saw it was larger than any I had seen before and a hundredfold more aggressive than the animals that lay supine on the sandbanks of the Tay. Silver coloured, with mottled dark markings, it was at least nine feet long, with a body three times as thick as a man, and when it opened its mouth it displayed rows of sharp yellow fangs.

'Captain…' I protested, but Pratt had obeyed orders and was already moving forward, swinging the great spiked seal club.

'Come on you great bladdernose bastard!' Pratt roared, but even as he advanced, the seal lunged forward, swinging its head. Pratt reared back, cursing, but the fangs ripped across his face, drawing bright blood and sending him reeling back, one hand to the wound as he yelled his pain. He crouched for an instant, making low gargling noises, with both hands covering his face and the club lying neglected on the ice, but Captain Milne was not finished with him yet.

'Try again, Pratt,' Captain Milne ordered, but it was obvious that the man was badly injured and I snatched the Martini-Henry from Donaldson. I fired, once, gasped at the massive recoil, worked the lever as I had seen Mackie do, thrust in one of the clutch of cartridges passed by a willing hand and fired again, this time steeling myself for the kick. Moving closer so I was between the seal and the wailing Pratt, I continued to fire, shot after shot until the seal subsided on the ice.

Still living but bleeding from half a dozen wounds, the bladdernose slumped, and then three of the hunters were on top, clubs swinging madly as they sought to crush out its life. Thoms stood on the massive back, crashing down his club until the spike jammed in the seal's massive skull.

'Got you, you murderous bastard! Bite John would you?' He wrestled the spike free and smashed down again, panting and swearing in his anger and horror.

Captain Milne watched with the clouds clearing from his eyes. 'You'll pay for these cartridges, Doctor! They were Sir Melville's property and he doesn't like waste, by Christ! That's the price of five bullets deducted from your wages!'

'Pratt!' Ignoring Captain Milne, I dropped the rifle and held the bleeding man. He writhed in my arms, clutching his face. 'Take away your hands so I can see. Take your hands from your face!'

Holding his mittens close, Pratt shook his head. Blood had already soaked through the thick wool and was dripping onto the ice. He was whining, high pitched and horrible.

'You must let me see, John,' I tried to pull the man's hands away but Pratt held them tight, shaking his head. 'Right, Mr Pratt, we're going back to the ship. Come on.'

Captain Milne looked over, his face impassive. 'That's twice you've failed to obey orders Pratt. I told you to kill it, not play with it. And you too, Doctor. I said no firing. I won't forget this day, Mr Cosgrove; you may be assured of that.'

I looked up, feeling anger deeper than I had ever experienced as I held the captain's bitter green eyes. 'Nor will I, Captain Milne, nor will I. This man might have been killed...'

'This is a man's job, Doctor. He knew that when he signed articles with the ship. It's mutiny or duty, remember.' Captain Milne sharpened his voice. 'Now take him away from my sight and stitch him up like a baby. When you're done, send him back to work. Thoms, you and Torrie go with the doctor.'

'Why?' Torrie, young and truculent, demanded.

'In case there are more bloody bears!'

Pratt staggered on the way back, making small mewing noises of pain as he tried to hold his ripped face together. Blood seeped through his fingers to drip on the ice, leaving our trail polka dotted with crimson. The flow increased as we walked and I wondered how to cope with such an obviously dangerous loss of blood.

'What's happened?' Learmonth was waiting to help us on board Lady Balgay.

'Bladdernose,' Thoms said shortly, as Learmonth looked at me with an I-told-you-so expression on his face.

'Get him down to my cabin,' I ordered, surprised that I could take charge so easily. 'And you two get back to the sealing.'

'But the captain said...' Thoms looked to Pratt.

'This man is not going back to work today,' I told him. 'Not judging by the amount of blood he has lost.' There was a crimson smear stretching across the deck, to match the blood that spattered all along our trail from the seals.

Settling Pratt on the bunk, I looked around the cramped and unsanitary surroundings and swore. My medical training at Edinburgh University had not prepared me for working in such primitive conditions, but there was no help for it. Taking a deep breath to settle my jangled nerves, I touched Pratt's hand. The sealer whined and tried to move away.

'Right, Mr Pratt. I'm going to have a look at your face.'

Pratt whimpered.

'Come on now, John.' I hardened his tone. 'If I look at it, I can help. If not, you could get gangrene, the wound will become poisoned and your whole face will be infected. If I don't treat you, John, you most certainly will die.'

The whimpering increased for a moment, but then Pratt slowly lowered his hands. He looked up through eyes desperate with fear and pain. His nose was smashed and a mask of bubbling blood concealed everything else. In short, his face was a mess.

I took another deep breath. 'All right. That doesn't look so bad. I'm going to clean away the blood and see what I can do. Prepare yourself, John.'

A word to Ross brought warm water from the engine room, but I had to ignore Pratt's howls as I washed the wound. The seal's teeth had gouged across both cheeks and broken his nose, leaving a gaping wound that poured with blood. Shaking my head, I set to work, allowing Pratt a generous tot of brandy to nerve him for the ordeal.

'This will sting a little,' I warned, knowing that the iodine would double the agony. 'Here's more brandy.'

Pratt swallowed the spirit like water, his eyes pleading for relief. As I began work he yelled as shrilly as a child, writhing on the bed at every touch of the iodine.

'Don't! Please stop!'

I sighed and stepped back. 'Try to lie still, John. There's no help for it, I'm afraid. We have to clean the wound thoroughly, for we do not know what sort of dirt is on the teeth of that seal. I don't want you to die.'

Learmonth thrust through the door. 'John's not the bravest of men' he said quietly. 'Come on. I'll hold him.'

With Learmonth's help, I swabbed deeper, ensuring there could be no possible infection from the animal's teeth. 'Right, Mr Pratt. That's the worst over.' Looking at my hands, I realised I was shaking, but whether with retained anger from the captain's sadistic order or worry at working in such primitive conditions, I was not sure. For a moment I eyed the brandy bottle, but at that time I had enough sense not to fall into that temptation. I could not let down this surprisingly vulnerable man whose big eyes followed me everywhere, pleading for release from pain.

'All right, John. Hold still now.' I tried to ignore the fear in Pratt's face as he prepared himself for renewed agony.

It was easy enough to bandage the broken nose, but difficult to stitch the face with my patient twitching and wincing with every prick of the needle. 'Hold still, man and it will be over quicker.'

Pratt nodded pathetically. 'Yes, Doctor I'll try.'

At last it was complete and Pratt lay on the bunk with his face swelling and bruised, crossed by a livid stitched scar. The terror in his eyes had not diminished.

'Will I die, Mr Cosgrove? Will I catch gangrene and die?'

I shook my head and looked as reassuring as I could. After Learmonth's display of stoicism, I was shocked to see such open fear. It was another insight into surgery, something my lecturers in Edinburgh had never mentioned. 'No. We managed to clean the wound. It'll swell more, and it will give you some pain for a few days, but that's all.'

Sitting up on the bed, Pratt took hold of both of my hands in his. 'Thank you, Doctor. Thank you.'

Embarrassed by this sudden display of gratitude, I shook my head. 'I am just doing my job. Now get hold of yourself and recover. I suggest you return to your own bunk in the foc'sle.'

Pratt shook his head. 'I have to get back on to the ice, Doctor. Captain's orders.' He was obviously more scared of Captain Milne than he had been of gangrene or the bladdernose seal.

'In medical matters, Mr Pratt, my orders supersede the captain's. That's the law.'

'The law? All right then, Doctor.' Pratt nodded meekly and rose from the bunk to slouch unsteadily forward.

'You've made a friend there,' Learmonth said quietly, and glanced at his own hand. 'That's two injuries now, and the second much more serious than the first. Who will be next?'

'Next?' I asked. I was still shaking but tried to look competent and professional.

'This ship is damned,' Learmonth reminded without a hint of jocularity. 'It will get us all eventually.'

I shook his head. 'I'm not superstitious,' I tried to block the memory of that woman from my mind. That was an anomaly, a delusion created by the unusual hardships of my present situation and augmented by my recent marriage: nothing else.

'You're not superstitious? Well, wait until you've been as long at sea as I have. There are no atheists in a storm, Doctor, and no seaman will scorn anything that may save him when the ice begins to nip.'

I looked at him with my disdainful laugh cut dead. 'So let's hope that does not happen.'

Learmonth shook his head. 'I've heard things on this boat, Doctor, things that are not right. I've heard footsteps where there are no people and voices down below when all hands were aloft. This is a bad ship, and that's a fact.' Putting out a hand the size of a small tabletop, he patted my shoulder. 'You take care, son, and get home safely to your wife.'

I did not laugh. He expected such words from superstitious oldsters such as Pratt, whose nerves had been frayed by decades in a hostile environment, but Learmonth was a steady and responsible man with about as much imagination as a lump of Cairngorm granite. When he started to speak in such a manner, things were not as they should be.

'Thank you, Bosun,' I said. 'I fully intend to.'

The laugh came from nowhere; drifting into the tiny cabin that now smelled of blood and iodine but when I looked around there was only myself and Learmonth present. The woman was in the cabin, her presence felt but not seen as she mocked my scepticism. Taking a deep breath, I consciously thought about Jennifer and once again heard those words, so softly spoken but filled with such meaning.

'In the gloaming, oh my darling
When the lights are soft and low
Will you think of me and love me
As you did once long ago?'

I looked up as the song slid the sensation of another woman from the room. Only Jennifer's memory remained, and I smiled, remembering her touch and her scent and her unexpected but always welcome mischief. I would see her again in a few months, but I wished fervently that I were with her now, holding her secure in the dim lights of Balgay House with all our life stretching before us.

'I'll be getting on then, Mr Cosgrove,' Learmonth said, but his face had somehow altered. The hard features had softened, the thin lips filled out and the eyes taunted him with their message of disquiet.

The mysterious woman had not vanished, merely altered her image as she merged with the bosun. Her laughter mocked my dreams as I began cleaning up the reeking mess in the cabin.

Chapter Twelve

GREENLAND SEA
APRIL 1914

No accounts whatever have been had of the ship George Dempster,
*whence it is inferred that she must have foundered at sea on her
outward voyage'*
Montrose Customs and Excise Records, 2nd February 1795

'Captain! Out there on the ice!' Thoms pointed with a gloved hand.
'Can you see them?'

Snapping open his telescope, Captain Milne focussed on the objects.
'Of course I can see them, Thoms. More polar bears, but we don't have
time to hunt them just now.'

'No, sir. That's not polar bear. That's people!'

We had spent a week killing seals, turning the once pristine ice into
a slaughterhouse of blood and broken bodies, and then spent another
week hacking off the skin and blubber and dragging the bloodied mess
back to *Lady Balgay*. I had thought that the killing was bad, but the
butchery of the actual skinning, or flensing as the men termed it, was
worse. It had been sickening, if professionally interesting, to see the
Greenlandmen remove the skin and blubber in a single dripping piece,

and throw the remnants of the seal aside. Drawn by the free meal, hundreds of birds added to the bedlam. On one occasion the seal was not quite dead and I had watched as a dozen birds had pecked at the still quivering body; the hands had callously ignored the creature's suffering. I think it was Shakespeare that wrote the quality of mercy was not strained; up here in the ice, mercy simply did not exist.

Despite my disgust, I could not help but be impressed as the seamen-turned- hunters proved expert butchers as they sliced and hacked at the bloody corpses, but amidst the shambles they also ensured that the actual skins were undamaged. This was a time to make the voyage profitable, for in a few months these skins would be sold in reputable shops up and down the country. Five shillings each, I think was the going price for a raw sealskin, but once dressed they would be turned into coats for wealthy women or fancy covers for travelling cases or anything else that fashion demanded.

Yet the skins were only incidental, for the blubber was the Green-landmen's prime concern; boiled down into oil, it would soften the raw jute that the factories of the Hilltown, Scouringburn and Dens Road would make into sacks, bagging and tarpaulins. Although the killing had lowered my already morbid spirits, I realised that the past murderous two weeks raised those of everybody else on board; Captain Milne, of course, mentally rubbed his hands with glee as he saw the seal skins being laced together and dragged over the ice, each one leaving a broad bloody smear.

'That's profit, Mr Cosgrove,' he gloated. 'That's wages for you and me. That's rent for the wives, food for the children and drink for the boys.'

What had been a huge colony of seals, bulls, cows and cubs was now a slaughterhouse stinking of blood, with skinned bodies left for the gathering birds and the Greenlandmen crimson with gore and spattered with fat.

At that time I wondered if I was in danger of becoming inured to slaughter, it was already so commonplace. With *Lady Balgay* part loaded, Pratt, bandaged and with his face so swollen he was unrecognisable, was hauling each skin over a flensing board before he carefully sliced off the blubber. Thoms was beside him, cutting the blubber into cubes and sending it down a canvas chute into the hold, where it was thrust into casks for the voyage home. Learmonth should have performed the flensing, but his hand had not sufficiently healed so he could only supervise and curse the money that his injury had cost him. I could not help in any of these operations, but listened to the conversations in a somewhat desultory fashion, for my mind was with Jennifer.

'If we make it back to Dundee, Leerie,' Pratt said in one of the rare occasions that there was a break in the work, 'I'll buy you a pint in Dock Street.' He returned to his skinning, his knife a bloodied silver smear as he ripped through the blubber of another seal. He looked up quickly, saw that Captain Milne was safely out of hearing on the ice and said softly. 'It was the ballast.'

'Keep your voice down,' Learmonth glanced over the side, as if Captain Milne was listening to everything said on board Lady Balgay.

'You know as well as I do that it was the ballast, eh?' Pratt looked toward the hold and shivered. 'I should tell everybody the story.'

'You should keep your mouth shut!' Learmonth said. 'Was the bladdernose not enough for you?'

I came closer as my curiosity overcame my natural desire to keep aloof from the hands, but Pratt touched a hand to his face and ducked sullenly away as the rest of the crew jealously counted each sealskin and every barrel of oil. Paid a meagre monthly amount, the oil money supplemented their wages so after a successful voyage they would have no need to work for the remainder of the year. That was one appeal of the Arctic, but it had been a long time since these men had tasted success and winters had meant voyages down the east coast or to Europe rather than time spent with their wives or in Dundee's roaring pubs. Ignoring Pratt's mumbles, they concentrated on storing up their wages, until Thoms' hail disturbed their routine of skinning and flensing and stuffing blubber into barrels. Each man looked up as

Thoms gave his verdict on the distant figures approaching across the bloodied ice.

'That's people, Captain; maybe survivors from some shipwreck.'

'Survivors from which shipwreck? There's no wreck. We haven't sighted a ship since the Prussian.' Captain Milne extended his telescope again and focussed carefully as every man in *Lady Balgay* hurried to the rail to stare and give his opinion.

I could see the two figures, but distance made them so miniscule I could not determine what they were. They might be men heavily bundled in furs, but they could equally well be polar bears, a mother and her cub.

'They're following the trail of blood,' Pratt pointed out quietly. 'They're following the blood to *Lady Balgay*.' He began to stroke his scrimshaw mermaid.

Of that there was no dispute. The sealers had left a distinctive broad smear across the ice, along which the two figures were walking. I shivered as I once again experienced the image of a voluptuous women drifting toward me on a silken crimson sea. The hunters had turned the frozen sea crimson with blood and now here was someone, or something, moving slowly toward us. I closed my eyes, surprised that the woman did not appear but alarmed that her absence now seemed as sinister as her presence had always been.

'Get away from here, Captain,' Pratt warned suddenly. 'Cut the lines and run before these things reach us. Leave them here, whoever or whatever they are.'

'Leave them here?' Captain Milne snapped shut his telescope. His look was poisonous. 'I'll do no such thing, Pratt. If these are men, I'll not leave them to die in such a desolate place, and if they're beasts we'll shoot them and sell the skins.' He spat over the side. 'Besides, if they're men they can help with the work, now that Learmonth's got himself injured.'

'Captain!' Pratt stopped and placed a hand to his face. Speaking stretched the stitches and caused him a great deal of pain.

'Aye, Captain. And don't you forget it.' Milne raised his voice. 'Thoms, Soutar, get onto the ice and see what these two are. Take a rifle too, for I'm not yet convinced they're human.' He shook his head. 'I can't quite make them out.'

The song returned then, the words low and yearning, as they had been when Jennifer last whispered them in my ear, and I closed my eyes, seeing her anxious, loving face as she had clung to me in that dark Dundee street.

> *'In the gloaming, oh my darling*
> *When the lights are soft and low*
> *Will you think of me and love me*
> *As you did once long ago?'*

Oh God, but I was thinking of her, wishing that I was with her in that splendid house in West Ferry with the view across to the fertile fields of Fife and the spring flowers bursting life into the garden. Instead I was stuck with these shaggy, fundamental Greenlandmen amidst the frost and with the smell of blood raw in the wind as these two mysterious figures slithered slowly closer. I peered across the distance, but some veil seemed to obscure the images, as if there was a haze lifting from the ice to deliberately blur my vision. If Captain Milne could not make them out with his telescope, what chance had I without one?

'Could they indeed be survivors, Mr Pratt?'

When Pratt looked at me, there was such horror in his eyes that I wondered if the attack by the seal had unhinged his mind. 'God, Doctor, sir, I hope that's what they are.'

'But from where have they come, Mr Pratt? We haven't seen a ship in weeks. There's nothing out here but us!'

Pratt's face creased with concentration. 'They might have come from some old wreck, Doctor, sir. Maybe they were stranded last season or even the season before. It happens out here sometimes; ships go down and people live with the Yakkies for months until they are picked up by another vessel.'

It was the longest speech that Pratt had ever made and I nodded my appreciation. 'Thank you Mr Pratt.'

'No, sir, don't thank me.' The gloved hand closed on my arm, nearly crushing any feeling away as Pratt made his point. 'You have nothing to thank me for, but I owe you my life, Doctor Sir, and I won't forget.'

'They're not bears. They're men! They are survivors!' The words spread through the ship as the hands clustered at the rail. There were stares and cheers, men pointing and gasps of astonishment that two people should be still able to walk after what must have been an appalling ordeal on the ice.

The two small parties gradually came closer and I watched as they met Thoms and Soutar. Thoms was a tall man but one of the survivors topped him by a good two inches, while the other looked short, almost childlike in comparison. There was a bout of hand shaking and what must have been emotional greetings before all four headed for *Lady Balgay*.

Picking up the mouth trumpet with which he communicated during foul weather, Captain Milne shouted across the ice, 'bring them aboard!' He looked around *Lady Balgay*, frowning, and dropped his voice. 'Although God alone knows where we are going to squeeze them in.'

The taller of the survivors clambered on deck first; his face damp with emotion as he stared upward at the two masts and stroked the upended dinghy. Within seconds a circle of astonished sealers surrounded him, asking a score of questions that he seemed quite unable to answer.

'Give him room!' I ordered, donning my doctor's hat. 'He must have been through hell out there! Give him some space!'

Pushing through the crowd, Captain Milne ordered that hot food should be prepared, and clean clothes procured from the ship's slop chest.

'You can work off the cost during the voyage' he said, and I grunted. I guessed he was worried in case any of his men thought he was becoming soft.

I raised my voice again. 'I had better examine them. They might need medical attention.'

The taller man spoke, his voice carrying the lilting accent of Orkney, so different from the harsh cadences of Dundee. 'There is no need, sir. We are both in good health.'

'Good health?' Captain Milne sounded suspicious. 'How can you be in good health out here? Where is your ship, mister, and what happened to you?'

'We were on board a foreign vessel,' the tall man said. '*Fortuna Gretel* from Greifswald in Prussia. A storm blew her too far north and she was nipped in the ice.' He waved his hand vaguely. 'We were not prepared for such a disaster. The master sent everybody out in small boats while he remained in case the ship got free.'

Learmonth glanced at Captain Milne. 'That was the Prussian that we got the rum from, Captain. She was out here, right enough.'

'Aye, I remember!' There was venom in Captain Milne's voice. 'So you deserted your ship and abandoned her master.' He spat over the side. 'What happened to the others in your boat, mister? And the boat itself?'

'We came on to the ice to spend the night and when we woke they were all gone.' The tall man shrugged. 'There was a thick fog so maybe they could not see us.'

'No?' Captain Milne moderated his tone. 'Or maybe they're just foreigners; as much seamen as I am a ballet dancer.' He glanced at the small man, who had remained quiet within his cocoon of furs. 'And how about you? Are you some sort of mute? Can't you speak?'

'He doesn't talk much Captain.' The tall man excused his companion. 'It was tough out there. We had just about given up hope when we heard your voices and followed the trail you left.'

'Aye.' For a second Milne looked dubious, and then he shrugged. 'Well, if you say so, mister, but the doctor's right, for once. Get below at once and let him look at you. I want a full report, Doctor. I want to hear that both men are fit for duty. More hands, more work, more seals killed.' He looked at the deck, with the bloody footprints.

'Pratt! Get this pigsty cleaned up! You might think you can shirk work by sticking your face in a seal's mouth, but not in my ship by God!'

'Aye, sir,' the bandages muffled Pratt's words, but he obeyed at once, looking at the survivors with something akin to fear. The smaller man turned toward him, his deep fur hood hiding his features, but there was no mistaking the intensity of his eyes.

'We don't need medically examined,' the tall man said. 'We can start work right away, sir.'

Captain Milne frowned. 'Did you not hear my orders, mister?' His voice was ominously quiet. 'I said report below with the doctor and get yourselves examined.' Stepping back, he flicked his clouded green eyes up and down the tall man. 'And when the doctor has passed you fit, report to my cabin, Mister...what did you say your name was?'

'Sinclair,' the man said softly. 'Isaac Sinclair. And this is...'he hesitated for a second, 'Jemmy Isbister.'

'Sinclair and Isbister,' Milne nodded. 'I'll write you into the muster books.' He withdrew aft a pace and abruptly glared around the rest of the crew. 'What the hell are you men hanging around for? Do you think seals skin themselves? Get back to work! Bring the last of the seals on board and smart! This good weather will not last forever.'

'This way,' I guided the survivors down the companionway to my cabin, where they stood hunch-shouldered, dripping melting ice on to the deck.

The design of *Lady Balgay* had put my cabin and the storeroom directly above the engine room, so the heat from the boiler eased through the deck, making it one of the warmest parts of the ship. I had been thankful for this small degree of comfort at many times during the voyage, but it was also helpful on a medical level.

'Strip, please,' I ordered casually. 'I want to make a proper examination.'

'There's really no need,' Sinclair said, 'we're perfectly fine. It's only been a few days...'

'No arguments, now.' I was determined not to have my authority questioned by a couple of strangers. I told myself that I was a qualified medical doctor, socially far above any sealing mariner, and I would be obeyed; 'strip!'

When Sinclair continued to protest, small Isbister shook his head and put a surprisingly delicate hand on my arm. 'Can we be seen separately?' his voice was quiet and low.

About to refuse, I considered for a second and nodded. This man might have some disease or injury that he found embarrassing, and it was a doctor's task to give confidential help with such things, even when on a sealing ketch hundreds of miles from civilisation. 'If you wish,' I allowed, and Isbister slipped quietly from the room.

Sinclair quickly shrugged off his clothing and stood stark while I probed and prodded, sounded his heart and felt his muscles. 'You're in surprisingly good condition for a man who was stranded on the ice,' I said, grudgingly. 'Indeed, you appear in better condition than most on board this ship.'

'I said I was,' Sinclair agreed. 'So there's no need to examine Isbister.'

'There's every need.' I contradicted. 'Send him in.'

'I'll wait here.'

'You'll wait outside,' I began, feeling genuine anger at such insolence from a man who should be grateful to be rescued, but on reflection I changed my mind. 'No, you'd better report to the captain as ordered. On this ship, you'll learn that Captain Milne is very much in command.' I had never expected to be glad of Milne's authoritarianism, but there was something about Sinclair I automatically disliked. The man was too self-assured and far too fit for the survivor of a shipwreck. 'Off you go.'

'Yes, Doctor.' Dressing slowly, Sinclair smiled and nodded as he left the cabin. I heard the murmur of voices outside and Isbister stepped in, still fully furred, with a thick hood covering his head and concealing most of his face.

'Right, Isbister. Strip please, and tell me what is bothering you.' Lowering my voice to be as approachable as possible without being too familiar, I patted Isbister's shoulder in an attempt to create trust. 'It's all right; there's no need to hide anything from me; confidentiality is part of my job.'

Isbister gave a light laugh, and pushed back his hood. The face that emerged was soft and delicate, with large brown eyes beneath long brown hair, and a small mouth that twitched into an amused smile.

I stared as Isbister continued to slowly undress, folding each item of clothing as neatly as possible until she stood naked, with both hands folded in front of her. About five foot four in height; she was shaped like Aphrodite, with generous hips and breasts that jutted their message of mature femininity. She faced me squarely, with her mouth undecided whether to smile or plead for help.

'Dear God,' I said, and sat on the bunk.

The sight of a woman standing unclothed and vulnerable within a sealing ketch crammed with some of the roughest seamen in Dundee was unnerving, but I knew I had other causes of unease. I tried to blink away that recurring vision of the brown haired woman floating toward me across a crimson sea and ensured my gaze did not stray from Isbister's eyes.

'You're a woman,' I said. I could not think what else to say.

'I know,' Isbister agreed, unfolding her hands and allowing them to fall loosely at her side. 'Isn't it lucky for us both that you are a doctor?'

The ambiguity of her words was not lost on me as I tried to view Isbister with professional detachment and speak to her only by her surname. I could not help but notice she was eminently and voluptuously desirable, with those thrusting breasts and wide, womanly hips. I looked away; this woman was a complete contrast to my tall, elegant Jennifer who was the only vibrant woman I had properly seen before. I shook my head to clear it from unsought and very disturbing images. Isbister's eyes, deep, brown and knowingly amused, were following mine.

'Miss Isbister...' I felt my words trail away. 'It is unusual for a woman to be on a sealing ship.'

'Yes,' Isbister agreed, without adding a word of explanation. Her smile was entrancing. 'Are you going to examine me, Doctor? Or am I to stand here in this condition all afternoon. This is not the warmest of cabins and...' She glanced over her shoulder, 'somebody might come in.'

'Of course,' I said, more than slightly flustered as I bent to my work. My attempts at maintaining professional detachment were nearly impossible with Isbister's shapely breasts stirring as she breathed and her hips pressing against me as I sounded her chest.

'You also seem in perfect health,' I controlled the harshness of my breathing, 'but I don't know what the captain will say when he hears he has a woman on board.'

Isbister smiled but made no move to dress. 'He'll say exactly what the master of *Fortuna Gretel* said.' Her voice was so calm that I guessed she knew of her power over men and how to exploit it to the full. 'He'll bluster and threaten to put me off the ship, and then he'll relent and become all paternal and caring. He'll look at me with a frown and allow me to stay because I'm a woman.' She accentuated her point with a slight, but shockingly disturbing movement of her hips. 'Of course, he will also insist that I keep myself apart from the crew and do not mingle.'

I sighed. She was right, of course. There was nothing that Captain Milne, or any other shipmaster, could do. In these latitudes it was impossible to put anyone ashore without condemning them to a freezing death, and there were no nearby ports where Isbister could be dropped off. The captain had no option but to allow her to stay.

'You seem very sure of yourself' I told her.

'I have to be; a lone woman in a ship full of men?' Isbister gave that disturbing quiver again. 'If I was not, goodness only knows what the consequences would be.'

'Indeed,' I agreed, nodding slowly. 'Goodness only knows.' Unable to help myself, I watched as Isbister slowly dressed. I was aware that she was also studying me beneath hooded eyes, and knew there was more amusement than friendship in her smile, but I still remained seated, transfixed.

Now there were three women in my head, and two of them could lead only to trouble.

Chapter Thirteen

A rather romantic incident has occurred on board the Flying Venus
in the harbour of Bombay. The captain shipped a young fellow un-
der the name of Thomas Brown, as a seaman, and after serving for
a considerable time on board the ship, it was only the other day
discovered that she was a woman.
  East of Fife Record, January 24 1868

'All hands on deck. Prepare for a stormy time!'

As always, the words created confusion as those men not already
working tumbled from their bunks and staggered the few steps to
the deck. I joined them, pulling on the great fur trousers and the fur
hat that was necessary for protection against the worst of the bitter
weather. All the same when I stepped on deck I could not resist my
astonished gasp. *Lady Balgay* was easing into a wide fjord, backed by
bleakly gaunt mountains still smeared with fields of snow. Floes of a
hundred shapes and sizes welcomed us, some shining under the morning sun, others shaded by mist as we slithered slowly on the surface
of the sea.

'More icebergs.' I shivered as the heights funnelled a bitter wind toward *Lady Balgay.*

'What did you expect?' Soutar snorted from his position at the wheel, 'bloody palm trees?'

Quickly closing my mouth, I stared at our surroundings. The mountains provided shelter but Lady *Balgay* still rocked slowly on steeply chopped waves as eider ducks, red throated divers and geese darted over and under the water as they examined this intruder into their world.

'We'll have the sails down, Bosun,' Captain Milne ordered quietly. 'And drop the anchor. We'll be here for a while.'

I remembered that last time the captain gave that order, Learmonth had sliced his hand, but now he was more careful, balancing himself foursquare on deck as he supervised *Lady Balgay* coming to rest. I watched carefully until satisfied he was safe, wondering at the change that had come over *Lady Balgay* since the two survivors had come on board. The atmosphere had altered; always tense, it had become nearly brittle, with men snapping at each other for no reason and heated arguments more common. Paradoxically, I had slept far better; that shaded, sensuous woman seemed to have completely disappeared from my mind, so I felt quite alert as I inspected our gaunt surroundings.

For the second time in our voyage I realised that there was beauty here, of a desolate sort. It was not the pastoral beauty of Angus or Fife, or the romantic landscapes of the Highlands with crumbling castles and shaggy cattle, but something more savage, untouched; primeval even, as if man had no place here.

This home of the seal and the frost seemed to invoke an uneasy restlessness from deep inside my soul. When a shaft of sunshine highlighted snow covered ice and the bird life of an Arctic spring, I knew I would never forget my time up here in the north; I suddenly understood a little of why men returned to the sealing year after year. Although I had vowed never to come back, I acknowledged a grudging admiration for…for what? I did not know. For something, surely, something that appealed to a different, more elemental, side of me, a side that I had not experienced before.

Jennifer suddenly seemed very far away.

'It's a fine view, Doctor.'

My start was involuntary; Isbister had approached so silently I had not been aware of her presence until she spoke.

'Yes. Yes it is.' Those expressive brown eyes were taunting me so I had to continue the conversation. 'How are your quarters, Miss Isbister?'

Captain Milne had cleared a cubicle for Isbister in the storeroom, segregated her behind a stiff canvas screen and guarded her with ferocious orders. She was not allowed to mingle with the crew, but could speak with the officers, and, grudgingly, with Isaac Sinclair. 'Adequate,' Isbister said, smiling very slightly.

I nodded, uncomfortable in her presence but unable to look away.

'You appear distracted.' Isbister was so close that I could feel her breath on my face, but it was her eyes that held my attention. They were deep and as dark and mysterious as a wishing well. But for what was I wishing? I stirred, not sure if I wanted to admit the truth even to myself.

'I was thinking about my wife.' That was a lie, but it was intended to warn Isbister off.

'And I'll wager that she is also thinking of you.' She replied easily. 'She will be all alone in Dundee, will she not?' She was smiling again, sharp teeth gleaming white against red lips.

I cursed inwardly. There was no place for women up here in the high latitudes. They were only a distraction from the work, and a temptation to men long separated from wives and sweethearts. 'Yes,' I replied shortly.

'You'll both be glad when you're back then.' Isbister's smile was as innocent as the hiss of a viper.

'I will indeed. If you'll excuse me?' I slid away, 'I have to speak with the captain.' Normally I would have avoided Captain Milne but anything was better than keeping company with this alarmingly captivating woman. I could feel her eyes following me as I ran aft, where Captain Milne was checking the rudder head.

'I thought you would be sealing, Captain, but the men appear to be scraping paint from the hull.'

'I do not like a shabby ship,' Milne explained quietly. 'So we will take off the ugly flaking green and paint her black.'

'I see.' I shrugged. I did not care what was happening, as long as it kept me away from Isbister's disturbing presence. 'But are there no seals here?'

'There are a few seals,' Milne pointed to half a dozen dog-like heads that bobbed amongst the glistening ice, 'and the longer we are here without unsettling them, the more will gather. Once they trust us, we'll capture them.' He shook his head, eyes shrewd. 'You've already seen a seal hunt, Mr Cosgrove. Did the blood and slaughter not cause you concern?'

'I did not enjoy it,' I admitted.

'I recall you had no qualms about shooting the bladdernose though,' Milne said dryly. 'However, I doubt your supposed squeamishness will prevent you scraping paint. Even a greeting faced girl can do that.'

Pratt's injured face was a constant reminder of the penalty of arguing with Captain Milne so within ten minutes I was over the side, scraper in hand and feet dangling a few inches above the chilled water of the fjord. I knew it was incompatible with the dignity of my situation, but strangely, I felt better there than I had when face to face with the seductive Isbister.

With most of the crew engaged in scraping, the work continued with some speed, and flakes of dry paint were soon floating amongst the brash ice and small washing pieces that clinked musically together around the ketch.

'Scraping when we should be sealing,' Thoms grumbled, scrubbing furiously, 'the captain has finally gone crazy.'

Trying to hold the scraper in hands made clumsy with huge mittens, I could only agree.

'Some bloody wages we'll earn this trip,' Thom continued, 'when we're wasting our time decorating when we could be making money. The Captain's gone soft. He's more concerned with making the boat look pretty than in doing his job.' He looked upward, where Isbister leaned over the rail, watching. 'It's that bloody woman of course. He's trying to impress her!'

In other circumstances I might have smiled at the thought of the irascible Captain Milne being influenced in any way by Isbister. When I glanced up she was looking directly at me, not smiling but with secret depths in her eyes, and I returned to my work, no longer certain of anything. I wished fervently that we had a hold full of oil and were steaming hard for the Tay.

'Here!' the cry came from the stern, where Mackie was working beside Donaldson. 'There's another name here, under the paint.'

'Another name?' Pratt sucked in his teeth. 'It's bad luck to rename a ship,'

'I thought it might be,' I murmured, trying to concentrate on my work. Everything seemed to be bad luck on this ship.

'What name is it?' Pratt called out, and asked Donaldson to repeat his words. 'Frigg? What sort of name is that?'

'A stupid name,' Donaldson responded; 'something foreign.'

'You're an educated man, Doctor Cosgrove,' Soutar reminded him. 'What does Frigg mean?'

'Nothing that I know.' Already glad of the break from menial work, I placed my scraper on the deck, climbed over the rail and walked aft. 'Show me.' I leaned over the taffrail, momentarily forgetting Isbister, who had sauntered behind me.

The name was in white letters, faded by salt water and foul weather, but still visible on the green hull. 'It's not Frigg,' I said, 'there are more letters under the paint.' Fetching my scraper, I removed the remaining few fragments of green. 'Her name was *Frigga*,' I read, casually.

'Frigga,' Donaldson repeated, rolling the syllables around his tongue. 'Frigga.' He giggled childishly. 'It sounds a swear word, eh?

Oh Frigga, the pub's run out of beer!' He stared shallowly at me. 'But what does that mean, eh?'

'Frigga was a Norse goddess,' I took the opportunity to display my knowledge to these mariners who had repeatedly shamed me with their skill, strength and endurance. 'Indeed, she would have ruled these parts, when the Vikings were here. That must be good luck, surely.'

Pratt grunted and shook his head. 'It's still wrong to change the ship's name, though. What sort of fool would do that?' He hawked and spat overboard. 'It's a stupid name, Frigga.'

'Not at all.' Now that I had begun to show my knowledge I was keen on continuing. 'It's a name we use every week.'

'What?' Instantly suspicious, Donaldson glowered at me. 'Maybe you use it every week, Doctor, but I've never said Frigga in my life; until now.'

'Yes you have,' I corrected. I knew that Captain Milne was frowning and shaking his head, but stupidly I continued. 'We all do. Friday was named after the god Frigga.'

'Oh Jesus,' Pratt stared at him. 'So the ship's called Friday?' He stepped back, nearly overbalancing as the rail caught the back of his legs.

'Dear God Doctor' Captain Milne's eyes were poisonous as they glared at me. 'Don't you ever bloody think before you talk?'

'Friday!' Pratt recovered and stared at me, with the blood draining from his face. 'We're sailing in a boat called Friday. That's the unluckiest day of the week; nobody sails on a bloody Friday.'

'Nonsense!' I was becoming tired with the superstitions of these men. 'It's only a name.' I pointed forward. 'That figurehead is probably meant to be Frigga herself, guiding us through the ice.'

The silence was suddenly acute as all the men within hearing range stopped to look at me. Surprisingly it was Soutar and not Pratt who spoke first. 'You mean we have Frigga, Friday, with us here? On the ship?' He looked forward. 'That's Frigga there?'

'We've all touched her for luck,' I reminded, knowing I was being foolish but determined to squash this superstition once and for all. This was 1914, for God's sake, and we were civilized Britons of the new, industrial age. 'Remember at the very start of the voyage we all fondled her bottom?' I smiled at the memory. 'Young Robert even kissed it, if I recall.'

'Oh sweet Lord, what have we done?' Pratt looked at his hands, his mouth open and lips trembling. 'We've touched Friday! We asked the unluckiest day for its help.' He looked at me, his face twisted with genuine fear. 'You're right, Doctor, young Mitchell did kiss her arse. We laughed at the time, but she'll get him back for his cheek; you mark my words!'

'What? How?' Mitchell's head appeared over the rail, his mouth wide open. 'What will she do, John?'

'Nothing,' Isbister put a comforting hand on his shoulder. 'It's all right, Robert. Mr Pratt is only jesting with you.' She smiled to me, her eyes warning. 'Isn't that right, Doctor?'

For the first time since I had met her, I felt a small glow of liking for Isbister, but Pratt was not finished yet. His voice sunk to a low whisper that I could hardly hear above the sharp clink of ice and the constant moaning of the wind.

'Nobody's jesting. This ship is doubly damned. Nobody will get home from this voyage!'

That was the first time I remembered the words of Mrs Adams, the gypsy woman who had told my fortune. She had promised I would return, and I felt a tiny nugget of gratitude for her words.

'Get back to your work or I'll show you damned, Pratt!' With his fur cap pulled forward so the peak was almost level with the tip of his nose, Captain Milne shoved Pratt hard against the taffrail. 'And if anybody else mentions any such superstitious claptrap again, by God I'll maroon the bastard right here and now!'

There was a general movement of heads to the surrounding land. The stark, snow streaked slopes and bitter grey-blue water was even less appealing than a voyage in Lady Balgay.

'No, Captain,' Soutar shook his head. 'You can't blame the lads. You know me, Captain. I'm not a wild man, but I've followed the sea all my life and I know it's bad luck to rename a ship, and nobody wants to sail on a Friday yet alone *in* a Friday.' His shiver had nothing to do with the cold. 'We'll have to change our luck somehow.'

When Thoms and Donaldson nodded their agreement, Isbister leaned against the mizzen, smiling to Captain Milne until he glared at her, when she moved slowly forward, not quite brushing against him in passing. Milne frowned, watched her for a second and sighed, as though making a momentous decision.

'You get that paint scraped off, and I'll remove any memory of *Lady Balgay's* last name, boys.' Milne's tone was suddenly fatherly. 'Now we know why the owner had her name changed, but I'll wager my luck against any long dead Norse woman, on any ocean of the world.' He looked around. 'Mitchell! Don't listen to those prattling old fools. You and the doctor come with me!'

Wondering, I followed Milne forward, with young Mitchell padding nervously at his side. The captain stopped at the bowsprit. 'Nip down to the stores and get a couple of axes, Mitchell, and we'll hack this bloody thing off the ship.'

'Captain?' Mitchell looked momentarily shocked.

'I mean the figurehead, Robert. If it is causing distress to my lads, then we'll get rid of it.' He raised his voice so everybody on board could hear him. 'If some Norwegian goddess thinks she can rule my ship, by Christ I'll prove her wrong!'

'Yes, sir.'

'And you can help too, Doctor. You caused all this trouble with your prattling tongue, so you can help put things right. Young Robert here is too young to be much affected, but some of those old salts have lived with superstition so long they believe it all. This is a new age now, of electricity and the telephone and heliographs. There's no space for old gods and suchlike rubbish. Come with me.'

I was aware of the crew watching, analysing every word Captain Milne spoke. I was just abaft of the bowsprit, within a short spit of the figurehead's rounded bottom as the captain gave his orders and thrust an axe into my suddenly sweating palm.

'Crawl out there, Mr Surgeon! Crawl if you don't want to be marooned on this damned island. Blasted Norse goddess, eh? Well, she's going off my ship, woman or no. Hack her down, Mitchell! Hack her down!'

'Yes, sir,' Mitchell sounded unhappy. He glanced aft, where Pratt and Soutar were watching, and hefted his axe.

Although the figurehead was attached to *Lady Balgay* by only a slender wooden stem, lack of space prevented a decent swing, so Mitchell could only manage a short chop that barely raised a splinter.

'You can do better, Doctor,' Captain Milne ordered. 'Go on; use these soft muscles of yours!'

Taking alternate swings, I competed with Mitchell, feeling the blisters rise on my palms as I worked, and very aware of Pratt's dismayed gasps. I stopped after ten minutes, more to catch my breath than to ask a genuine question.

'Is this wise, Captain? Meddling with the men's fears?'

Captain Milne grunted. 'You are a doctor, are you not?'

I nodded.

'And if there was a growth inside one of these men, something that gave them pain, what would you do?'

'Why, I'd cut it out,' I said.

'Exactly so, Doctor. Think of *Lady Balgay* and her crew as a single living creature and this figurehead as a growth. If we cut it out, the whole body should be healthier.'

The comparison was apt; I realised, and swung again, wondering if maybe Captain Milne was more intelligent than I had thought.

'Come on, Doctor! Put some beef into it!'

Even with both of us working, it took forty sweated minutes before the Naked Lady toppled over on one side, hanging by a sliver of wood and leaving a base of jagged splinters and the raw scars of our axes.

'There she goes!' Mitchell crowed, wiping perspiration from his forehead. 'Watch this!' Leaning forward he gave a final push with the head of his axe and the Naked Lady creaked forward. She hung for a second as if reluctant to finally fall, and then plunged downward. I had a brief glimpse of the figurehead poised like a diver, her arms outstretched as she arrowed into the water. The splash seemed to rebound throughout the length of the fjord and the ripples washed along the hull of *Lady Balgay*.

Only then did I realise that everyone in the crew was watching, and only Isbister did not look strained; she gave a few short claps of her hand.

'Well done, Captain. That took courage. And well done Robert; you handled that axe like an expert.'

Mitchell grinned his embarrassed pleasure at her.

'Fifteen are you, Robert?' Isbister flicked her eyes over him. 'My, but I'll wager the ladies skip after you, with that cute little face and the heart and body of a man.'

Captain Milne gave her a long glare before raising his voice. 'That's her gone now. No more Frigga, no more Friday. We're free of her, lads!' His shout echoed from the surrounding slopes. 'We're free of any bad luck!'

Only the birds replied as the crew looked at him in silence. Pratt held his scrimshaw mermaid as if his soul depended on it. Soutar openly prayed.

'Bugger you all then!' Milne said softly. 'Fetch paint from the stores and we'll have this ship black before night. I want her fresh painted, boys, and then we're after the seals again. Oil money, my bullies! We'll earn oil money for the pubs of Dock Street!'

There was no immediate response but gradually, one by one, the crew returned to work, slapping black paint on to the scraped hull of *Lady Balgay* as if furious effort could erase the memory of their presumed curse. I thought it significant that nobody came forward to the bows, and no seaman laid his brush on the raw scar where the Naked Lady had been. I looked over the side but the water was smooth and undisturbed; the figurehead had vanished as if spirited away. Even though she was made of wood, the Naked Lady had not floated alongside.

Chapter Fourteen

JAN MAYEN LAND
JUNE 1914

I haled me a woman from the street,
Shameless, but, oh. So fair!
I bade her sit in the model's seat,
And I painted her sitting there.'
  Robert Service: My Madonna

With none of the caustic banter that I had come to expect, the atmosphere was dull, until Sinclair began to sing a psalm so anciently obscure that only Pratt could accompany him, desperately clinging to any message of reassurance.

The tune sounded flat in the fjord but as they picked up the words, some of the others joined in. 'That's better, boys!' Captain Milne donated his fine tenor to the day. 'Sing, lads. Sing for the seals!'

As if they understood, some of the seals began to moan, so seal song intertwined with the human voices in an ululation more melancholic than tuneful but which seemed fitting for the time and place. To my nearly tone deaf ears it was like damned souls pleading for release, but when I tried to recall Jennifer's parting melody, I could not; the eerie combination of psalm and seals had driven both words and tune from my memory.

'Oh Jennifer,' I apologised, 'I haven't forgotten you, only the song,' I closed my eyes to recall her features, just as the Naked Lady bobbed up a cable's length to starboard, pointing her long finger accusingly.

'Oh Jesus,' Pratt cringed against the hull, 'Oh Jesus save us all.'

The figurehead spun in some unseen current, with the finger gesturing now to the ship, now to the surrounding mountains, and then it turned a slow somersault and slid softly beneath the surface, so the last glimpse we had was the rounded, white painted buttocks, taunting us with undeniable insult.

'She's going in front,' somebody said. 'She's preparing the way to Davy Jones' locker for us all.'

There was an instant of silence, and then Isbister laughed. 'What nonsense! Are all you brave strong men really so afraid of women that even a wooden carving can frighten you?'

Mitchell's laughter was forced, but most of the others joined in and for the second time I warmed toward Isbister. Only Pratt remained downcast, but nobody really expected anything else from him.

It was Captain Milne who slid over the stern with the ship's only pot of white paint, and he inscribed the name *Lady Balgay* in large, bold letters exactly over the place where *Frigga* had been painted. 'There now! There's our ship back! No figurehead and no foreign goddess. We're *Lady Balgay* from Dundee and that's the way it will stay.' He looked up, with white paint smeared across his face and his eyes aquamarine and unreadable. 'Right lads; we'll have an easy night tonight. Cards and a bottle eh? Get the spirits up?'

I nodded. I did not consider that anything could quickly restore the morale of these men, but Captain Milne had been managing whaling crews for years and he knew just what to do. Learmonth grinned and nudged Soutar. 'There we go, Sooty, rum tonight.'

Rubbing the back of his neck, Soutar looked at the spot where the Naked Lady had curtseyed and danced. 'Aye, there's rum, Walter, but not much celebrating, I fear. Not now.'

'All the same,' Thoms grinned to him. 'We'll drink the rum.' When he looked at me, he dropped his eyes. 'And so will you Doctor, tonight.'

In a small ketch like *Lady Balgay* there was no cabin large enough to accommodate all the crew so we gathered around the mainmast, some perched on the upturned boats, others leaning against the illusionary warmth of the funnel. With the surrounding heights shadowing even the summer light of the Arctic, Captain Milne ordered seal oil lanterns placed around the deck and *Lady Balgay's* reflection undulated prettily on the glittering water.

'Jennifer would like this,' I told Learmonth, 'it could be romantic with the clinking ice and moaning seals for music.'

'Drink the rum, Doctor, Learmonth advised, 'and set the romance aside. We're a long way from home yet.' He gave a small, bleak smile. 'Out here, thinking of your wife will only bring frustration and madness.'

I nodded; sometimes these uneducated men revealed more wisdom than any lettered professor secure in his bubble of academia.

Captain Milne had provided two bottles of rum and the keg of gin; Soutar brought a deck of cards and Learmonth, winking at me, provided a banjo with songs and tales from his time as a Klondike miner, while Ross the engineer spoke of the Boer War and high jinks on the veldt.

'This is a pleasant evening,' Captain Milne said, as he dealt the cards and we played pontoon and a simple variety of whist.

'All it lacks is some female company,' Soutar said casually, and everybody looked to the captain, who sighed and relented.

'Why not, Soots? We may as well have all the crew here, as long as you promise to behave yourselves.' He pulled at a chipped stoneware mug that contained three fingers of rum. 'But if there is any impropriety, any at all, I'll end this jollity and send you all to scrubbing the deck.' He glanced at Sinclair, who had fitted into the crew like a Greenlandman to a Dundee pub. 'Well off you go then, man! It's not right leaving her all alone while we have a holiday!'

'Right, Captain,' Sinclair rose at once.

'Leerie!' The captain emptied his mug in a single swallow, refilled it and leaned his back against the mainmast. 'Give us a song! Make it something lively, though, not one of your long dirges. It's weary enough up here, for Christ's sake.'

The notes of the banjo plucked at them, bringing memories of home and family, of other voyages and past days that they spoke of as the rum loosened their inhibitions.

'Isaac said I could join you, Captain.' Isbister waited for Captain Milne's permission, but as soon as he gave a nod and a rare smile, she slipped between Mitchell and Soutar, wriggling her bottom to get a more comfortable seat. 'This is a happy gathering,' she said, looking around her.

'All the better for having you here, my dear,' Captain Milne agreed, passing along a clean mug and a bottle in which dark liquid sloshed invitingly.

'Why, thank you, sir,' Isbister gave him a smile that would have charmed the growl from a polar bear, poured herself a miniscule tot of rum and tasted it, screwing up her face.

'That's not a drink! That's only a dirty glass!' Moving closer, the captain poured more into her mug. 'We've nothing suitable for ladies I'm afraid, and no fancy glasses.'

'A mug is as good as a glass to a thirsty woman,' Isbister excused him, and did not object to the larger measure. Nor did she screw up her face on her second tasting, and her hand lingered on the captain's arm as he withdrew. 'Thank you, Captain. I never did thank you properly for rescuing us from the ice.'

'There was no need then and no need now,' Captain Milne was surprisingly chivalrous, and I wondered if he had been misled when Sir Melville had warned me about his drinking habits; the alcohol seemed to make him mellower. Perhaps Sir Melville had only assumed that drink and Captain Milne were poor bedfellows. I tasted my own rum, decided that it was too strong but suited the situation and drank some more. The night seemed all the better for it.

Pratt glanced toward me and ran his gaze over the assembled crew, swore in soft desperation and looked away. I could see his hand trembling as he tasted the rum.

'Are you all right, Mr Pratt?' Isbister seemed concerned as she stretched over. She would have touched his arm if Pratt had not reared away. 'Don't you like women?' Her smile hovered between mockery and concern, with those dark eyes laughing to him.

'I like women well enough,' Pratt spoke without looking at her.

'Oh good. I am sure that your wife is pleased to hear that.' When Isbister spoke, everybody else stopped to listen, and she was aware that every male eye, except those of Pratt, was fixed on her.

'John never got married.' Ross said seriously.

'Oh, that's a shame,' Isbister lowered her voice and her eyes. 'And him with such a love of women, too. Maybe we could do something about that at the end of this voyage, John.' She looked away, sighing. 'But you'll be bound to have a sweetheart already, though? You'll have somebody who cares for you?'

'John never had a sweetheart either,' Ross continued. 'Although there was a seal that gave him a little nibble once!' Some of the more inebriated joined in the laughter, but Thoms glowered at Ross.

'There's no need for that, Dode. This is a friendly gathering.'

'We're only in fun, Tommy. John knows that. Don't you, Johnny boy? You know that me and you are good pals!' Flinging his arm around Pratt's shoulders, Ross hugged him briefly, to the raucous delight of the others.

'There's still time to find a wife, John,' Isbister said quietly. 'Why, a handsome man like you...'

'There's no time,' Pratt edged backward until he was jammed against the rail. 'There is no more time, Miss Isbister, and you of all people know that.'

There was a moment's silence before Ross gave a cruel laugh and Torrie joined in. 'What do you mean, there's no more time, Johnny boy? Have you been reading H. G. Wells?' Ross's smile was not pleasant. 'Is that what you do when you should be on watch? Immerse yourself in *The Time Machine*?'

'Not him,' Torrie scoffed. 'Johnnie Pratt can't read!'

'He can't read and he hasn't got a wife; what do you do when you're ashore, John? What do you get up to?' Ross leaned closer. 'Maybe you prefer boys, eh?'

'Enough, lads! Leave the man alone,' I tried to smooth things over, but Torrie glared at me, curling his lip in contempt.

Pratt shook his head. 'I can't help it if I can't read.'

'No, Mr Pratt,' I gave him all the support I could. 'And it really doesn't matter a two-penny damn!'

'Quite right, Doctor,' Isbister approved, 'it's all right, Mr Pratt, I'm only in fun.' She turned her attention and those tantalising eyes to Mitchell.

'You'll have a sweetheart, Robert, won't you? A good-looking young lad like you, always busy about the ship. You must have a dozen young women in tow, more's the pity.'

'More's the pity?' Mitchell raised his eyebrows, glancing to Torrie, the next youngest on the ship, for support. 'How do you mean, more's the pity?'

Torrie grinned and made an obscene gesture with his hand, to which Mitchell did not respond.

'Well.' Ignoring the by-play, Isbister favoured Mitchell with an open smile. 'If you had not got so many other girls, then you would be free for me.'

As the older men chuckled and nudged each other, Mitchell visibly coloured. 'I haven't anybody special...' he began.

'No? Well that's good news for me!' Isbister glanced at Ross, who was grinning, 'then we'll have to arrange to meet sometime, once we are back in Dundee.'

'Well,' Mitchell glanced around the men, obviously embarrassed and confused but not willing to forgo the opportunity to act the man. 'I might. But there's Mr Sinclair...'

'Me? Oh no,' Sinclair leaned back, waving a hand in front of him dismissively. 'I don't want to meet you in Dundee, Rab. Not unless you're paying for the drink.'

The chuckle deepened Mitchell's embarrassment. 'No, I mean, you and Miss Isbister are together.'

'Not at all,' Sinclair shook his head in emphatic denial. 'We just happened to be on the same ship together. That's all.'

'So there we are, Robert. Or may I call you Rob?' Isbister wriggled closer so her hips were pressing against those of Mitchell. 'Rob would be more companionable. I don't really like Rab.'

There was more rough laughter as Mitchell coloured further, but was unable to move away in the press of bodies.

I looked at Milne, hoping he would intervene, but he was too absorbed in opening another bottle of rum to notice what was happening. 'Will we be resuming the sealing tomorrow, Captain?'

Milne looked up and pushed his fur cap to the back of his head. 'You're surely desperate to see the slaughter, Doctor, but aye, tomorrow or the next day. It depends how the lads are after tonight.' He grinned around the deck. 'There will be a few sore heads, I wager, as this night is yet young.' He raised his voice. 'Pratt! Stoke the boilers, man! Put more oil in these lanterns!'

'Yes, Mr Pratt, let's have more light. You never know what Rob here might get up to in the dark!' Isbister had an arm around Mitchell now, and stretched to smile over the heads of the men on either side.

Grumbling, Pratt poured more oil into the lanterns, muttering about the waste when the Arctic night was nearly light as day, and then he thrust himself beside me.

'Shift over Dr Cosgrove, please.'

I obeyed, finding more space on the deck. 'This is a good idea of the captain's, Mr Pratt.'

'Is it? Count the heads, Mr Cosgrove.' Pratt spoke in a harsh, urgent whisper. 'Count the heads!'

I did so, wondering. 'There are ten of the original crew, including me, plus the captain and the two survivors.'

'How many is that?' Pratt answered his own question. 'That's thirteen, Doctor Cosgrove. Thirteen people on a damned, damned ship, and one of them's a woman!'

'Lucky thirteen, Mr Pratt,' I tried to lighten the conversation.

'It's the worst of luck to bring a woman to sea. It's the worst possible luck!'

Isbister leaned closer, her hand hot on my ankle. 'What are you whispering at, Mr Pratt? I hope you're not telling the doctor how attracted you are to me?' Her comments raised another laugh, and Pratt relapsed into miserable silence. I was embarrassed for the old seaman and looked away, but immediately wished I had not.

For the first time since the survivors came on board, the shadowy woman was back. She eased around the circle of men, touching one here, brushing past one there, and finally stopped behind Mitchell. I fought my fear as I watched her, knowing that she portended bad news but not understanding who or what she was. I tried to rise, to speak, to warn Mitchell, but the woman merely glanced at me and I could not move. And then, as suddenly as she had appeared she was gone, as if she slid inside Mitchell.

Isbister was speaking, with the men treasuring her woman's words as if they were oral gold. 'Tell us another story, George. Tell us about the strange goings-on in South Africa!'

Ross smiled into her eyes, obviously enjoying her company as he began a tale of a run ashore in Durban that had the whole company in stitches.

Captain Milne downed another mug of rum and held the bottle upside down. Only a single drip fell out. 'That's another dead soldier,' he said, and tossed it over the side, shouting 'Mitchell! Pour some gin!'

'Yes Captain.' Disentangling himself from Isbister's enfolding arm, Mitchell ran to the keg and splashed the clear liquid into half a dozen eagerly proffered mugs.

'Good lad! Get back to your place beside Jemmie now, and continue your education.'

I smiled, realising that Sir Melville had been completely mistaken. He had said that Milne was 'a splendid mariner, as long as you keep him away from the bottle,' but rather than causing violence or disaster, I now knew that rum brought a rare streak of humanity to the captain. It was another lesson in human nature that I tucked away for future reference.

Isbister welcomed Mitchell with a high giggle and a smacking kiss on his cheek that raised a cheer from some of the men, while others looked on sourly. Torrie grunted and began a private conversation with Ross.

'There'll be trouble later,' Thoms said seriously. He looked over to me. 'As ship's doctor, should you not limit the amount of drink?'

I sipped at my rum. Now I was used to the taste I found the sensation quite pleasant. 'It can't do much harm,' I said, nodding to the slowly smiling captain. At that moment I was much more concerned about the return of that shadowy woman. Who was she and from what misunderstood quarter of my brain had she emerged? I drank more rum, welcoming the oblivion I hoped it would bring. 'It might even do some good.'

'I hope you are right,' Thoms said. 'By God I hope you're right, but there'll be sore heads tomorrow.'

The singing grew louder and the jokes more crude as the night progressed, but Isbister joined in with the others, fending off any straying hands with a sharp slap and light banter. It was Pratt who was first to leave, stumbling forward to the jeers and catcalls of his fellows, but I was not far behind. Mingling with drunken sealers was amusing for a while, but even through the fog of alcohol I ultimately recalled my position as surgeon of the vessel, and son-in-law to the owner and decided it would be best to withdraw. Only Isbister seemed to notice my departure, but her smile was friendly as she waved me goodbye.

Desperately hoping that the vivacious woman would not stray into my head that night, I slid into my damply cold bunk. I closed my eyes, wondering how *Lady Balgay* managed to sway even in the sheltered waters of the fjord, but it was the loud scream that wakened me and I jumped up, cringed at the splitting agony of my head.

'What in God's name was that?'

Chapter Fifteen

JAN MAYEN LAND
JUNE 1914

Some die in the wayside, some drop down on the streets, the poor sucking hobs and starving for want of milk which the empty breasts of their mothers cannot give them. Everyone can see Death in the faces of the poor.

Robert Sibbald, eyewitness to King William's Ill Years, Scotland, mid 1690s

'What the devil is happening?' I emerged on deck and looked around. The lamps must have guttered out in smoke and stink hours before, and the pale Arctic night had lightened into the greyness of day. Everything was still and dismal, with *Lady Balgay* swinging softly to her anchor in the solemnity of the fjord.

The scream sounded again, more drawn out, ending in a horrifying bubble of despair that raised the small hairs on the back of his skull.

'Jesus.' I raised my voice to a shout. 'Who's that? It's me! The doctor! Where are you?'

After the screaming came the silence, so intense and so thick I felt as if I could hack it into chunks and pack it in the blubber barrels.

With my head thick and throbbing and my breathing a painful rasp in my throat I looked around, but I could see nothing unusual amongst the coiled cables and ordered gear of *Lady Balgay*. In the few moments since I had staggered on deck the light had already altered, turning sickly green so everything, from the sky to the neatly furled sails, was tinged and discoloured. Still dressed in nothing more than long woollen underwear I shivered uncontrollably as the gaunt slopes gloomed all around and the seal call haunted the sullen sea.

'It's begun,' Pratt had emerged from the deckhouse that passed for a foc'sle with his skinning knife in his hand and fear on his face. 'It's begun now.'

'What's begun now?'

Pratt shook his head, glancing around him. 'Who was it, Doctor Cosgrove?'

'I don't know.' I raised my voice again. 'This is the doctor! Who was screaming? Who's hurt? What's happened?'

Donaldson burst from the foc'sle with a sealing club in his hand and murder in his eyes. 'Mr Cosgrove! Did you hear that?'

'I did! Who was it?'

Donaldson shook his head as others followed him; some as sparsely clad as I was, others in full furs and ready to go on watch. Mackie was giggling as he took Donaldson's club. 'It's the Naked Lady come to get us,' he said, and vomited on the deck.

'Drunken bastard,' Donaldson said without heat, but made no move to help him.

'Who is missing?' Learmonth glanced around, 'only the captain, the woman and the boy.'

'Aye, we can guess what the woman and young Rab were up to,' Thoms said soberly. 'She was all over him like a dose of crabs, which is just what he'll get if he's not careful.'

'Aye, if he's lucky that's all he'll get.' Pratt raised his voice. 'Mitchell! Where are you, you dirty wee bastard! Come here!'

'What's all the noise?' Isbister emerged on deck with her hair a tousled mess and her eyes bleary. She put a hand to her forehead, as if she was suffering. 'What's happening here, Doctor?'

'Was that you screaming?' Learmonth was brusque.

'Screaming? I didn't hear anybody screaming.' Isbister blinked across to him, and then at the array of men in their underwear. 'You might make the effort to be decent in the presence of a lady.'

'Ladies don't come on board sealing ships,' Learmonth gave her pretensions short shrift. 'And we've no time for niceties. Where's young Mitchell? Where's the boy? Is he with you?'

'With me?' Isbister shook her head, the sudden movement obviously causing her pain. 'Why on earth would he be with me?'

'He was with you last night.' Learmonth said grimly as he pushed down the companionway to look inside her quarters. 'It's a bloody mess but Mitchell's not there.'

'Of course not...' Isbister began, but Learmonth ignored her.

'Thoms, Soutar, Pratt, you search the ship. Ross and Torrie, check the engine room. Doctor, get your medical kit ready, just in case, and I'll wake the captain.' He hesitated for a second. 'He had quite a bit to drink last night so he might not be in the best of fettle.'

Accepting that as a warning to keep out of the captain's way, I withdrew to my cabin and got my medical bag ready, checking for bandages, lint and anything else that might be needed. The screams had sounded terrible, but there were no follow-up noises, so perhaps I had imagined the intensity. Possibly it had been a yell of surprise rather than pain. Taking a deep breath, I tried to ease the pounding of my heart; I freely admit that the atmosphere on this ship unnerved me, together with the superstitious nonsense from old men such as Pratt.

'Oh Jesus! Rab!' That was Thoms' voice, raised in concern. 'We've found him! Doctor! Come here quickly!'

Mitchell lay face down on the ballast in the dim greyness of the main hold. His legs were at an acute angle, his left arm was twisted beneath him, his right was thrown out and blood coated him from his skull to his knees. Scrambling down the ladder, I pushed Thoms aside and knelt at the boy's side. The initial examination took only seconds. Mitchell was not breathing, his neck was clean broken and he was dead.

The vision came unbidden and terrifyingly clear. Last night that shadowy woman had returned. She had stood behind Mitchell before gradually and insidiously merging with him. I flinched as the truth slammed into me. That enigmatic woman had culled him, as surely as these monsters from Norse mythology, the Choosers of the Slain, selected their victim. I closed my eyes as I recalled Pratt's fears about Frigga and the destruction of the figurehead. What would be dismissed as laughable superstition while safe in Dundee was quite different out on the ice.

Learmonth was kneeling beside Mitchell, holding his head very gently. 'He must have gone to the heads in the night and fallen down the hold.' His voice was quiet. 'Poor wee bugger, on his first voyage north.' Sighing, he looked up at me, his eyes hooded. 'He was a fisherman too, from Broughty. He had spent all his life in the fishing boats but he wanted some adventure before he settled down.'

'How could he fall down the hold?' I asked. 'He was the most agile man aboard! Remember how he danced on the bowsprit and was always playing up aloft?'

'More importantly,' Thoms wondered, 'who left the hatch cover off? The captain always insists it's battened down in case the weather turns foul.'

'Aye,' by that time I could swear as fluently as any Greenlandman and proved it, there and then. 'There's something not right here.' That woman was in there, in the hold beside me. I could feel her presence as she prowled among the blubber barrels, drifted across the shingle and gloated over the twisted corpse of Mitchell.

The boy accused us through wide staring eyes. He had been open and handsome in life but death made him ugly, his features twisted and his mouth gaping in a scream that I knew would live forever in my memory.

'All this way for adventure,' Learmonth repeated, 'to end up falling down the hold.'

'Well,' Thoms said, looking at the body. 'He's had all the adventure he's going to get. That's the end of Robert Mitchell.'

'Let me see him properly.' I ordered. 'Bring a light!'

Clambering down to the hold, Captain Milne held the lantern high so the flickering light bounced shadows across the shingle ballast and stacked casks. I knelt down and straightened the body before I examined the boy's wounds. What I found only increased my feelings of unease.

'Jesus,' I blasphemed, 'something's been chewing at him.'

'Oh sweet God!' Pratt had joined me, one hand closed on his scrimshaw mermaid. 'Chewing?'

'Look at this!' I lifted Mitchell's right arm to show where the boy's sleeve had been gnawed through; there were raw puncture wounds on the flesh beneath. 'These are teeth marks.'

'Rats,' Captain Milne gave his verdict, as Pratt stepped back, making small sounds of terror. 'Every ship is overrun with rats.'

'No Captain,' Pratt shook his head, clutching his scrimshaw as if it would save his life. 'It wasn't rats!'

'Shut your mouth!' Milne hissed. 'And keep it shut, Pratt, or I'll sling you overboard and make you swim back to the Tay. Rats chewed at young Mitchell. All right?'

'Yes, Captain,' Pratt glanced at Milne, and for a moment I wondered who scared him more, the captain or the creatures that had so mangled Mitchell's arm.

'Bring him on deck,' Captain Milne spoke thickly, as if in pain, 'and we'll do what's necessary.'

When I lifted the body, Mitchell's tightly closed fist opened on its own, and something trickled out.

'That's unusual,' I said, and looked closer to see what had fallen. He had held a few small stones together with a brittle fragment of something smooth and white. Thinking it was only a seashell, I was about to throw it away when Pratt took a deep breath.

'Oh God, Doctor! See what the lad was holding!'

'A piece of shell,' I said, carelessly, but looked again when I saw the horror on Pratt's face. I had been mistaken; the white object was not a shell. 'No, it's not. It's a bone. It looks like a piece of a human skull; the eye socket, I think.' Holding it closer to the lantern, I examined it more closely. 'Yes, it might be a human eye socket. I wonder how that got here.'

'Don't touch it!' Backing against the blubber barrels, Pratt was absolutely petrified, one hand stretched before him and the other clutching his scrimshaw mermaid. 'Throw it away, doctor, if you value your life! Oh God, oh my God. They're coming for us!' He began to sob, with great tears rolling down his cheeks.

'It's all right, Mr Pratt,' I tried to soothe him, dropping the piece of bone back onto the shingle. 'Whoever it belonged to is long dead now. It's more important to take care of poor Robert here.'

'No, no, no. That won't help. They're coming. It's the ballast!'

'Ballast my arse!' Pushing Pratt contemptuously aside, Captain Milne swung a mighty kick. 'Get over there, you snivelling wreck! Go and help with your mate!'

While Pratt began to whimper, Learmonth stooped closer. 'Come on, John. It's only a piece of bone. It's probably from some drowned seaman washed ashore on the skerry.' Patting Pratt's shoulder, he looked up at the circle of faces that surrounded the hold. 'Right lads, let's get poor wee Rab on deck and get him ready.'

Some of the hands came down willingly; others hung back, unwilling to touch the dead body of a boy they had known so well in life, but it was Torrie who looked most upset.

'He wouldn't have just fallen, not Rab. He was sure footed as a goat.' He lowered his voice, glowering around the deck. 'Some bastard must have pushed him. Maybe it was one of the survivors!' He pointed to Sinclair. 'Where were you when Rab fell?'

Sinclair stepped back. 'How should I know where I was when the lad fell? When did he fall? Anyway, I spent the night in the foc'sle with everybody else.'

'He was with us,' Donaldson nodded in vigorous agreement. 'Snoring his bloody head off.'

'Aye,' Mackie agreed. 'It wasn't Sinky.'

'It must have been the woman then. Where the hell is she anyway?'

'God knows. Give a hand here!'

With Captain Milne supervising, the broken body of Mitchell was hoisted up and laid gently on the deck. The men gathered around, most with expressions of grief but Mackie with a terrible excitement in his eyes.

'I've never seen a dead man before,' he said.

'He was pushed,' Torrie said, and suddenly pointed. 'She pushed him!'

Isbister was standing alone beside the mizzenmast.

'Why would she do that?' Captain Milne asked. 'Don't be stupid, Torrie. It was an accident and he fell in the dark. It was ugly, tragic but simple. These things happen at sea.'

'Not to Rab they wouldn't.' Torrie lifted his chin in defiance but suddenly all his anger disappeared. One minute he was a savage, muscular young man, all ire and fury, but the next he was sobbing, his shoulders shaking as he knelt beside the dead body of the boy who was the nearest thing to a friend he had on board. 'Rab!'

It was Isbister who reached him first, pulling him close and leading him away from the inarticulate sympathy of the men. 'Come on, Albert. He's gone now. You can't help him.'

'But he was my friend.' Torrie had dropped any pretence at insensitivity. 'I didn't want him to die.'

'Nobody did. Come on now. He was my friend too.'

'Leave them,' I took control as gently as I could, stopping Ross when he moved toward Torrie. 'A woman's touch will do him good.' I was pleasantly surprised at my own insight, but amazingly and unexpectedly grateful that Isbister was comforting Torrie. At that moment, other matters demanded my attention.

When I examined Mitchell properly I found his neck, femur and left arm were all fractured, and he had two cracked ribs. All these could be caused by a fall into the hold from the deck, but I paid particular attention to the teeth marks on his forearm. 'These aren't rat bites,' I pointed out as quietly as I could. 'They're far too large.'

'Robert Mitchell fell into the hold and broke his neck.' Captain Milne ignored my comments. 'That's what happened. Put that on your piece of paper Doctor, and we'll all be satisfied.'

'Aye, Captain,' I had no doubt about the cause of death, only the reason and what happened afterward. I refused to withdraw, despite Milne's vicious look. 'I heard two screams and he couldn't have fallen twice. The second scream was long; it lasted for about five seconds, as if he was in great pain. He couldn't have screamed after he died.' I shivered, remembering the horror of that memory.

Frowning from the aftermath of two bottles of rum, Captain Milne thrust a stubby finger into my stomach. 'What did he die of?'

'A broken neck, Captain.'

'Then that's what you write. You're no Sherlock Holmes, Doctor; so don't try to be too clever. I only heard one scream and I've far better hearing than you have. Your ears must be playing tricks on you. Broken neck – write it!'

What choice did I have? I had to record the cause of death and, as the captain said, Mitchell had died of a broken neck. My pen spluttered as I recorded the facts, but we both knew were things unsaid. 'And the second scream? And the bite marks?'

'As nobody except you claims to have heard the second scream, Doctor, we can discount it. You were hearing things. Perhaps you were having a nightmare.' Milne leaned closer. 'Do you have nightmares, Dr Cosgrove?'

'Well yes,' I thought of that veiled woman.

'There you are then; it was a nightmare.' Captain Milne turned aside.

'I was awake when I heard that second scream,' I was surprised at my own stubbornness, 'and what about the teeth marks?'

'Rats.' Milne abruptly stepped closer so his breath was warm and foetid on my face and his eyes green and viciously boring into mine. 'What else could it have been?'

I closed my mouth and said nothing. I could not speak of the woman that slid in and out of my consciousness and had slithered inside Mitchell's body, or the feeling of horror that lived constantly with me. A man did not mention such things, and I had come north partly to prove myself as a man.

'So finish scribbling on your bit paper, Doctor and I'll make the necessary arrangements.'

Chapter Sixteen

Confronting a storm is like fighting God. All the powers in the universe seem to be against you and, in an extraordinary way, your irrelevance is at the same time both humbling and exalting
  Franciose LeGrande

We buried Mitchell at the side of the fjord, scraping a shallow grave in the frozen ground and covering the body with stones to keep it safe from any prowling animals. Captain Milne gave a short service and the crew ducked their heads and sang a mournful hymn. Few spoke to each other, but most patted Torrie on the shoulder in unspoken sympathy. The young fireman was white faced and clearly shocked, occasionally shaking his head as he mechanically sang, although it was obvious that the words gave him no comfort.

I noticed that Isbister stood apart until the service began, but stepped close to Torrie immediately we covered the body. Pratt stood alone the whole time, watching Isbister and Sinclair like a rabbit with a stoat. Even in the plunging temperatures of the Arctic, I could see the sweat beading his face. The sound of shovels on the gravelled shingle of the frozen shore was something from the seventh pit of hell.

'All right.' Captain Milne stepped back from the grave immediately the final stone was laid. 'Rab Mitchell was a nice lad but he's gone now.' He looked around his crew. 'We've wasted enough time, so let's do what we're here for. Let's capture some seals and get home.'

'And now there are twelve.' Pratt came behind me as I stood watching the final batch of sealskins dragged aboard. When *Lady Balgay* had arrived the fjord was a place of peace and solitude; now it was a slaughterhouse and the water was greasy with blood.

'Aye. Twelve, Mr Pratt.' I glanced at the lonely grave, already covered by a wreath of snow. Robert Mitchell's parents would have wanted the boy taken home, but he would lie here forever, alone with the remnants of the animals he had come to hunt.

'Can I speak to you, please, Dr. Cosgrove?'

'Of course.' Since the encounter with the bladdernose seal, I had come to understand Pratt. Beneath the quivering superstition there was a high imagination and sensitiveness unusual among these sealers. In different circumstances Pratt might have made something of himself, but there was little chance of advancement for an illiterate seaman dragged up on Dundee's dockside. In a moment of introspection, I wondered how I would have fared if my background had been different. Probably no better than Pratt, I decided, and shivered at the thought.

'The captain said that I wasn't to say anything, but I've been thinking, Doctor, especially after Mitchell's death...' Pratt looked at me for support.

'I understand.' Expecting Pratt to speak about his sorrow, I held his eyes. 'You can tell me anything you like, Mr Pratt. We know each other well enough now.'

'Yes, Doctor. It was the ballast that killed young Rab.'

There had been no visions in the seven days of hunting since Mitchell's death, but those few words of Pratt's immediately reawakened the fear that shadowed my mind. I tried to adopt the pose of a stern, educated man. 'I hope this is not more of your superstitious nonsense, Mr Pratt.'

'No, Doctor. This is true. Please…' there were nearly tears in Pratt's eyes and he implored me with an outstretched hand. 'Please listen, Dr Cosgrove.'

Taking a deep breath, I nodded reluctantly, wondering if I could fight my own fears by concentrating on those of others. 'Carry on.'

'It was the ballast, Doctor. Everybody knows that Gass Skerries is an unlucky place. Nobody goes there. Even the local fishermen avoid it.'

Torn between my duty to help my patient and my desire to block out fears I knew to be irrational, I hesitated, but years of training triumphed. 'Why is that?' I swallowed hard, trying to control the terror that lurked at the fringe of my sane mind. 'You'll have to tell me everything, John, so we can clear this away.'

'Yes, Doctor.' Pratt's arm felt like a steel hawser when he wrapped it around my shoulder and guided me to the lee of the mainmast.

I noticed Isbister watching, but turned my back in the hope she would take the hint and keep her distance. 'Carry on, Mr Pratt.'

'It's not good to take ballast from Gass Skerries.' Pratt hesitated, obviously hoping for encouragement.

'Why is that, John?' I knew I was delving deeper than I really wished to go, but I thought that if I could remove some of Pratt's fears, I might find a way to deal with my own. Already I could feel that phantom stirring, emerging from the fringe of my consciousness. I shivered, but tried to concentrate on Pratt; my duty as a doctor was to help my patient recover from the death of Mitchell. My own mental welfare came second.

'You won't know the story, sir.' Pratt exhaled slowly, with the resulting moisture freezing on his beard. His hands shook as he produced a stubby pipe and thrust it in his mouth, sucking out of habit, for there was no tobacco in the bowl.

'Not at all,' I admitted, wishing that I could ignore this old man and run. But where could I go? There is nowhere to hide on a fifty-eight ton ketch in the Arctic.

'It's called Gass Skerries, but the original name was Gallows Skerries because there was a hanging there,' Pratt sucked noisily and looked at me, to ensure I was still listening. 'You see, hundreds of years ago there was a great famine in Scotland. King William's Ill Years, they called it, because King William was on the throne and it lasted for years.'

'I understand,' I vaguely recalled the term from my school days. It had been at the end of the seventeenth century, and thousands of people had died of hunger and disease. If I remembered correctly, the famine had occurred at the same time as a trade depression and had been a factor in driving Scotland into the Union with England. 'It was a terrible time.'

'It was,' Pratt agreed sadly, as if he had experienced the famine in person. 'Well, it hit Orkney as badly as anywhere else, except for one married couple at Tormiston, on the east coast of the Orkney mainland. They stayed fit despite the deaths all around them. In these old days people began to suspect witchcraft, and they sent over the minister to see what was happening.' Pratt paused for a moment, again checking to see if I was paying attention.

I shivered as a chill wind slid from the gaunt slopes on either side. These stark hills seemed to be watching, resenting this small vessel that had marred their island with death.

'And that was the last they saw of the minister.' Pratt spoke louder to hold my interest. 'He was never seen again. So the people got even more worried, and three of them armed themselves with staves and swords and marched across the moor to the farm at Tormiston. After a day only one returned, and he was half mad with fear.'

A gust of wind struck *Lady Balgay*, howling through the rigging like a tormented soul so that I looked up in increasing fear. My eye caught Isbister just as the wind flattened the bulky furs against her body. For a second I remembered the occasion when she had stood naked before me, and I shamefully but vividly recalled every curve and swell of her figure.

'No!' I tried to deny the vision, but the brief, guilty memory had already prompted the memories I hoped to repress and that dark headed woman encroached across my imagination, hips swaying tantalisingly and her allure undoubted and unrestrained. I strained to see her face, but Pratt was waiting for a response, his harsh breathing shattering my train of thought.

'The man who returned was half mad with fear,' Pratt repeated, urging me to listen.

'What had happened?' I allowed Pratt time to relax a little, knowing that the woman was also waiting; waiting with the patience of the damned.

'Well, sir,' Pratt shook his head. 'We'll never know for sure, of course, but that sole survivor told of horrible things, of a cottage with human limbs hanging up, and of people eating human flesh.'

'Cannibals!' I was not sure whether to be shocked or amused. I had heard of such things happening in the Pacific Islands and such like remote places, but knew they could never occur in a Christian country like Scotland. Confining Pratt's tale to complete fantasy, I pretended to be outraged. 'No wonder the man was upset. What happened next, John?'

Pratt gripped his scrimshaw mermaid as if for security. 'All the people of the area gathered together and marched to Tormiston. There was a great mob of them, men and women together, with sticks and rocks and whatever weapons they could find, and as they marched they sang psalms to give them strength. Of course, once the cannibals saw them they tried to run away, but the people captured them and held them tight.' Pratt looked down at the deck with his body trembling as if he had actually witnessed the events he described.

'They examined the cannibals, and found they were fit and far healthier than anybody else in that time of dearth, and then they looked inside the farmhouse.' Pratt lowered his voice to little more than a whisper. 'They found the remains of men and women hanging from the rafters, legs and arms and other things. It was horrible, Dr Cosgrove, horrible…'

'Yes, John,' I placed a reassuring hand on his shoulder. 'But it was all a long time ago, if it happened at all.'

'Yes, Dr. Cosgrove.' Taking a deep breath, Pratt continued. 'The people pronounced sentence and they dragged the cannibals to the point and hanged them there and then, right on the tip.' He looked at me, as if for condemnation.

'I can understand that,' I said, struggling to push aside the woman who stepped into the realms of my conscious mind. She was no longer alone, for a man stood at her side and both smiled at me with teeth stained with blood.

Encouraged, Pratt finished his story. 'Some were going to throw the dead bodies in the sea, others wanted to burn them, but instead they buried them there, on unconsecrated ground under the shingle, so that they can never get rest. The people built a cairn over the graves as a reminder of the terrible sins, and it remained as a shingle spit for decades. It was about forty years later, about 1739 that a high tide and a storm changed the coastline forever so the spit became a skerry.'

'Gass Skerry?'

'Gallows Skerry, it was known as,' Pratt corrected sternly, 'but eventually the name was shortened to Gass. And now that skerry is cursed. No local will ever go there and nobody will ever go near the cairn that was built over the cannibal's bodies.'

I shuddered involuntarily: it was that same cairn from which I had taken a shovelful of ballast, the same cairn that Pratt had refused to go near. I nodded as the images in my mind altered. Where before there had been a single female wraith, now there were two much more substantial figures, smiling with bloody teeth as I learned their story, laughing as they emerged from the anonymity of the shingle mound and basked in the freedom of exposure.

'Nonsense,' I tried to dismiss my imaginings. I knew I was only augmenting my own fantasies with those of Pratt, but after hearing the story, and being aware of Pratt's deep superstition, I could understand his reluctance to take ballast from the cairn. I took a deep breath and looked away; if I concentrated on Jennifer, I could push the two ethereal images from my mind, forcing them back step by bloodstained step. Jennifer would be my saviour. 'That's some story,' I said at last.

'It's a true story,' Pratt insisted, 'and some of the boys are unhappy that we took ballast from the skerry. It's unlucky, and we had thirteen people for that gathering, and one a woman, on a ship named after Friday.' His voice rose as the hysteria took control of him. 'Doctor! We're all cursed! We must put back the ballast!' Lunging forward, he grabbed my arms, thrusting his face forward. 'It's the ballast, Doctor Cosgrave!'

'John! John!' I wrestled free from Pratt's grip and held him secure. 'It's all right!' I waited until some of the madness cleared from his eyes before I continued. 'Now listen. We've changed the name, Mr Pratt, and got rid of the figurehead. The Friday thing is gone! And there are no longer thirteen on board. That's why young Rab left; he was trying to help us, John.' I guessed that logic would not work against Pratt's superstition, so I had to ease his fears by other methods. 'We only have to catch a few score more seals and we'll be heading back home. Think of that, Mr Pratt. Dundee is waiting for us.'

'Aye, sir,' Pratt sounded doubtful. 'And so are these cannibals.' His eyes looked directly into mine, wild as any devil-worshipping heathen. 'We'll never see Dundee, Dr Cosgrove, not with that ballast on board. There are too many evil things happening on this boat,' he shook his head, looking old and suddenly, terribly, weary. 'Far too many things, Doctor.'

I struggled to sleep that night, lying in that bunk that reeked of damp and with Pratt's words echoing and re-echoing around my head. I thought of the name, *Frigga*, and of the crew of thirteen; I thought of the death of Mitchell and the tale of the ballast, and although I knew each item on its own could be explained away, the combination was far more potent than the sum of its component parts. And always there was that shadowy figure, the image of voluptuous femininity fused with a hidden horror with which I knew I could not cope.

I sat up suddenly as the feeling of chill dread returned, many times stronger than before. They were here; the woman and the man; I could feel their presence on *Lady Balgay*, even in this cabin. I looked up, fighting the fear as both figures lingered near the cabin door.

'What do you want?' I failed to conceal the quaver in my voice.

They did not speak, but I knew I was to follow them as they drifted through the ship, their feet noiseless on the deck but leaving a red smear that could only be blood. *Lady Balgay* was quiet save for the normal creaks and groans and the constant whistle of wind through her rigging, and I knew that the crew could neither hear nor see us, although I do not think I was sleeping.

Nevertheless, despite my fear, I confess to being interested in this strange shift of the mind, and resolved to write a paper on the psychological effects of worry and danger as soon as I returned to Dundee. If I remained logical and did not allow this strange mental aberration to take complete control, I could chronicle these occurrences, but rationality was difficult when one was coping with personifications dredged from a combination of recent experiences and one's own imagination.

The images ushered me forward, past the canvas screen that concealed Isbister, past the storerooms and into the foc'sle. When I saw the entire crew sleeping there, the logical part of my mind confirmed that this occurrence was imaginary, for I knew there would be men constantly on watch, but the two figures were my guides and I must do as they willed. It was strange that I now felt no personal fear. I knew, somehow, that I was in no immediate danger, although I sensed great evil.

The realisation that my mind could create such wickedness was immensely disturbing; I would have to explore this new side to my personality. Much more importantly, I would have to ensure it never escaped to harm Jennifer.

The men lay in their bunks, some snoring noiselessly, others, such as Pratt, curled up in foetal balls and twitching as nightmares roamed their minds. When the woman looked at me, her eyes were ensnaring caverns in a featureless face, and she eased casually past me to fondle the sea chests. Most had decorated lids, lovingly painted pictures of a clipper ship, the face of a wife, or initials carved with pride. The seaman spent hours on such artistry in order to retain some individuality in an environment where they were powerless cogs, human machines with a function to work the ship and not people with a past, present and slow-fading hopes for a future. Although I could not see the woman's face, I knew she was smiling as she examined the chests for a long moment before moving off, toward the sleeping crew.

Ignoring Torrie, who lay with both hands snug in the cradle of his upper thighs, and Thoms, who looked so peaceful it was hard to believe that he barely took breath between complaints, the man stopped where Soutar lay in an untidy heap. With a telling glance at me, the man leaned over and slowly, nearly lovingly, kissed the helmsman full on the mouth. Looking sideways at me, he lay on top of Soutar and then gradually the two bodies became one in an obscene parody of the act of love.

More intrigued than disgusted, I said nothing as the female figure beckoned to me before withdrawing from the foc'sle. I followed, easing back through the sleeping ship with the woman throwing occasional glances over her shoulder as if to ensure I was still there. She brought me to my own cabin, where Learmonth lay on the bunk, his brows furrowed in concentration as he dreamed us safely back to Dundee. The woman gave that light, terrible laugh and slid beside him, gyrating her curves until she merged with the bosun, and then disappeared, leaving me alone with my horror.

'No, please, no!' Remembering the cull of young Mitchell, I shook my head, denying what I had seen. 'Don't take Leerie!'

The shadows lifted, gradually but inexorably and I was on the chair, with my medical bag on my knee and the sound of Learmonth's snores battling the creaks from *Lady Balgay*. I did not understand much of what had happened, but knew there were worse times ahead.

'Doctor!' Captain Milne was glaring at me. 'What the hell are you playing at? It's your watch! You should be on deck, damn your idleness!'

As the summer days passed, Captain Milne headed northward, where the mature, well-blubbered seals spent the season, but bad weather followed *Lady Balgay* like avaricious mourners behind the hearse of a wealthy man. Day after day the wind came from the north east, driving us further from our intended destination of Spitsbergen and toward the distant coast of Greenland, and although Captain Milne burned bunker coal recklessly as he tried to battle north, the wind drove us westward as persistently as a politician's prevarication.

'Lift to them, old lady, up my bonnie lass!' Captain Milne stood by the helmsman with his frustration at *Lady Balgay's* sideways progress causing him to adulterate his encouragement with frustrated threats, 'come on you old hussie, steer for your Daddy or I'll sell you for scrap!'

'It's no good, Captain!' Lashed to the wheel for safety, Soutar had to shout above the roaring of the gale. 'She won't go against this storm.'

'Well damn and blast and bugger her!' Milne shook a fist at the malignant wind that stopped him from hunting his prey. 'I'll not be defeated! I want to hunt seals! Hold her steady, Soutar, by God, and we'll run the engine until there's no coal left!' Turning forward, he kicked the mizzenmast. 'My luck hasn't turned yet, mister! This is my last voyage and we'll come back full or we'll come back dead!'

'Maybe Mr Soutar's right, sir,' I shouted, but I knew Captain Milne would ignore my voice of inexperience.

Blowing into the voice tube that led to the engine room, Captain Milne shouted his orders. 'Keep shuffling in the coal, Torrie, lad, and keep these engines thumping, chief!'

With all sails furled so she was under bare masts and the screw howling its protest every time it lifted clear of the sea, *Lady Balgay* fought the wind, dipping her bowsprit into the waves, alternately lifting her screaming screw clear of the waves and plunging it deep into the sucking green water. The ketch accepted the hundreds of gallons of bitter cold sea that cascaded on board but each time she shook herself free, she was slightly more sluggish, and each time she was slightly more reluctant to answer the helm.

'We could jettison the ballast now,' Learmonth yelled his advice. 'Lighten her a bit.' He was always on deck in bad weather, ready to lend a hand.

'Then she'd be skittish as a young colt, Leerie. We need the weight to keep her stable.'

Red eyed from a sixteen-hour stint at the wheel, Soutar staggered as a fresh wave crashed over the bows and swept the length of the deck, cascading against the upturned boats and hammering at the door of the deckhouse like Satan's knock of doom. 'Captain!' He looked up, the sinews of his forearms straining to hold the vessel secure. 'She can't take much more of this!'

He looked aft and I saw his eyes widening in horror as we both saw the rogue wave. It rose far above the sluggish *Lady Balgay*, hissing with menace, mottled green and white. With its tip curled level with the mizzen mast it hung over us ominously for a long half minute, dripping bucket loads of iced water and with spindrift blowing like the breath of the kraken. We watched it as it began to drop and Soutar closed his eyes in resigned surrender, praying hopelessly. The wave exploded on the stern, thundering thousands of gallons of the North Atlantic on to the tiny ketch. The force of the wave knocked away his feet and threw him forward into the spinning spokes of the wheel, splintering two of his ribs and sending him spiralling on to the deck.

'Sooty!' I stretched helplessly for him, too slow and too late to be of any use.

Soutar screamed once, in horror and agony as the sea embraced him, carrying him kicking to the rail, but, faster than I ever could be, Learmonth lunged forward, one hand on the lifeline and the other snatching at Soutar's sou'wester.

'Sooty! Hold on, Sooty! I'm here!'

For a moment both men stared at each other, eyes meeting eyes in a brief acceptance of a friendship that neither man had acknowledged, but both had understood. In that second I knew they were as close as any two people could be, linked by fear and companionship and flesh amidst the worst horror the sea could throw up. It was the culmination of their lives as they linked hands, and I could do nothing but watch.

I stared at the horrendous scene as a succession of giant waves reared the height of the mizzen mast, the tops hissing and spraying spindrift before they broke in a welter of white fangs that cascaded down toward the heaving, twisting deck. I saw Learmonth gripping Soutar's hand, both men lying full length on the bucking deck with the sea smashing on top of them.

'Hold on, man! I've got you!' Learmonth was screaming; his eyes fixed on Soutar.

'But the ship!' Soutar looked up, his face contorted with a combination of agony and fear for the predicament of *Lady Balgay*, but alight with the sudden realisation that Learmonth had risked everything for him. 'Get the wheel!' He looked upward and whispered, 'God save us.'

The wave thundered on to the deck so one moment there were four men struggling for survival and the next only Captain Milne and I remained, staring at the twisted rail and the gap where Learmonth and Soutar, two of the best and steadiest seamen on board, had once been.

'Sweet Jesus in heaven! No!' I had known it would happen, for the figures had warned me. They had emerged from the shades of my mind, but whether to inform or to select, I did not know. But I did know that I had been warned and I had done nothing to help. The torment of failure added to the agony of loss.

And now there were only ten left on board *Lady Balgay*.

That fatal wave proved to be the worst, for having completed its prescribed mission, the storm subsided, with the wind easing to fitful gusts and each battering wave smaller than its predecessor. I remained on deck, paralysed by the numbness of shock as Captain Milne took the helm and *Lady Balgay* gradually stabilised, two hundred miles to the westward of her intended position.

Huddled wordless beside the mainmast, I did not remove Isbister's hand when she placed it on my shoulder.

'You could not help it,' she said softly, her lilting accent now as homely as anything from Dundee.

I inched instinctively closer, knowing that although Jennifer would listen with sympathy to my stories of the Arctic, she would never fully understand as Isbister, who had lived through the same experiences, would. At that moment I was closer to Isbister than to my wife, and I hated the world for forcing me to accept that truth.

'It's just life up here.' Isbister shook her head and I allowed her to speak.

The female figure was smiling to me, her eyes soft with empathy and her body more a comfort than a temptation. She was no longer trapped in the fringe of my subconscious but had emerged from that shadowy periphery into the cognisant, but she was not yet completed. However rounded her body, however deep the eyes, there was still a hazing there, a quality I could not define and I instinctively knew that there would be other sacrifices before my voyage was complete. The unwanted insight made me feel physically sick.

I looked at Isbister, but my painful insight had already altered our incipient relationship. She might understand life out here, but she was still not Jennifer. I wanted my wife back. I wanted desperately to go home.

Chapter Seventeen

GREENLAND SEA

JUNE – JULY 1914

The bear, unable to make much resistance, opened his mouth however, sufficiently wide to swallow the man, and bellowed like thunder.
    'Capture of a Polar Bear,' Banffshire Journal, 25th May 1852.

'And then there were ten,' Pratt seemed calmer now, as if he were resigned to his doom. He stared at the waves that stretched quietly to infinity. 'I knew Sooty for twelve years,' he said, 'and the bosun for eight. Good men. We won't get many more of their quality.'

'Perhaps not.' I was still sobered by the completeness of their death. In these latitudes there was no point in searching for their bodies; the sea had reached out and plucked them as easily as a man picking a raspberry from a cane. It had been their time and that was that.

'It was the ballast,' Pratt said quietly. He looked behind him where Isbister stood near the stern, speaking with Captain Milne, 'and that woman.'

'It was the sea,' I was unsure if I was trying to convince Pratt or myself, 'and nothing but the sea.' Despite my words I followed Pratt's eyes. My conscious, reasoning self knew it had not been Isbister, but I could now fully understand how the superstitious Pratt could link the coincidence of her arrival with the story of the cannibals on Gass Skerries. The certainties of city life were missing out here, and things that might elsewhere be rationally explained were ambiguous and distorted.

Up here, death waited in a shadow's guise, and temptation took the form of an imaginary female or the contents of a bottle, so a man's mind could easily veer from what was considered conventional to the irrational fears that the primitive had always harboured. Hardship and fear were bitter educators, and the lessons they taught would not always be recognised in the more comfortable and secure environments of Academia or even in the damp streets of a Scottish city.

'It was the ballast,' Pratt repeated. 'And what it contained.'

'What it contained?' I reflected on the psychological process that had created images from my mind to select Learmonth and Soutar for sacrifice, but the practical Pratt had a more direct focus.

'Remember when we found young Rab?'

'Of course,' I nodded.

'He was holding a piece of bone.' Pratt faced me, obviously fighting his fear as he gave his unbelievable points in a logical and controlled manner. 'That bone came from one of the cannibals that were buried on Gass Skerry. It could not have come from anywhere else. By taking that bone on board, Doctor, we have set them loose. They're here, on *Lady Balgay*, and they're killing us one by one.' His hand was shaking as he thrust his empty pipe between stained teeth. 'Remember how Rab's arm was all chewed? That was them.'

'That was rats,' I tried to sound reasonable. 'The hold is full of them.' I did not mention the size of the tooth marks, or the second, terrible scream. I did not mention my own imagined images, or the sweated fear with which I viewed my bunk every evening, in case they were waiting.

'And then these two,' Pratt jerked a thumb toward Isbister, 'came on board. We'll have to get rid of them, Dr Cosgrove, and we'll only do that by returning the bones to their grave. They must go back to the exact same spot.' He hesitated and then his urgent hand gripped my sleeve. 'Please tell the captain, Doctor! He'll listen to you.'

A few weeks earlier, I would have laughed Pratt off the deck, but my recent experiences had made me much more sympathetic. 'Well, Mr Pratt, perhaps you are correct, at least about the ballast.' I knew that a pile of stones, even a huddle of splintered bones, could not be blamed for the three deaths, but my own psychological torment had brought some empathetic enlightenment to Pratt's beliefs. Where I had reasoned that the immense strain of this voyage that had somehow granted me this terrible insight into death, the ultimate enemy of the medical profession, the less educated Pratt would see things on a different plane, but with the same objective.

We both knew that there was something wrong on *Lady Balgay*, but we dealt with it in a manner that suited our own training and experience. While I subconsciously sought to ease my troubled mind with nightmare imaginings, Pratt wanted to remove a supposed supernatural blight with a physical action. I considered what response would best help my patient.

'I think we maybe should ask Captain Milne to call at the Gass Skerry on our return journey,' I said. 'And we can dump all the ballast.'

'It's only the bones that matter...' Pratt began, but I stopped him with a raised hand.

'It would be easier to dump the lot,' I pointed out. 'The captain would never agree to sift through ten tons of stones.'

'No,' Pratt was shaking, nearly collapsing with relief. 'No, you're right, sir.' Taking hold of my hand with both his own, he shook so hard that I felt my wrist creak. 'Thank you, Doctor. Thank you! The captain will listen to you, but never to me.' He was laughing hysterically, his eyes bright with relieved tears and I could neither object nor free myself when he suddenly took me in a rough hug.

'My, Doctor Cosgrove,' Isbister had arrived very quietly and stood watching, her head tilted to the side. 'Whatever would your wife say?' She opened her eyes wide, smiled and walked away, swaying her hips in a manner frighteningly reminiscent of the dark woman from the shadows.

'Maybe now the captain will think about taking us home,' I was unable to prevent myself from watching the retreating Isbister. 'We can't stay up here much longer.'

'God, I hope you're right, doctor,' Pratt took a long breath to control his sobbing.

Captain Milne, however, was not so easily defeated. When he called us all together just after dawn the next day, I felt a surge of hope. I could nearly see the green slopes of Dundee Law lifting over the horizon and hear Jennifer's melodious voice as she called me home. I stood side by side with Pratt, trembling with excitement at the thought of going home.

'Right lads,' Captain Milne addressed the assembled crew from his position beside the wheel. 'We are all saddened by the loss of Learmonth and Soutar. Coming on top of Mitchell's accident it was a grievous blow, but we're all seamen and we know that such things happen at sea. We must just make the best of it. For the sake of them both, and to make some money for their widows, we will make one last attempt to fill our holds'

Pratt looked at me, his obvious dread mirroring the lack of enthusiasm in the crew. They were subdued, disheartened by the deaths; nobody cheered the prospect of another seal hunt. Although it was obvious that the majority just wanted to go home, I knew with a sick slide of dismay that nobody would protest when Captain Milne scanned them with those smoky green eyes.

'We'll anchor soon and spend a day or two on the ice. I know there are seals nearby; I can sense them, hiding among the floes, and if there are seals, then there's profit for us. It will mean higher wages boys, oil money for your wives and the publicans of Dock Street.'

This time there was neither enthusiasm nor excitement, but what was left of the crew quietly made ready the seal clubs and rifles, following Captain Milne's orders as they had since they left Victoria Dock. Only Mackie and Donaldson retained something of the fervour of their earlier hunts, exchanging bawdy banter and boasting how many seals they would kill.

'Five shillings says I'll beat your total, Macks!' Donaldson swung his club, the savage weapon swishing through the air.

'You're on, Billy. So that's five shillings less in your pay already!' They grinned at each other, oblivious to the sullen silence of the remainder of the men.

Captain Milne also ignored the mood of his crew. 'Thoms! You're the bosun now; and Donaldson,' Milne gestured to the club swinging man. 'You and Ross are in charge of the ship. I want Torrie with us; his muscles will come in handy.'

Albert Torrie gave a small smile, as Milne had no doubt intended. At eighteen the fireman was now the youngest person on board but his work in the engine room had massively developed his chest and arm muscles. Donaldson was less happy, glancing at Mackie before he voiced loud protest.

'Captain! Macks and I always work together. Anyway, I'm one of the best sealers you've got while Torrie is only a fireman! Leave the doctor on board; he's as much use as a fart in a gale!'

'You shut your mouth, Donaldson!' Captain Milne was in no mood to listen to arguments. 'I need two men left on board and one has to be a seaman. That's all there is to it. The rest of you, get to work!'

With heads low and shoulders hunched, we trailed from *Lady Balgay* and on to the ice. Captain Milne was in front, with Pratt at the rear and the rest of us in between, a straggling group of seven men, for the captain had insisted that I come along in case of injury. 'Head up, Mr Pratt,' I whispered. 'If we kill enough seals this time, we can get back home.'

'Yes, Dr Cosgrove,' Pratt agreed sulkily, 'but I want to get those bones back right now!'

I could not reply as I bowed my head to the inevitable and trudged into the wilderness ahead.

Unlike our previous expedition, we were not on a continuous plateau of ice but on a much less stable scattering of flat floes and hummocks, separated by chasms of unpredictable depth that we had to leap across. I hesitated as I stepped from one floe onto the next, with the sea glinting dark below, but when I realised that the Greenlandmen were unconcerned I could only follow, even though the chasms would sometimes close together, or widen alarmingly as the floes drifted apart.

'This is ugly work,' I grunted my concerns to Captain Milne, who glowered in reply.

'I did not design the ice, mister, and we must take what we are offered.'

When a foolhardy seal thrust its head through holes in the ice, Mackie would yell, 'there's another one!' and a man would immediately shoot it, or use the club if it was too small a prize for a bullet. The bodies were dragged on to the ice and left there, oozing blood.

'We'll come back and skin them later,' Captain Milne decided. 'Just now we hunt.'

With the first few kills behind them the spirits of the men rose, although there were many references to the loss of Soutar and Learmonth, but the thought of seal oil and an easy winter at home helped ease the pain.

'I wish I was in the Arctic Bar,' Thoms said, 'with a dirty great pint in my hand.'

'We'll get there,' Torrie promised, throwing a chest as befitted a hunting man. 'And I'll buy the first round.'

'Will they let you in?' Thoms asked bitterly. 'You're barely away from your mammy's reins!'

Torrie flushed as the others laughed, but there was no denying his strength as he crushed the skull of the next seal. By midday we had killed upward of forty and were far into the ice.

'I wish Billy was here,' Mackie said, holding up his club and watching the blood run onto his glove. 'But this is what it's all about, eh boys?'

When there was no response I guessed that even these hunters had had their fill of slaughter. I watched Mackie for a second, seeing him as a suddenly indistinct form among the ice, with a vague, shadowy shape behind him. 'Macks?'

That shadow slid free, took its dreadful shape of a woman and glanced in my direction as if willing me to watch.

'Oh no!' I could barely watch as the figure merged slowly with Mackie. 'Oh Jesus; Macks!' I slid forward as the full implications came to me. Every time I had seen these terrible figures fuse with somebody, death had followed, and now they were out here on the ice and Mackie was the next to die.

'What?' Mackie looked at me, with his mouth hovering between a smile and a sarcastic comment. 'What's the matter, Doctor?' He stepped closer, just as a crack opened in the ice at his feet.

'Mackie!' I lunged forward, but it was Thoms who grabbed hold of his arm and dragged him clear. We stood for a moment, gaping at the expanding chasm and the unfathomably deep water beneath.

'Jesus! Thanks, Doc, but how did you know that was going to happen?'

I shook my head, feeling the rapid patter of my heart. 'Instinct, I suppose. I just knew that something was wrong.'

'Well Doctor Cosgrove, you're useless at the hunting, but we'll make a Greenlandman of you yet.' Thoms slapped me resoundingly on the back as Mackie laughed hollowly and began to shake with reaction.

I smiled weakly; a bit dizzy as I wondered if I had won. Had I defeated death by saving Mackie's life? I stared into the wastes around, the home of the seal and the great white bear, but where that shadowy figure had also appeared as comfortable as it had on *Lady Balgay*. Was there anywhere safe from death? It had taken me some weeks but I had finally discerned the meaning of these images, these creations of my own imagination, and now I could calculate how to use them. They were not enemies, but allies in my fight against death. Ignoring the astonished stares of the Greenlandmen, I began to laugh; perhaps that was the secret of a good doctor, realising that people were close to death and finding out how to help?

If so, then this voyage had given me some remarkable insight. It may not have advanced my career by providing the surgical experience I had expected, but the psychological perception, in however unorthodox a manner it had arrived, would be invaluable.

'Oh God you work in incalculable ways your wonders to perform.' I laughed louder as I realised how I had completely misunderstood. The figures represented a message of help, not a threat.

'Are you all right, Doctor?' When Pratt placed a concerned hand on my arm I hurriedly closed my mouth, belatedly recognising the hysteria in my laughter. Taking a deep breath that threatened to freeze my lungs, I forced myself back to my present situation, where the men were clustered around the captain.

'It will take some time to get back to the ship,' Thoms was saying quietly. 'And the weather is going to change.'

'I want a hundred captures,' Captain Milne told him. 'Anything less is a waste of a day.'

'But Captain; the weather.' Mackie pointed to the heavy sky, but Milne ignored him and walked in the opposite direction from where *Lady Balgay* lay.

'A hundred captures, boys. No less.'

'Aye, Captain,' Thoms nodded. 'Come on, lads. The captain will see us right.' Shoulders bowed, we followed, walking into a finely falling snow that coated us white and blurred our footprints in seconds. After half an hour the captain stopped, lifting his head.

'I hear them, Captain!' Pratt pointed forward. 'Seals!'

'I hear them too, Pratt. Christ, man even the Doctor can hear them and he's got house bricks for ears!'

I gave a brisk nod, unwilling to admit that I could not hear anything but the whine of the wind and the pad of feet on the snow-covered ice. I had watched the seal killing with little emotion, for after the loss of Soutar and Learmonth a few seals counted for nothing, but now, as each step took us further from *Lady Balgay*, I wished I was safely in my bunk. Strangely, it was once again of Isbister that I thought rather than Jennifer, for Dundee seemed so far away it belonged to a different world. At that moment I could hardly remember my wife's face; it seemed that all there was in life was ice and snow, murderous waves and the bloody mess a club left of a seal cub's skull.

'I'll get the first one!' Mackie was laughing, enjoying the thought of massacre for its own sake. Hefting his rifle he moved ahead, jumping over a crack that appeared in the ice. He slithered on the far side, recovered and stumbled on until he was barely visible in the whirling snow. 'I can hear them, Captain!'

After more than three months in the north, I was used to the rapid shifts in Arctic weather and was not surprised when the wind suddenly dropped, taking the snow with it. The seal appeared almost immediately, shoving its great whiskered head through a hole in the ice and looking around with an expression of bemusement that always seemed to entertain the hunters.

'He's looking for us,' Thoms looked for an appreciative audience for his weak joke.

'Here I am!' Mackie obliged as he worked the lever of his Martini-Henry.

Waiting until the seal had hauled its long body onto the ice; he pressed the muzzle of the rifle against the seal's head and pressed the trigger. The shot sounded hollow, but the entire skull exploded, spraying blood, brains and splinters of bone all around. The seal reared back, stone dead, and slumped on to the ice. Blood pooled.

'That's another one, Captain!' Mackie waved his rifle aloft. 'That's fifteen I've killed today!' He was the only man among the crew who kept a reckoning of his personal kills, noting them carefully in a small black notebook that sat under his bunk. He called it his tally book, and boasted that 'all the nobs did the same.' Remembering Sir Melville's trophy room in Balgay House, I could not criticise him; the only differences were the type of animal and method of murder, not the fact of hunting and killing.

'The weather's worsening, Captain,' Thoms nodded ahead, where a thicker cloud of snow was approaching.

'Aye, you're right Alex. Damn it to hell and gone but we'll have to stop now!' Captain Milne raised his voice. 'That's it for the day, boys. Skin our captures and we'll drag them back to the ship. We'll return for more when the weather clears.'

Pratt glanced at me, frowning. He did not speak but the message was obvious; he wanted desperately to head home, to dump the ballast and get back safely to Dundee. I could only give a helpless shrug; I could not approach Captain Milne out here, but I might try again when we were back on board.

Mackie was laughing as he slipped the great skinning knife from his belt and started work on his last kill, taking both skin and the layer of blubber at a single stroke. It was a skilled job, and I could only wonder at the speed of these butchers, but within a few minutes Mackie had shoved aside the useless body and was dragging the skin across the ice. 'That's a few more pounds of blubber for the ship, Captain!'

The northerly wind increased, blowing the snow on to our backs as we trudged over the ice. Within fifteen minutes we were staggering under the weight of the seals we had killed and cursing the effort of hauling them over terrain that was rapidly becoming more treacherous.

'Captain,' Thoms jerked his head to indicate the curtain of snow that concealed our route back. 'Maybe the seals will have to wait.'

Captain Milne looked up, grunted, and made a rapid decision. 'We'll leave the sealskins in a heap here, boys, and come back for them tomorrow. The weather is deteriorating fast.'

'We can't leave our captures, Captain,' Mackie said. 'I've got a score to keep.'

'They'll be safe enough here,' Milne managed a wry smile. 'There's nobody around to steal them. Just obey my orders, Mackie. I don't want to lose any more men.'

'I'll just get that last one, then!' Mackie pointed to a seal he had shot earlier. The animal lay beside a distinctive hump of ice a few score yards to the north.

'No!' Milne roared, but Mackie was already sliding away, his knife held point upward as he prepared for the skinning. After three months in their company, I knew that of all the crew, Mackie was perhaps the most unlikeable, but also the most natural hunter. It was the kill he enjoyed even more than the profit. He was here for the thrill of the hunt and the tally, the feel of the dead bodies under his knife and the smell of blood. Mackie was a predator: he belonged in this unrelenting environment.

'You fool, Mackie!' Captain Milne yelled, but turned his attention to the others. 'You lads keep together now. Mackie's an old hand, he'll be all right.'

Remembering the merging ethereal figure, I was not so sure. I glanced over his shoulder, but the snow had already cut Mackie off from my vision as if he were in a different land, rather than just a few hundred yards across the ice.

Chapter Eighteen

*Staggering blind through the storm-whirl, stumbling mad through
the snow*
Frozen stiff in the ice pack, brittle and bent like a bow;
Featureless, formless, forsaken, scented by wolves in their flight,
*Left for the wind to make music through ribs that are glittering
white;*
   Robert Service

'Doctor!' Pratt loomed up, as shaggy and solid as any polar bear. 'We're
moving. Keep up!' He took up position at my side, acting as escort
through the Arctic wilderness.

   Leaving the sealskins piled in a bloody heap, Captain Milne led us
back over ice that seemed even more dangerous than before. The ice
holes were more frequent and larger, while the crevasses and chasms
seemed wider, and harder to see through snow that drove horizontally
across that terrible landscape.

   'I hope Macks is all right, eh?' Pratt had to shout over the scream
of the wind.

I kept my head down, uncaring of anybody else's suffering. Amidst the howling gale and the veil of snow I could not think about Mackie; I could only concentrate on the next step, following the shape of the man in front and hoping that Captain Milne was leading us in the right direction. Narrowing my eyes, I peered into the hypnotic vortex of snow that disappeared into the distance. It felt as if I was staring down a long tunnel edged with a maelstrom of white flakes that spun and moved and enticed me on, while the wind thumped my back, pushing me endlessly into oblivion.

'Doctor!' I was suddenly aware that Pratt was shouting in my ear and tugging at me; 'it's this way!'

We had altered our route to avoid a new crevasse, but with my sense of direction completely lost in the snow, I allowed Pratt to guide me. I slogged on, miserable, hating everything, with my mind almost supine. I nodded as Pratt helped me around an ice hole, slipped, swore and nearly fell as we crested a hummock and negotiated the other side. Why had I ever come out here? This world was composed entirely on ice and snow, of misery and fear. Why had I left Dundee?

'There she is, Doctor. There's the old *Lady Balgay.*'

The sight of the ketch was like the light of salvation. She sat there, her masts alternatively appearing and disappearing as the snow shifted direction, but her black hull remained a smudge of sanity in this frigid white nothingness. 'Thank God,' I said, and meant it. Now I understood something of the feelings seamen could have for their ship. *Lady Balgay* was not just a place of safety and warmth; she also represented familiarity, hope, home and comradeship.

'But where's Mackie?' Screwing up his eyes against the stinging snow, Pratt looked over his shoulder. 'I haven't seen him for a while.' He counted the men. 'Aye, everybody's here save Mackie.'

Captain Milne cursed. 'I told the fool not to go back,' he excused himself. 'He should have known better, but he's an experienced man. He'll be all right.'

'I could go and look for him,' Pratt volunteered, but Captain Milne snorted.

'Then I'd be two fools short and not just one. Get on board, Pratt.'

Donaldson was waiting for us with hot coffee and a strained smile, and I was glad to feel the planking of *Lady Balgay* under my nearly-numb feet again. Sheltering behind the funnel, Isbister smiled to everybody, but it was Torrie she welcomed with a broad wink and a sensual swing of her hips that had the fireman's mouth dropping.

'Where's Macks?' Donaldson asked. He peered into the whirling snow. 'I'll bet he's killing one last seal!'

'He's coming,' Thoms said and paused. 'We hope.'

'Hope?' Donaldson stared at him. 'What do you mean, hope?'

'He lagged behind a bit,' Thoms explained. 'As you said, trying for one last seal.'

'And you all left him?' Donaldson's voice rose. 'Out there?' He pointed northwards, where the snow now blasted in intermittent violent flurries, so one moment visibility was virtually nil, and then the ice was abruptly clear for half a mile.

Now we were safe on board, we shared a general shame at having left Mackie behind, so we lined the rail and peered into the ice, searching and calling for our missing colleague.

'There he is!' Thoms was first to see the dark figure emerging from the white haze, and everybody cheered. Mackie was not the most popular man on board but he was one of us, a skilled hunter and a man who shared their hardships and triumphs. At that distance he looked tiny, an insignificant figure belligerently thrusting homeward with his rifle balanced on his shoulder and his head held low.

'Who's that with him?' Isbister said quietly. She stood between me and Torrie, erect in her furs. 'He's not alone.'

'There is nobody else,' Thoms said quietly. 'He's the last.'

'I must be mistaken then,' Isbister apologised, 'but I thought I saw somebody else.'

'Oh God,' I closed my eyes, remembering again that shadowy figure merging with Mackie and hoping against hope that I was wrong. I looked up, muttering to myself as anxiety replaced the stiff upper lip that phlegmatism and educational discipline had imposed upon me for so long. 'Come on Mackie, get here safely.'

'Come on Macks!' Donaldson heard me and began to shout and wave, with the rest of the crew joining in as though they had not seen Mackie for months, rather than a few hours. The sound must have reached Mackie out on the ice, for he waved back, holding the rifle aloft. He fired a shot as a signal, the sound flat, muted in this vast terrain, and then Thoms pointed again. 'Jemmy was right. There is somebody else.'

Feeling sick with fear, I squinted into the snow. A flurry blocked my view, but when it cleared I could see there were definitely two figures there, one was Mackie, walking forward again, sliding on the ice but thrusting stubbornly for *Lady Balgay*. The second was taller and further away back but moving faster, as if the conditions were not a hindrance at all.

'It's a giant, an ogre,' Pratt sounded afraid. When he looked at me his eyes pleaded that I would make everything better.

'It's a bear,' Thoms corrected. His voice was flat calm. 'And Macks hasn't seen it yet.' He began to shout. 'Who's got a rifle? Rifles, lads! Macks is in trouble there!'

The bear was two hundred yards behind Mackie but closing, dropping to all fours as it advanced.

'Jesus, Mackie! Run!' Thoms yelled the words, but the distance was too great, the sound of the wind too loud and the muffling effect of layers of fur around Mackie's head too difficult to penetrate.

'Fire a gun, somebody! Warn him, for Christ's own sake!'

There was a volley of shots as every man with a rifle fired into the air, hoping that Mackie would look around, but instead he raised his own rifle, and pressed the trigger, glorying in the sound as he worked the lever, pressed in another cartridge and fired again in response to what he probably assumed was a greeting.

'Jesus!' Donaldson bellowed. 'Jesus, Macks, there's a bear!' He was screaming his fear, hopping on the deck in his agitation. 'Rifle! Give me a rifle!'

'Here!' Thoms threw the Lee-Enfield across to him. 'The magazine is full!'

Gasping, Donaldson hefted the rifle and clambered on to the boom, leaping on to the ice as the others shrieked unheard messages to Mackie.

I began to pray but the words were a meaningless gabble until I cleared my mind of everything but the drama on the ice, and then I prayed for Mackie's life harder than I had ever asked for anything before. I watched Donaldson slithering toward Mackie, trying to run but only succeeding in lumbering clumsily, like a drunk weaving his way home from the pub.

The crew fell silent, some covering their mouths as the bear drew closer to Mackie on one side while Donaldson was still hundreds of yards away on the other. We heard, carried high with the wind, Donaldson's warning.

'Macks! Look behind you! It's a bear!'

Perhaps some inner instinct made Mackie turn, but he moved awkwardly, slowed by cold and the thick furs that he wore, and he flinched when he saw the bear.

'Now he can shoot it,' Thoms said, as Mackie pointed the rifle and squeezed the trigger.

'The thing's empty,' Thoms reminded them quietly. 'He fired off his bullets.'

I could see Mackie fumbling within his furs, presumably for cartridges, but as the bear lurched closer, he panicked. Without attempting to reload, he dropped the rifle and began to run, with the bear now fifty yards behind and increasing its speed to a lumbering trot.

'Run Macks! Run!' Every man in the crew was yelling, trying to encourage Mackie to greater effort, but he was exhausted after a day's hunting and his legs were blundering and slack.

'Yes, run, Mackie.' Isbister spoke quietly as she watched, but I saw that her eyes never left the running man. Her mouth remained open, with her breath coming in shallow pants that clouded and frosted on her fur collar. Her tongue was very red between white, sharp teeth.

Two hundred yards in front of Mackie, Donaldson tried to race across the ice and aim his rifle simultaneously, but was unable to fire in case he shot his friend.

'Run, Macks; please run!' Thoms' hands were gripping the rail so tightly that I thought he would twist the solid teak in his frustration.

As the bear closed, Mackie quickly stripped off his outer coat and dropped it on the ground. He ran on, slipping sideways, recovering with his arms flailing wide, and running desperately onward toward us.

'That's an old trick,' Pratt murmured quietly to Iain. 'The bear might stop to chew the furs and Macks will have time to escape.'

When the bear slowed to sniff at the furs Mackie increased his lead, but the animal was not fooled for long. After only a few seconds, it lumbered into motion, huge legs pounding over the frozen ground as Mackie dropped item after item of clothing. Within a few moments Mackie was running in his woollen underclothes, with the bear now just twenty yards behind him.

'He'll make it!' Pratt said. 'He's going to make it! Look!'

Donaldson was also approaching, now only fifty yards away. He knelt on the ice, levelled the rifle and waved for Mackie to move aside but the sealer's fear was so great he could only run in a desperately straight line.

'Drop, Macks!' Donaldson's roar came faintly to us. 'Macks, please drop so I can have a clear shot!'

It was Pratt who heard the sound first, and blasphemed desperately. 'Oh sweet Jesus, no!' He looked at me and I knew he was on the point of tears. 'It's the ice, Doctor, it's splitting!'

I nodded. Even I could hear it now; the distinctive, horrible crackling of breaking ice as the crevasse opened. Twenty yards in front of Mackie, it began to split, slowly at first, but then rapidly widened to form a moat between him and safety. Within thirty seconds of the sound reaching us, the entire outer rim of the ice shelf eased clear of the main mass.

'Macks! Jump!' Donaldson fired a hasty shot that went nowhere and ran forward, halting helplessly at the edge of the growing gap. Teetering there, he shouted, waving his hands hopelessly. 'Macks!'

The crevasse was too wide to leap and Mackie, now a palely naked figure on the ice, sank to his knees and lifted both hands to heaven in tragic supplication. He looked utterly vulnerable, a man lost in a hostile environment, a soul exposed to the freezing hell of the north.

'Oh sweet Jesus,' Pratt said as I continued to pray, harder and harder as the words left my lips at an increasing rate.

Donaldson fired again and again, working the bolt until he had no bullets left. He reached for a magazine in an empty pocket, and then he could only watch, twenty yards from Mackie but distant as the moon as the bear continued to advance, ponderous now, as if it realised its prey could not escape.

The great mouth was open, the hooked claws extended as Mackie finally turned and a terrible slant of wind brought his initial scream to us. Desperate, high-pitched, that wail sliced deep into my heart as I stopped praying. I could only watch, horrified, as the bear slashed hooked claws across Mackie's chest, throwing him to the ground, and then it lowered its head and began to chew him as he lay writhing and screaming on the ice.

'Oh Jesus! Shoot it somebody, please shoot it!'

Those of the crew who had guns aimed, but did not fire.

'I might hit Macks,' Pratt wailed.

'You'll be doing him a service,' Thoms told him quietly.

Mackie's screams continued endlessly as the bear tore at him, ripping off a mouthful of fingers and then burrowing its head into his intestines.

'Fire! For the love of Christ! Shoot it!'

Mackie lived longer than I thought possible, and probably longer than he wanted as the bear began to eat him alive, piece by ripped off piece. Pratt emptied his magazine and reloaded, while Thoms ran on to the ice for better aim, but as the outer floe detached itself, he was further away with each shot and the bear continued with its ponderous killing.

It was dark before the last of the noises ended, and the shocked crew hunched back to the foc'sle. I joined them, slumping onto a sea chest with my shoulders bowed and my mouth as slack as the others.

'And then there were nine,' Pratt looked at me with resignation battling the horror in his eyes. 'I wonder if any of us will get back.'

I shook my head. I did not know, but I dreaded each visit of that shadowy woman, and I begged a bottle of gin from the captain before I retired. I did not expect to sleep that night, but if I did, I wanted the oblivion of alcohol rather than the fearfulness of the images from the shadows.

'Who's next?' I sobbed openly, sitting on the bunk and holding the bottle as if it were a child. 'Who's next?' I stared at the door, waiting for the woman to enter as the tears rolled down my cheeks.

My Jennifer would not have thought much of her husband then, but I was no longer the brave young man who had teased her in the garden.

Chapter Nineteen

GREENLAND SEA
JULY 1914

Our men are very superstitious and attribute our ill luck to various causes. One day it is put down to a comb which is universally used by all in the cabin... another day it is to a small pig
    Captain A.H. Markham RN: '*A Whaling Cruise to Baffin's Bay and the Gulf of Boothia and an Account of the Rescue of the Crew of the Polaris*' (London 1874) page 44

The snow continued all day and well into the night, swathing *Lady Balgay* with a white cover that muffled all noise but could not erase the memory of Mackie's death. What was left of the crew remained in the foc'sle, huddled together for warmth and what comfort they could find in each other's company, while I sat in the cabin I now shared with Thoms, wrestled fearfully with my imaginings and said little. I recalled having promised to write Jennifer a journal, but I could not then face putting pen to paper, not with such a tale of tragedy and loss.

Although there was one empty bottle rolling on the deck and the level of gin in the next was falling, I felt as sober as a Free Church minister on a Sabbath morning.

'Strange that Mackie should get killed by a bear,' Thoms said at last, after a silence that had dragged on like a November Sunday.

'Strange? In what way is it strange?' I looked up. The tiny lantern did not give any heat and its light created uncanny shadows that bounced around the varnished plank bulkheads. I could hear the wind whining outside, and the creaking of the ship. I was so used to the constant throb of the engine that the sound hardly registered, but I knew that the heat of the boiler kept *Lady Balgay* at a bearable temperature.

'Well, everybody else killed seals as a job, but Mackie enjoyed hunting. He was the only man who killed for fun. You saw him with those polar bears a few weeks ago.'

I nodded. I remembered Mackie's pleasure in killing the cubs. He had decapitated them later and cut off the paws, which he had stowed at the bottom of his sea chest. 'He was a born hunter.'

'Aye, and the only man I've ever known to be killed by a bear.' Thoms sat on the chair and stared into the lamp. 'I think that's strange.'

'Pratt would say it was because we're damned,' I said, no longer mocking.

'Pratt's a superstitious old fool,' Thoms replied. 'He's been saying things like that for the past ten years, and probably before. He sees meaning in everything. Oh, there's a crow – that's bad luck. Oh, there's a ring around the moon – that's bad luck. Oh, there's a star – that's bad luck.' Thoms shook his head. 'Don't listen to Pratt, and just hope that the rest of the lads don't either.'

I tried to smile, but the memory of Mackie's death was too vivid. 'Do you think we'll go home now?'

'It depends on how badly the captain wants these seal skins,' Thoms shrugged. 'If it was up to me, I'd have turned for home the day we lost Leerie and Sooty, but it's the captain's decision.' He lay back on the bunk and folded his hands behind his head. 'Mind you, Doctor, and between us only, Pratt has a point. I've never known a voyage like this before, with so many men lost in different ways.'

'So you think Pratt's right and we are damned?' I asked, uncaring if Thoms thought me a superstitious fool or not. I needed reassurance very badly.

'I did not say that,' Thoms replied quickly. 'I didn't say we were damned.'

We relapsed into silence again, until the wind and snow finally abated and we emerged from the cabin onto a ship whose image might have decorated any Christmas card. Seen in the pale light of the north, *Lady Balgay* must have been a beautiful sight for those who could appreciate it. With her deck under eighteen inches of snow and every line and spar gleaming white, she was like a nautical angel against a backdrop of virginal white. Once again I could understand something of the fascination of men for the Arctic, but still I longed for the damp factory streets of Dundee with their raucous people and flickering lights.

And I desperately missed Jennifer, if I could only remember her face. I tipped back the third bottle and allowed the gin to flow down my throat.

'Right lads, this is decision time.' We were becoming used to Captain Milne addressing us from the quarterdeck, and stood in sullen silence. Swathed in our furs, our forms were disguised, but looking around, I noted that all our faces shared the same symptoms of strain and fear. 'We can either go back for the seals we captured, or head for home. I don't know about you, but I would be inclined to leave them as a tribute to Mackie.'

'What about Macks' body¿Donaldson demanded truculently. 'We can't just leave him unburied.'

Captain Milne sighed when some of the crew mumbled their agreement.

'If we're going to bury Mackie, then we'll pick up the skins at the same time. I'll not see a journey wasted.' He looked pointedly at me. 'The owners still expect their profit and I expect the doctor will want to see the body. He'll want to make sure that Mackie is properly dead.'

I recognised their sudden hostility as misplaced grief when the hands all turned toward me. I kept my face expressionless even as I cursed the captain for redirecting his guilt at losing another man.

Mackie was indeed properly dead, but there was nothing much left of him to bury. Judging by the paw prints, there had been more than one bear at work, and between them they had eaten more than half the body, leaving a splintered mess of bone and entrails, with pieces of raw meat among the bloodied snow.

'Bastards!' Donaldson hugged his rifle, looking around for a bear on which to take his revenge, but the prints, although partly obscured by fresh snowfall, led in three different directions.

'Just animals and surely no worse than us,' I told him, unforgiving of the love for slaughter that had rebounded on these men. All the same, I had taken the precaution of thrusting Sir Melville's revolver through my belt. After witnessing the strength of these polar bears, I did not expect a pistol bullet to be effective against its mass of bone and muscle, but I felt marginally safer carrying a weapon. Sir Melville had been correct; if you needed a gun, you needed it desperately.

I knelt beside the remains of Mackie and began to pull the pieces together. It was nauseating work, touching the bloodied remnants of what only yesterday had been my colleague, but that was my duty. No doubt the bears had dragged away a few chunks of Mackie to eat at leisure, and other fragments would be buried under the snow, but I had no intention of digging around too much.

'I can help,' Sinclair was a quiet man, but he showed little distaste as he helped me collect what was left of Mackie, lifting splintered bone and bloodied entrails with as much detachment as if they were pieces of dead seal.

'You're a cool one,' Thoms commented, but Sinclair simply shrugged.

'It's only meat,' he said. 'Mackie's gone now.'

'What do you mean, only meat?' Donaldson worked the bolt of his rifle. 'That's Macks! That was my pal!'

When Sinclair stood erect he was five inches taller than Donald-son. 'I liked Mackie as well, Billy, but he's dead. This...' his gesture included every splinter of bone and tattered piece of gut, 'this isn't Mackie. This is just the body he walked around in.'

'You're fucking peculiar, you are,' Donaldson stepped back, his face twisted in disgust and confusion. 'Of course that's Macks; who else would it be?' He raised his voice, appealing for support. 'Did you hear that? Sinclair here said that Macks was only meat!'

'What?' The remaining crew gathered round; frustrated and fearful, they wanted desperately to hit back at the fate that had turned their sealing voyage into a nightmare.

'Meat?' Torrie pushed his fists together, staring at the tall man. 'What does that mean?'

'I mean his soul has departed from his body,' Sinclair tried to explain, but the crew were too hurt to listen to reason.

'That's not what you said.' Pratt was at the back of the crowd, mut-tering under his breath but never looking directly at Sinclair. 'You said he was only meat.'

I took a deep breath before intervening. 'Break it up now, lads. We need to do something with Mackie's' body and arguing won't help any. Let's all pull together in this.' I could sense the incipient violence as the men searched for a victim, something or somebody on whom they could vent their anger. It was only human nature to pick on the outsider, a man who had come last to the crew and who had a different accent from the others.

'Pull together? He said that Macks was only meat!' Donaldson pointed to Sinclair. 'That's what he said. He said that Macks was only meat!'

'Come on now; we all say things we don't mean!' I looked around desperately for help; I knew I did not have the ability to quell a fight between these angry and work-hardened men. 'Is that not right, Cap-tain?'

'The doctor's right boys,' Captain Milne tucked away the bottle he had been holding. 'It's been a bad time but let's not squabble, eh?' He lowered his voice to a sinister hiss, glaring at them with these smoky green eyes. 'That was an order.'

Still giving Sinclair poisonous looks, the men nodded and backed reluctantly down.

'Sinclair, help the doctor.' Captain Milne said quietly. 'You other lads follow me.'

While Captain Milne grudgingly abandoned the search for sealskins that were now buried under a foot of snow, I bundled what remained of Mackie into a tarpaulin and with Sinclair's help, dragged it to the water's edge. Neither of us spoke of what had happened, and I thought lovingly of the bottle that sat under my bunk. An alcoholic stupor was the easiest escape from this never ending horror.

Mackie was buried at sea, with a brief prayer and a savagely sung hymn that was all the more meaningful because of the fear and brooding resentment of the men. Not even Captain Milne mentioned the skins we left behind as we filed back on board *Lady Balgay*. I listened intently to make sure Ross got steam up, for I was sure that many more days up here would destroy the last vestiges of my sanity.

'Good bye Macks,' Pratt said quietly, but nobody disturbed Donaldson as he stared over the rail.

'Steer south by east,' Milne said with a shake in his voice. 'We're going back to Dundee and I for one am never coming this way again.'

'Oh, thank God,' Pratt closed his eyes. 'We're going home.'

One or two of the hands cheered, and they obeyed the captain's orders to raise sails with a willingness that I had not witnessed for weeks. I began to wonder if I might even see Jennifer again, and hear her voice and walk in that lovely garden in West Ferry with the avenue of fruit trees that would now be bursting with life. Leaning over the rail I thought of Macks, Sooty, Leerie and young Rab Mitchell and fought the tears that threatened to publicly unman me.

I was going home, as I had promised. I was going home to Jennifer. So why did that brown haired headed woman still float toward me over a crimson sea? Why did these images continue to haunt me, waiting to emerge from my imagination? Perhaps now, with the ice already receding in the wake of *Lady Balgay,* I could remove the fear but retain this new, terrifying skill of identifying people in imminent danger of death.

Suddenly I felt old and wise but very lonely. I knew there were eight other people on board, but I was isolated from them by standing, temperament and intelligence. I was the sole university-educated man here, and Captain Milne only came close to my social class by virtue of his position. I missed Jennifer more than ever then, as I clung to the sanctuary of the rail and peered over the grey waves.

What had happened on this ship? My educated mind automatically dismissed Pratt's fantastic tales, but there was certainly something wrong. Yet nearly everything that had happened could be rationally explained. There was nothing supernatural about the wave that had swept Learmonth and Soutar away; such accidents happened at sea every week and it was sheer bad luck that both men had been killed together. Young Mitchell's death could also be explained as an unfortunate accident, save for that double scream that I had heard. But I seemed to have been the only person who heard it, so had I been at fault? Had I actually heard two screams, or was I imagining things? I knew that the shadowy figures were purely imaginary; that was just my mind's method of expressing nervous strain and my growing professional acumen.

Pratt's mauling by the seal was also unfortunate but certainly no more supernatural than Mackie's terrible death. Seals and bears were wild animals that could kill; of that there was no doubt.

No, I decided. I did not believe that anything supernatural had occurred. Despite my close proximity to these basic, superstitious men, I assured myself that I was a rational man of a scientific mind. Bogles, ghosts and things that went bump in the night did not affect me.

I sighed, having successfully reassured at least the rational part of my mind, but I swallowed hard as I watched a bank of bruised cloud gather on the horizon and rise slowly upward to occupy the entire sky. It was an army of a million trillion molecules of moisture, propelled by a wind of incalculable force; together they created an enemy that could destroy *Lady Balgay* in an instant, or a friend to speed her home. Only God knew which it would be, and maybe God had never cared much for this part of the world.

This voyage had changed me; I was certain of that. As well as witnessing hideous death and brutal life, I had experienced nocturnal longings and the physical temptation of Isbister's open flaunting of her body, but despite a period of natural wavering caused by weeks of enforced abstinence, I had remained faithful to Jennifer. If these incidents had been tests, then I had survived and was now a stronger man, tempered in adversity and ready for the softer, more prolonged trials of marriage.

If I closed my eyes I could picture my wife now, slim and elegant and with that mischievous glint in her eye. By concentrating on Jennifer I could block that other, voluptuous woman from my mind, but I knew she was still there, hovering, waiting for a window of weakness. I shook my head; I must never tell Jennifer of my experiences up here, and my medical peers must never learn of my fears and imaginings. Sitting safe in comfortable practises in Dundee or Edinburgh, they would never understand; they would disregard my words and deride my experiences.

'Wind's rising doctor.' Thoms moved to stand beside me, his face concerned. 'Please God it blows steady from the north.'

I replied absently. 'Why is that, Mr Thoms?'

'A northerly wind will send us home. Nobody wants to be trapped up here any longer. Not after so many deaths and ...other things.'

'Other things?' I took a deep breath. 'We have suffered a series of unfortunate accidents, Mr Thoms; nothing more. As soon as we are safely home we will view them in a more rational frame of mind and see that there was nothing supernatural about them. Despite what Mr Pratt may believe.'

Thoms looked at me through the side of his eyes. 'I don't know about that,' he said. 'It's not only John Pratt that's concerned.' He walked away, head down as I battled the new doubts in my so-far-still-rational mind.

Chapter Twenty

GREENLAND SEA
JULY 1914

It was with a happy heart that the good Odysseus spread his sail to
catch the wind and used his seamanship to keep his boat straight
with the steering-oar
Homer

The gale hit us ten minutes later, shrieking out of the north like the
Ride of the Valkyries and hammering at the sails as if determined to rip
them from the masts. But Captain Milne was a superb seaman and had
everything trussed up securely, so that *Lady Balgay* merely shuddered
beneath the assault and held on, her reinforced hull crashing through
the waves and her stern rising to meet the storm as if she had been
born to occasions such as this.

'Lift to them, old lady, up my bonnie lass!' Standing by the helm,
Captain Milne patted the taffrail. 'That's the way, my darling.'

'Aye, Her Ladyship can deal with this weather all right,' Pratt said.
'And coming from the north it will serve to drive us home all the faster.'
He glowered aft, where streaks of brutal red slashed the dark purple

sky and the waves reached higher than the mizzenmast, curling hungrily as they lunged at *Lady Balgay*. 'Thank God for some real sailoring after that inching about in the ice!' Grinning, he began to sing a few lines from an old Dundee whaling song.

> *'And the wind is on her quarter,*
> *And the sails are full and free*
> *There's not another whaler sailing on the Arctic sea'*

'You seem in top spirits,' I was surprised at Pratt's fine singing voice.

'Oh aye, doctor,' Pratt grinned to me, with the livid and still raw white scar writhing across his battered old face. 'We're going home.' He changed his song to the bawdier *Ratcliffe Highway*, roaring out the words in unison with the howling wind.

> *'Here's a health to the gal with the black, curly locks;*
> *Here's a health to the gal who ran me on the rocks,*
> *Here's a health to the quack, boys, who eased me from pain,*
> *If I meet that flash packet I'll board her again!'*

'I don't know that one!' Sheltering in the lee of the funnel, I could only smile at the double entendres, and wondered if I could repeat the words to Jennifer.

'It's a wee bit filthy, eh?' Pratt said. 'But we're going home. Back to bonny Dundee, eh?'

'Aye, back to Bonnie Dundee,' I agreed, meeting Pratt's grin.

The gale continued all that day and well into the next, bowling *Lady Balgay* homeward and improving the morale of the crew with every passing mile.

'Blow, you bastard,' Thoms spat his contempt into the wind. 'You can blow from Monday till Christmas but you won't upset the old Lady.' He patted the handrail as if the ketch was an old friend. I did not mention the earlier fear of the ship changing her name.

'This is sailoring!' Thoms said as *Lady Balgay* rose to a wave, hovered for a second and plunged down the opposite side. 'This is what separates the men from the boys.' He raised his voice. 'Come on you bastard! Do your worst!'

'No!' Abruptly halting the song, Pratt placed a hand on his arm. 'Don't tempt the sea god, Tommy!'

'Sea god?' Thoms shook his head. 'It's not the sea that's our enemy John. You and I both know that...' he looked at me and abruptly closed his mouth, as if he had said too much.

'What can happen now?' I asked. 'We're going home!'

As we approached the night the wind shifted a few points, coming from east of north, and then it shifted another, so Captain Milne ordered an alteration of course. 'We'll ride the wind, lads,' he shouted, as the atmosphere on board changed again. The grins and music ended as the men attended to the needs of the ship, now fighting the weather they had blessed so shortly before.

'Here we go again,' Pratt shouted, and the fear was back in his eyes as he looked at me. 'Oh Jesus help us now!'

All night *Lady Balgay* battled the wind, and all night it continued to veer round. It shifted from north to east until it was coming at right angles from its original direction and once more pressing us toward the coast of Greenland, three hundred miles to the west. It altered again the next day, easing east and then south, so we were forced, with great reluctance, backward, with the battered prow of *Lady Balgay* facing into a screaming hurricane that ripped away the final fragments of even our triple lashed sails and drove us north, yard by fighting yard.

'No! Not again! We're not going back north again!' Pratt stared into a day turned dark as a December midnight by the storm, then, in bitter frustration we watched the binnacle compass gyrate until the needle pointed the same way as *Lady Balgay* was headed. Shaking his head, Pratt looked pitifully at me as if I had the power to help him. 'It won't let us go, Doctor Cosgrove! It's not finished with us yet!' There was a break in his voice and his face crumpled like a distraught child.

Lashed to the mast with the water cascading from my sou' wester, I could only continue with my pretence, 'what won't let us go? What's not finished with us yet?' But I already knew the answer.

'It's the ballast! That ballast won't ever let us back!'

'No, John! That's not right! The ballast is only a pile of stones!' I tried to convince him, but my own doubt had returned, stronger and uglier than before.

'There are bones as well as stones, Mr Cosgrove; and the bones are from a cursed grave!'

There was no point in arguing with such entrenched superstition, so I just forced a twisted smile and shook my head. 'We'll get home,' I shouted, hearing my voice weak against the screaming wind.

But Pratt was correct in one thing; the storm would not let us go. It battered us for days, driving *Lady Balgay* ever north despite the torn muscles and aching backs of the crew, despite all the cunning of Captain Milne and the straining, throbbing engine, despite the engineering skill of Ross and Torrie's relentless toil of shovelling coal into the furnace. For everything we did, for every ounce of labour expended by the hands, the storm seemed to correspondingly increase its force, thrusting *Lady Balgay* back to where she had come.

Twice a day, I entered the captain's cabin and saw our erratic route marked on the chart. I could see how the pencil line, once crisp and clear, was becoming thicker and more blurred with each entry. Seven days after the storm began, the depleted crew was exhausted and even Captain Milne looked ready to drop. Staring at the chart, I saw we were being forced into a high latitude trap, with pack ice waiting to the north and the vicious coast of Greenland to the west. Unless the storm abated soon, we could be smashed to pieces and then nobody would be going home to Dundee.

'Iceberg, captain! Dead astern!' Thoms screamed the warning above the bedlam shriek of wind through the rigging and the roaring thunder of the sea.

'Jesus! We're all doomed! We're running hard against it!' Pratt clung to the lifeline, staring at the mountain of ice that stood squarely in our path. It was not the largest we had seen, perhaps ten times the bulk of *Lady Balgay* above the water and twice as high than the masts but the sea smashed against it, sending spray and spindrift right over the top for the wind to scatter to the uncaring heavens.

'Doomed? Not when I'm in command!' With his left hand gripping the lifeline, Milne flicked open his telescope and examined the berg. 'Do you know what this is, boys? It's a godsend, that's what it is!'

I stared at the captain, wondering if the strain of the voyage had toppled him over the edge of insanity. Too exhausted to ask questions, I waited for enlightenment.

'The iceberg is our harbour, boys! We'll anchor in its lee and get shelter. Tell Mr Ross to make sure his engines are running at full blast, Doctor. Thoms! Get all hands up here; I want one last effort to get us into safety. Come on men, move yourselves!'

The captain was right. With Ross running the forty-horsepower engine and Torrie slaving with his shovel to keep the furnace bright, *Lady Balgay* had just enough power to manoeuvre around the base of the berg. As soon as we eased into its lee, the wind magically dropped.

'You see? This berg is too big for the wind to force north.' With water cascading from his oilskins, Pratt looked exhausted. 'The captain's saved us again.' He secured a line with skill so casual he would have dismissed it with a shrug, looked fearfully north and added sycophantically. 'He's the best seaman in Dundee.'

'Cut engines, Mr Ross! Make her fast, boys! Ice anchors!' With his fur car sodden on his head, Captain Milne gave rapid orders that saw *Lady Balgay* attached to the berg, holding her secure to the ice mountain that protected us from the worst of the weather.

'There's more to this sailoring than meets the eye,' I gave a weary, but heartfelt opinion. Despite their foolish attachment to superstition, my respect for seamen had increased yet again. Education was the answer, I decided. If a good standard of education could be provided for every working class person, they would soon forget all the irrational fears and would become even more useful members of society.

'Come on, Doctor!' one of the hands broke my introspection. 'Stop daydreaming and lend a hand here! You're about as much use as a Bible in a brothel!'

With *Lady Balgay* tied and fast, we gathered on deck, nodding to each other in a mixture of relief and exhaustion. 'So what happens now?' I asked, staring at the blue-white mountain that could so easily have been our nemesis but instead had proved our saviour.

'Now we wait for the storm to blow itself out, Mr Cosgrove, and then we sail south once more.' Captain Milne glanced along the deck. 'Thoms! You and Sinclair are on watch. Wake me if anything happens. The rest of you grab a couple of hours rest before we clean up this pigsty.'

It felt surreal to stand in comparative shelter behind a giant island of ice with the wind howling like a thousand frustrated banshees, while a few cables lengths on either side the sea rose in savage waves that had the capacity to smash us to fragments. Knowing that I would never sleep in such conditions, I remained on deck, my shoulders hunched as I pondered our position.

We had nearly made it home. Just two more days of favourable wind would have seen us in the latitude of Shetland, and then we were within striking distance of the Scottish mainland. It was just blind bad luck that had seen us blown back north, but, as Captain Milne would say, such things happened at sea.

I grunted; I knew this experience would change me; witnessing the violent death of men I had known had removed most of my youthful certainties and created a different man. Now I was becoming much more philosophical. I felt older and much wiser than before, and hoped that Jennifer would appreciate the change.

But how had such a sequence of horrors happened in what should have been a routine sealing voyage? I shook my head; growing up in Dundee I had heard about the adventures of the whaling fleet and knew of the strange superstitions of the Greenlandmen, but I had never considered that these tales were created from hard fact. I had listened, slightly amused, and assumed they were manufactured, embellished, garnered with imagination for effect and elaborated with each alcoholic rambling. Now I knew differently; they were the result of terrible events occurring to simple, semi educated, basically decent but superstitious men.

And Jennifer? I was taking her loyalty for granted, but was she really still waiting for me in that comfortable house that was so unreal after the harshness of the North? At that moment I found it hard to imagine a landscape of soft grass and trees swaying in a gentle breeze, tended rolling fields and streets of people secure from ice and storms and danger. No; I told myself; it was all right; Jennifer would wait. In a world of shifting uncertainty, Jennifer's fidelity was a fixture. She would be there when I returned; of that I had no doubt.

And then they were back. This time there was no warning, no gradual realisation of unease; one moment my mind was occupied with Jennifer in Balgay House, the next the two figures dominated everything. They were crowding inside my brain, sliding from the unconscious and undetermined into the conscious and rational, seeping into my thoughts and influencing my actions so I cowered from every new sound and started at those that were unfamiliar.

'No!' I might have said the word out loud, but there was nobody to hear. 'No! Go away!'

They remained, pushing ever closer to me as their forms solidified. I could see them clearly now in all but feature. There was one man, tall and broad and potent; and one woman, so thrusting she might be a suffragette; yet so beguiling I could not look away. They waited until they captured my entire attention and then led me on that same appalling journey through the silent ship.

'I don't want to go,' I said, but they beckoned to me and I found myself drifting in their wake, hating myself and dreading the horrors I knew were to follow.

'I'm not here,' I told myself. 'This is not real.' But I could not withdraw as the two images slid from the deck to the crew's quarters. Once again I saw the hands, less in number now, but still sleeping in their various positions. The taller image stopped at the head of Sinclair's bunk and beckoned me closer, drawing me to him as easily as honey attracts a wasp. Sinclair slept like an innocent baby or a weary, work-worn Greenlandman, lying on his back with his legs apart and his head thrown back. The image stopped for a lingering, mocking second and then slowly descended to merge with the recumbent man.

'No! Don't take any more!' I shook my head in pointless denial. 'Please?'

Extending a hand, the female took hold of my sleeve and for one inconceivably terrifying moment I thought she would condemn me, but instead she conducted me away, aft through the ship, to the canvas screen behind which slept Isbister. The image smiled, the mouth too large for the shaded face, and brought me inexorably inside.

Isbister lay on her side, crammed into a make shift bunk of timber and sailcloth, facing away from me with her hands folded under her face. Although she slept cocooned in warm clothing, once more I saw her naked, and could not help my eyes roaming from the neat shoulders to the firm waist and the subtly wide flare of her hips. I lingered there for an aching moment, devouring the swell and texture of her buttocks, and then she rolled over, facing me, with her eyes gently closed and her mouth relaxed and nearly childlike in sleep. Her breasts were larger but even shapelier than I remembered, and her belly seductively smooth, guiding my eyes downward into even sterner temptation.

The image laughed and slid on top of Isbister, gradually disappearing until the two bodies were as one, and I watched as Isbister's mouth stretched into a smile that matched that of the intruder. She looked up, her eyes wide.

'Iain.' She said softly, but with neither surprise nor disapproval, and I jerked my attention away.

The rail was cold under my hands, the iceberg hostile in the reflection of a thousand stars, and I heard what may have been a seal moaning somewhere nearby.

'Oh God,' I prayed desperately. 'Not Jemmy Isbister. Please not her.'

I knew that in my imagination, Isbister had replaced Jennifer as my woman; she represented my fevered longings for my wife. If Isbister was to die, where did that leave Jennifer? Should I rush forward and wake her? The thought was instantly appealing, but what could I tell her? Could I tell her that I dreamed of her death? But that was not true; I had dreamed of her lying naked, which was a perfectly natural thing for any red-blooded man, deprived of his wife, to do. Once again I tried to rationalise the images. I was under strain, I was in a state of nervous collapse, and I was separated from Jennifer.

I knew all these things, but I also knew there was much more. There was too much for me to understand and I needed professional guidance that was not available out here. As I tried to rationalise the images, I learned to hate the wind that had driven us back north; I cursed it with more venom than I had ever felt before, and with a range of profanity I had not known I possessed. When all the spite and fire and gall was expunged from my body, I sunk my head in exhaustion and cried salt tears.

Would I ever see Jennifer again?

The voices drifted softly to me, the rumble of a man and the lighter cadence of a woman, intermixed with a high pitched giggle that I recognised instantly as belonging to Isbister. Stepping further away, I tried to block out the sounds of what seemed quite an intimate meeting. I frowned; it was obvious that Isbister was speaking with one of the crew although she was forbidden contact with anybody save Captain Milne and me. The voices were from below, where she lay, both in reality and in my imagination, and if I returned to my own quarters I would have to pass her screened-off cubbyhole.

I recognised my moral dilemma. Should I go below, which I was perfectly entitled to do, and disturb Isbister at what was probably an innocent, if illicit, meeting, or should I stay here? The recent disturbingly vivid images had upset the clarity of my thoughts so I could not make any decision. How would I have felt if somebody had walked in on my wedding night?

Even more importantly: what would Jennifer have felt?

That thought convinced me to remain where I was, hoping Isbister and her friend would soon finish and part company. In a way it was unfortunate that Isbister's cabin was so close to the engine room, so the relative warmth permitted such behaviour as I imagined. But I could not interrupt her enjoyment; I was a doctor, not a disciplinarian; it was not my job to interfere with the personal affairs of any member of the crew.

Moving astern, I reached into my pocket and pulled out a pipe. I had never smoked before this voyage, but Thoms had introduced me to the habit and had passed on his spare pipe. Although I was not yet an addict, I already found the process soothing at times of stress. When things were at their worst, most of the crew resorted to pipes or cigarettes and I had joined them. Now I lit up and drew smoke deep into my lungs before allowing it to trickle softly into the air as I listened to the waves hammering against the far side of the iceberg.

Whatever happened we were hostages to fate. We could do nothing until the storm blew itself out, and then Captain Milne must ascertain our position and sail south before the winter set in, or face months frozen into the ice. I could not suppress my shiver of fear, just as Isbister's voice rose in what was definitely a laugh of pleasure.

'That's Jemmy!' I had not noticed Sinclair a few yards from me, hunched beside the mizzenmast with hands thrust into massive mittens. 'That's Jemima!'

'Leave her,' I grunted. 'She's doing no harm and it sounds like she's having some fun. God knows we all need that.'

'What?' Sinclair was the only member of the crew taller than me, for Dundee seamen tended to be compact; broad rather than tall. When he shuffled closer and glowered downward he overtopped me by a good two inches. 'She's doing lots of harm. Jemmy's my bloody woman!'

'Wait!' My grasp failed to make contact as Sinclair plunged past. I cursed, remembering Pratt's claim that a woman on board was bad luck. Maybe the saying was based on sheer common sense rather than some fanciful superstition: when a woman was present, men tended to argue over her company. Instinctively, I followed Sinclair, to see him jerk open the canvas screen that sheltered Isbister's quarters. There was a shrill scream and a momentary glimpse of smooth female flesh, then a man's leg appeared and a brawny arm tugged the canvas back into place.

'What the hell are you doing?' That was Torrie's voice, raised in indignation. 'This is none of your business, Sinky!'

'It bloody is!' Sinclair grabbed the canvas and wrested it from Torrie's grip. 'You're a bastard Albert! You well know that Jemmy's my woman!'

'Your woman? She doesn't think so!' Struggling free of the cramped cubicle, Torrie stood face to face with the much taller man. 'Anyway, you told us you were just shipmates!'

Thrusting in, I pushed them apart, more by force of surprise than strength. Sinclair staggered against the bulkhead, blustering his outrage, while Torrie, stark naked and muscled like Hercules, took only a single step backward before standing with his chin aggressively outthrust.

'The captain told you to keep away from the woman!' I snarled at Torrie, too angry to be afraid. 'Did you not learn your lesson in Dundee?'

The reference to his supposed venereal disease did not seem to bother Torrie, who snorted and pushed me back. I slammed painfully against the bulkhead. 'The captain's already lost half his bloody crew, Doctor. Why should anybody listen to him?'

'And you, Isbister. I thought you had more sense!' I pointed to Isbister, who was shockingly enticingly, equally, naked, standing with her hands covering as much of her as she could but her eyes alight with excitement. She did not look afraid.

The image returned to me, that hideously faceless woman lowering herself onto Isbister's languid body, and I closed my eyes.

Misreading the signs, Isbister laughed. 'It's all right, Doctor. There's nothing you haven't seen before.'

'What?' Sinclair advanced. 'You too?' He glowered at Isbister, raising a massive hand. 'You bloody whore!'

Isbister easily dodged the slap. 'Don't be stupid, Isaac! During the medical examination, I mean.'

'Oh,' the reminder calmed Sinclair for only a second; he directed his anger back to Torrie. 'You thought we were just shipmates?' He thrust his hand against Torrie's bare chest, pushing him backward against the bulkhead. 'Are you a complete fool? Since when have you heard of a woman in the crew? Of course she's mine!'

At least ten years younger than Sinclair, Torrie was not inclined to give way. He pushed back, unbalancing the taller man, who staggered against me. 'Well, Isaac, she's chosen me tonight so you can bugger off and count the waves.'

I expected Sinclair's angry punch, but so did Torrie, who ducked and countered with a smashing blow to Sinclair's stomach. The older man roared and doubled up, but responded with a savage uppercut to Torrie's groin. Torrie squealed high-pitched, and Sinclair slapped him open handed on the back of the head, sending him to the ground, and began to kick into his ribs, grunting with every blow.

As I leaped to pull them apart, Sinclair's elbow unwittingly caught me in the face. I yelled and staggered back, clutching at anything for support and finding only Isbister's smooth flesh. We fell together, landing in a tangle of bare limbs and damp fur as Sinclair continued to kick at Torrie, who lay writhing and roaring on the deck.

'Enough!' I shouted, trying to rise, but failing as Isbister pressed against me. 'Sinclair! You'll kill him, man!'

Sinclair stopped, staring at me. His eyes were wild, his nostrils dilated and he panted through a gaping mouth. 'I'll do that, right enough,' he promised.

'Jesus!' Torrie crouched on all fours, retching green bile. 'I'll do for you, Sinclair.' he wiped the back of his hand across a bloody mouth. 'I'll fucking kill you for this.'

'There's been enough killing!' The second's respite gave me the opportunity to haul myself upright, and I stepped between them. 'Sinclair, get back on deck. You're meant to be on watch. And you Torrie, I'd better examine you. You've taken quite a beating there.'

'I'll kill him! I swear to God!'

The noise had attracted the rest of the crew, who gathered round, either asking questions or trying to act as peacemaker. When Donaldson openly eyed the still naked Isbister, Thoms ushered into her cabin with curt orders to dress. I had a brief glimpse of a pert bottom, then realised she was watching me over her shoulder and looked away in some confusion. Her laugh may have been directed at anybody, but I suspect it was intended for me.

'You bastard!' Still doubled over with pain, Torrie lifted the knife from Sinclair's belt and made a wild, futile slash. 'I'll kill you.'

'Not today, Albert!' Moving more swiftly, Ross thrust Torrie against the bulkhead, holding him there with a forearm rigid across his throat. 'Keep still! She's not worth the fuss. It's certainly not worth swinging for. There are plenty more of her type!'

Isbister pushed out of her quarters, now glaring. 'What do you mean, her type?'

'Keep quiet, you!' Ross glowered at her. 'You've caused enough trouble for one night.'

'That's my woman,' Sinclair repeated, but with Pratt and Thoms holding him back he could not advance on Torrie.

'Get back on deck, Sinclair,' I knew my authority was fragile at best, but I had to try and restore order.

'Where's the captain?' Thoms glanced around. 'He should sort this out. Donaldson, go and wake him, although God knows this lot were making enough racket to waken the bloody dead.'

'Right men, it's all finished.' Mention of the captain's name had calmed the situation and I took advantage of the lull. 'Everybody except Sinclair get back to the foc'sle; now. Isbister, for God's sake put some clothes on, and Torrie, come with me so I can look at your injuries.'

With a parting glance at Torrie, Isbister gave another small laugh and swayed back into her cabin, emphatically dragging shut the canvas flap. The rest of the men dispersed, with Sinclair repeating 'she's my woman' and throwing malevolent looks at Torrie, who retaliated with an obscene gesture that I chose not to notice. The situation had been unpleasant, but hardly unexpected on a small vessel in which there was so much tension, and I ushered Torrie into my cabin.

'You're bruised and battered, Albert,' I observed after a brief inspection. 'But there's nothing broken and no permanent damage. I'd keep away from Isbister for the remainder of this voyage, and avoid Sinclair too. I think he's a bit big for you to handle yet.'

Torrie scowled, curling his lip. 'I'll do for that bastard.'

'Maybe you will at that, Albert, but not today.' I looked pointedly at his rapidly purpling and swelling genitals. 'And I think Isbister is safe for a while too.' I watched Torrie slouch painfully away, wondering if that was the encounter of which the two shadowy figures had warned him and started when Donaldson tapped my shoulder.

'It's the captain, Dr Cosgrove. I think you had better have a look at him.'

Chapter Twenty One

GREENLAND SEA
JULY - AUGUST 1914

One of the men last night took a piece of his undergarment and committed it to the flames, saying at the same time "burn the witches'
Journal of a Voyage to Baffin Bay aboard the Ship *Thomas* Commanded by Alex Cooke, John Wanless, 8th November 1834

Captain Milne lay on his back with his head at an acute angle and his arms spread out. At first I thought he was dead, but then I smelled the sweet perfume of rum, heard the clink of empty bottles rolling under the bunk and realised he was merely drunk. Sir Melville's warning returned to me:

'Captain Milne is a good man too, Iain, the last of a long line of Dundee whalers. A splendid mariner, as long as you keep him away from the bottle.'

Jennifer's father had been right all along, and my self-congratulation on easing my passage with a display of generosity had backfired. I had failed in that simple task he had set me.

Sighing, I bent over the captain, loosened his clothing so he was more comfortable and removed every bottle from his cabin. 'Sleep tight, Captain,' I said, feeling the weight of guilt pressing down upon me. 'And when you wake up, I hope you are capable of taking us safely to Dundee.' I left the cabin, closing the door behind me.

'He'll be all right, Mr Donaldson, so long as we keep him away from anything to drink.'

'I see, Doctor.' Donaldson grinned, immediately understanding the situation. 'I think I'll get my head down now.'

'I think you should,' I agreed. 'I'll do the same.'

After so long fighting the storm it felt strange to lie in a bunk that did not toss and gyrate, and I stared at the deck beams above, listening to the howl of the wind around the iceberg as I wondered anew what would become of me. The fight had been nothing; an incident that was soon ended; I discounted Torrie's threats as the bluster of a shamed youth.

Captain Milne's drunkenness was far more important, for nobody else could properly control the crew. I sighed and resolved to try and keep him sober for the remainder of the voyage, which would not be an easy task given Milne's utter ruthlessness when it came to having his own way. But I had encouraged his drinking, so imposed upon myself the penance of controlling it.

I closed my eyes in near despair: there never seemed any peace on this voyage, just a succession of problems that materialised without warning and with no indication how best to deal with them. Suddenly I found myself grinning sardonically; perhaps that was a suitable beginning to married life?

Recognising my rising laughter as hysteria, I checked myself.

God, Jennifer, I hope you enjoy my company because once I return home I'll never leave your side again, that I'll swear on a stack of bibles.

Unable to alter the reality of my present situation I escaped into a daydream of a lifetime with Jennifer, with a growing brood of children, a successful practise and a quiet house in Broughty Ferry, when I became aware of the growing clamour. Before I could sit up, the door banged open and Isbister leaped in, screaming, with a half-dressed

Torrie a step behind and a press of men clustering in the corridor outside.

'Get her! Hold the witch!' With his injuries still troubling him, Torrie pointed from a half crouch and his left hand protecting his groin. His face was contorted with hatred.

'What in God's name?' I sat up, staring, half asleep and wholly disturbed. 'Torrie! What the hell is this?'

'Help me doctor! Please help me!' Dressed in a man's thick woollen underclothes, Isbister looked ludicrous but respectable as she cowered at the head of my bed. 'They're going to kill me.'

'What? Nobody's going to kill you, Jemmy! Torrie, explain yourself!' Dragging myself out of bed, I stood as upright as the limited space allowed.

Again, Torrie jabbed his forefinger toward Isbister. 'It's her that's been causing the trouble, Doctor. She's the one!'

'What one?' Standing between the cowering Isbister and truculent Torrie, I felt very vulnerable. 'It seems that she's scared of you, Torrie!'

'She's a witch, that's what she is!' Torrie jabbed the accusing finger. 'John told us the story...'

'The story?' I was unsure how Torrie could transform Pratt's tale of cannibalism at Gass Skerry into claiming Isbister was a witch. I swore as foully as any Greenlandman as my frustration took control. 'Ignore John Pratt!' I had to move quickly to block Torrie's lunge at Isbister. 'Pratt tells fairy tales for children, Albert! I'm surprised at you believing such things in this day and age! Pratt's an old fool!'

'She's a witch!' Torrie repeated.

I had long known that Torrie was a muscular young man, handsome as sin and undoubtedly popular with a certain type of woman, but nature had not blessed him with an abundance of brains. When somebody told him something, he tended to nurse that new knowledge until it became a fixed belief. Now that Pratt had informed him that Isbister was a witch, it would be hard to persuade him otherwise.

'You were the best of friends only an hour ago,' I reminded, trying to push Torrie back. It was like attempting to move a granite wall. 'Now leave her be.' I looked up, where Donaldson was hovering just outside the door. 'Billy! You know that Pratt just talks nonsense. There's no such thing as a witch. Tell Albert that Pratt's just an old fool!'

'Maybe not such an old fool,' Donaldson sounded worried. 'John's right you know. Since we took that ballast on board this trip has been a disaster, and where did these two come from? Sinclair and the woman, I mean? They just appeared on the ice, and whoever heard of a woman as a member of a crew?'

'And whoever heard of a witch up here? Or anywhere else for that matter?' I could sense the fear in these men. They resented the deaths of so many of their shipmates and wanted somebody to blame, and now that Pratt had spread his stories around, Isbister seemed the natural choice.

'She came with the ballast,' Torrie sounded sulky now. 'They both did; her and that big bastard Sinclair.'

'I shovelled the ballast on myself,' I shouted. I knew that was not strictly true, but it sounded better than saying I had supervised the work, 'and I swear to you that Jemmy Isbister was not hiding amongst the shingle.' I hoped for a laugh for that, something to ease the tension, but the mood of the men did not alter. They continued to stare at Isbister as she cowered at the far side of the cabin, showing far more concern than she had when she was utterly naked but in control of the situation.

'Listen,' Donaldson tried to persuade me with what passed for logic in his primitive mind. I made allowances, knowing he was still hurting after the terrible death of Mackie. 'There were two people hanged for witchcraft and cannibalism, eh?'

'So the story goes,' I agreed, 'but that was over two hundred years ago.'

'Aye; two people hanged; one man and one woman. And what came aboard? Two people; one man and one woman. They even admitted following the blood trail, and as soon as they arrive, wee Rab is killed.' Donaldson pointed to Isbister. 'And then just tonight, Sinclair admits that she is his woman; they're man and wife, just like they were on Orkney, eh? We can't keep her on the boat!'

'She's a witch,' Torrie repeated, sulkily, 'and we want her off the ship.'

'Off the ship?' I gestured to the bulkhead with my hand. 'Where would she go? On to the iceberg? Or maybe you want to cast her adrift in an open boat? She would not last a day out there; you know that!'

'So?' Donaldson shrugged in callous unconcern. 'She killed Macks.'

'A polar *bear* killed Mackie,' I tried to sound reasonable as I reminded him. 'We all saw it.'

'She's killing us all, one by one. John says so.' Torrie did not retreat an inch from his position. 'It's either her or us.'

'Look at her.' Taking a chance, I stepped aside and put my hand on Isbister's shoulder. It felt warm but she was shaking in fear. 'She's only a woman; a young woman, and just look at her! She's terrified! Have you ever heard of a frightened witch?'

'Aye,' Donaldson said, 'when they were burned, eh? Maybe we should burn her!'

Shockingly, Torrie and even Thoms nodded at that, and when Sinclair tried to protest, Thoms held his sealing knife to the tall man's throat.

'Maybe we should burn you too, Sinclair. You were quick to beat up young Albert there, but you're not so tough now, eh?' Thoms twisted the knife slightly, drawing a red bead of blood. 'Aye; you're every bit as bad as the woman and I'll gut you myself before I apply the match.' Thoms raised his voice. 'Come on boys, Billy's right. Let's burn the witches and get our luck back!'

I expected the men to scorn Thoms' words, but I realised with horror that Pratt and Donaldson were slowly nodding, and Torrie was grinning in savage delight.

'Aye, Tommy! They always burned witches in the past!' Pratt prodded Sinclair painfully in the ribs, 'maybe if they had burned these two when young Rab was murdered, Leerie and Sooty would still be alive! Aye, and Macks as well. The bastards came from the ballast!'

I pushed forward, still with one hand holding Isbister. She was trembling so violently I wondered how she could stand. 'No! Don't be a fool, Thoms! That would be murder of the worst kind! For God's sake, man! It's been a bad voyage but it's hardly the fault of these two. They're survivors of a shipwreck!'

The men began to murmur, but Thoms kept his knife at Sinclair's throat.

'I understand what you are trying to do, Dr Cosgrove,' Pratt spoke slowly and with the raw scar on his face working hideously with each word. 'But listen to this.'

'I'm listening,' I put my arm protectively around Isbister's shoulder. It was shivering, but with fear or cold I did not know.

'You already know the story of Gass Skerry. A man and woman were hanged there for cannibalism and witchcraft.'

'You've told us that.' I reminded, 'but that was hundreds of years ago...'

'Aye,' Pratt held up a broad hand. 'I know that, Doctor. But listen; please listen. We loaded ballast from beneath the burial cairn, and there were bones in it. Remember that young Rab was holding a handful of bones when we found him dead.'

'He had one small piece of bone in his hand,' I reluctantly allowed, 'but we cannot prove a connection.'

'Where else would they come from?' Torrie asked forcibly. 'The witches were buried there, and we find the bones, eh? They must be the witches' bones, and then these two appear and folk start to die, eh? No connection, the doctor says. Every connection, I would say.'

There was a murmur from the men as they nodded their heads. Frightened faces turned to Isbister. 'Whoever heard of a woman working on a ship?' Thoms curled his lip contemptuously and gave his pronouncement. 'Aye. She's a witch.'

'A witch,' Pratt echoed. 'So Dr Cosgrove, I know you're just trying to help, as you helped my face,' he put a hand to his scar. 'You did a good job Doctor, and saved my life, but this time you're wrong.'

The men nodded, but Isbister's courage broke and she began to weep, her sobs acting as background to Pratt's words.

'After that we sailed north, and there was an accident to Learmonth when he cut himself, and you patched it up. Correct?'

I nodded, holding Isbister as close as I could. She pressed against me for protection.

'Aye. And some of the men had strange dreams after that. Young Torrie here said he dreamed of a woman,' Pratt pointed to Isbister. 'It was that woman there, a big breasted brunette, walking across blood.'

Oh God. The vision returned, as forcibly as ever; the salacious woman gliding across the crimson sea, her body inviting, her face veiled and the atmosphere of menace combined with intense seduction. So I had not been alone in my imaginings, and it was not the medical insight I had hoped, but something else. What? Could it have been a mass hallucination, something that appeared to everybody? I raised my voice. 'Did anybody else apart from Torrie dream about a woman walking across blood?'

There was a moment's silence but the men shook their heads. Then slowly, reluctantly, one by one, they admitted to unusual dreams. Some had dreamed of a man with a knife, or a whale overturning a small boat, but only Torrie and I had seen the woman. Why would she appear to Torrie? What connection could there be?

The answer was crushingly obvious. I was newly married, with my first sexual encounter with Jennifer just behind me, and Torrie was a Romeo, a man whose life, and no doubt his head, was filled with the pursuit of women. The other men would dream about something important to them; work, home or family; whatever that image was, it seemed to connect to a fundamental need or fear or desire. If I had more time I could investigate this phenomenon and perhaps see a pattern. I might find a cure for what appeared a psychological requirement, but Pratt was speaking again, his voice flat and menacing.

'And then we had the seal hunting, Doctor, remember? I was bitten and these two appeared. They followed the trail of blood to our ship. Is that not exactly what cannibals would do?' Pratt waited for a moment to allow his words to sink in. He may have been illiterate but there was a strong sense of the dramatic about Pratt, combined with a healthy dollop of native wit.

I closed my eyes in fear; perhaps if I had a few moments of peace I could create a logical defence for these two survivors, something that would convince the Greenlandmen of their innocence, but there was no time. The crew were fearful, impatient for revenge. All I could do was bluster. 'You're talking nonsense, Mr Pratt.'

'I'm not,' Pratt insisted. 'The first smell of blood awakened them from the ballast and the gallons of seal blood brought them in person. They're both witches and cannibals.'

'What?' I glanced at Isbister who cuddled against me, weeping unrestrainedly, and Sinclair, standing white faced with Thoms' knife pressing against his throat. 'Cannibals eat people, Mr Pratt. All these two have eaten is ordinary rations!'

'What are their names, Mr Cosgrove?' He answered his own question: 'Sinclair and Isbister, eh? Both are Orkney names, the same as the cannibals that were hanged. And when we picked them up, were they half-starved and frostbitten like survivors always are, eh? No!' He leered his triumph around the crowded cabin. 'You examined them Doctor, and you said yourself they were fit and healthy! But how could they be, after surviving days or weeks on the ice?'

'That proves nothing!' I said. Isbister was trembling so violently she had to hold me for support, while I saw Sinclair's Adam's apple jump as he swallowed.

'It proves everything, Doctor,' Thoms had taken the lead in the group, pushing forward his opinion by virtue of experience. 'I was wrecked in the ice once, and I was out in an open boat for three days. When I was rescued I could hardly stand, and I lost two toes. How many toes did these two lose?'

'None,' I admitted, 'but they were very well clothed.'

'I'll bet they were,' Thoms said.

'And then we found out about the ship's old name and got rid of the figurehead, remember?' Pratt was pushing now, recalling every detail of the voyage.

'I remember,' I said wearily.

'And that same night wee Rab was killed, pushed down the hold.' Torrie glared at Isbister. 'She pushed him.'

'He fell in the night,' I heard the despair in my voice. 'Nobody pushed him.'

'He was murdered. And then his arm was chewed too, if you remember?' Pratt backed up Torrie.

'Rats,' now I was beginning to panic, for I knew no rats had chewed Robert Mitchell. 'Rats chewing the body.'

'Cannibals,' Pratt contradicted. 'These two are cannibals and they came aboard with the ballast from Gass Skerry.'

I shook my head, frantically searching for words that might turn these men from their course. 'I liked Rab Mitchell too, John, but he died in an accident. As the captain says, such things happen at sea.'

But where was Captain Milne now? He was lying drunk in his bunk with rum that I paid for. I shuddered at the inevitability of it all; my grasp at popularity had contributed to this nightmare. Sir Melville, that wise, cunning man, had been right while I, in my arrogant inexperience, had only added to the troubles of this ship of the damned.

'They're cannibals and witches,' Torrie gave his opinion from the distilled wisdom of all his eighteen years. 'And witches should be burned.'

When the rush came it was so sudden that I was nearly overwhelmed. I just managed to block Torrie's path as he reached for Isbister, and his face, distorted with hatred or fear, glared into mine as he reached for the woman. The fireman was all muscle and bone, with neither ingenuity nor guile, so I managed to duck his roundhouse punch and ram a merciless knee into his already damaged groin. Torrie screamed and doubled up, clutching frantically at himself and retching in his agony.

'Doctor!' Ross was staring, but the few seconds' hesitation gave me time to grab for the revolver that Sir Melville had given me so many months ago.

'Back! Back! Get out of my cabin!'

Chapter Twenty Two

GREENLAND SEA
JULY - AUGUST 1914

A dead woman bites not
· Patrick, 6th Lord Gray (d 1612)

I waved the revolver at the leading men and they withdrew a reluctant step. They remained crowded in the entrance to my claustrophobic cabin, filled with sullen anger as I waved the weapon around, unsure if I could actually pull the trigger and shoot one of my own shipmates, but certain I could not let them grab Isbister. 'If anybody puts a single finger on this woman I swear to God I'll put a bullet in his brain, sure as death!'

The men retreated another inch and, encouraged, I stepped forward. 'Sinclair, you come in here where you're safe.' I presented the revolver again, feeling it heavy in my hand. 'Get in, man!'

'They're in it together!' It was Donaldson that broke the impasse, grabbing hold of Sinclair even as Thoms relaxed the knife.

'No!' Smashing an elbow into Donaldson's face, Sinclair leaped for the sanctuary of my cabin as what had been a situation nearly under control degenerated into quick chaos. Somebody threw a flensing knife, which clattered off the bulkhead behind me, Pratt shouted and balled fists like hammers and Isbister began to scream.

'Get the woman!' Torrie shouted, plunging forward.

'Stop!' I ordered, and fired a warning shot above their heads, the sound deafening in the confined space and the bullet crashing into the woodwork of the bulkhead. There was a second of shocked silence, but before the echoes ended Torrie and Pratt grabbed for the hysterical Isbister and Donaldson was again wrestling with Sinclair. Pratt's muscular body slammed into me, but whether by accident or design I do not know.

'Leave her,' I yelled, falling backward as Isbister continued to scream, high pitched and terrible.

I saw Ross, the practical, down-to- earth engineer staring at the back of the crowd and yelled for help. 'Mr Ross! Lend a hand here, for the love of God,' but Ross had also been affected by the general madness and roared as he lunged through the press and on top of me, grappling for the gun. I tried to fire again but his sinewy fingers locked around the trigger.

'Ross!'

The combined weight of Ross and Pratt bore me downward onto the bunk, and my cabin was like something more normally seen on a Saturday night in Dock Street. The throng of struggling men rolled around with me in the centre, punching, gouging, sobbing and butting in their hatred and fury and overpowering fear.

I fought harder than I had ever fought in my life, but although I was the taller and heavier, a lifetime dealing with recalcitrant machinery had braced Ross's arms with sinewy muscles, while the sealers were hardened hunters buoyed by terror. I was outmatched, overpowered and held down.

'Leave them be!' I yelled, but somebody elbowed me under the jaw and I yelled at the sudden explosion of pain and slid off the bed. A boot made sickeningly impact into my stomach, but Pratt stepped forward.

'None of that! Don't hurt the doctor. He saved my life!'

'Tie him up,' Thoms ordered, and within seconds I was thrown face down on the bunk while skilled seamen wound a line around my ankles and another around my wrists. They pulled cruelly tight into my flesh and somebody, possibly Torrie delivered a sharp cuff to the back of my head.

'I said: none of that!' Pratt intervened again, but did not suggest releasing me.

I heard Isbister screaming for mercy, heard Sinclair's cursing abruptly cut short and then the men left the cabin and dragged their captives outside and up on to the bitter deck.

I heard the thunder of their feet, the terrified protests of Isbister and the low growls of Sinclair.

'You can't do this!' I yelled. 'Tommy! John! For God's sake think what you're doing!' I heard Isbister's screams rise to a long drawn, terrified wail that bristled the small hairs at the back of my head.

'No! Please, please, don't!'

The screaming continued for a few minutes, then subsided to a hysterical sobbing that was every bit as bad to hear.

Perhaps fifteen minutes later Donaldson and Torrie returned and Donaldson at least was laughing. Grabbing me in un-gentle hands, they hauled me face up on the bunk.

'We want you to watch this, doctor,' Donaldson said. He was grinning, with the same terrible joy in his eyes as when he hunted the seals.

'What are you going to do?' I could hardly bear to hear the answer.

'Burn the witches,' Donaldson leaned closer. 'And you're going to watch.'

'No,' I shook my head in disbelief and horror. 'You can't do that. You can't; they're not witches, they're just survivors! They did not cause Rab Mitchell to fall, or the bear to kill Mackie, or the sea to take Soutar and Learmonth. It was not their fault!'

'We say it was,' Donaldson contradicted. 'And Macks was my friend.' Reaching down, he dragged me roughly off the bed, and with Torrie helping, hauled me carelessly up to the deck. They deposited me there as if I were a sack of potatoes.

'Look at that, doctor.' Donaldson was still grinning, 'and watch how we deal with witches.'

'Oh Jesus,' I shrunk away, trying to escape from the horror. 'Oh good God in heaven!' I widened my eyes, trying to wake from this new nightmare, hoping that the figures from his imagination would appear so I knew I was sleeping, but instead Torrie slapped my face.

'Watch, Doctor.' His voice was soft. 'Watch when you're told.'

It was a surreal spectacle, an incubus that could have erupted from the brush of Hieronymus Bosch, so terrible that I shook my head in disbelief. Behind us was the iceberg, taller than *Lady Balgay*, with a double pinnacle of ice stretching to a sky of pale grey from which the occasional flurry of snow cascaded. *Lady Balgay* herself was demi-white, with frost in the more shaded parts and those exposed now damp and dark and greasy. Her canvas hung in shredded tatters from spars that wind and weather had stripped of most of the varnish, leaving the wood patched and bare.

Beneath the masts the crew were mustered in a frenzied group, Thoms was swearing and gesticulating, Donaldson laughing high pitched and Pratt trembling, but all clustered around two large barrels. Cubes of seal blubber slithering on the once scrubbed planking of the deck showed that the barrels had been emptied of the contents that had taken so much effort to collect, while mollies jumped and pecked at the blubber, their harsh calls adding to the hallucinatory image.

'Put tar and some of the blubber inside the kegs,' Donaldson had taken charge, his eyes brilliant. 'Put in enough to burn, but not too quickly!'

Torrie was first to obey, grinning to Sinclair. 'I told you I'd kill you, you big bastard! I told you, eh?' The others followed, pouring in tar and dropping greasy cubes of blubber into the barrels until Donaldson was satisfied.

'That's the way, lads. Now, in with them!'

Bloodied and bruised, securely tied, but with their mouths free to scream, Isbister and Sinclair lay wriggling beside the mizzenmast. They looked toward me, pleading for the help that I could not provide.

'Oh God, no! Please! We didn't do anything!' Crying and protesting their innocence, they struggled as eager hands lifted them clear of the deck and thrust them feet first toward the barrels. Perhaps because she was smaller, Isbister managed to free her ankles and she straddled the barrel, one foot on either side, until Donaldson punched the back of each knee so she involuntarily folded her legs.

'In with her,' he ordered and slapped her hard across the face, 'the murderous witch!'

'Tie them in!' Thoms ordered. 'Lash them tight so they can never escape again!'

'Jesus, no! You can't do this! You're mad!' Sinclair fought the sealers, swearing mightily. 'I'm a whaler, a Greenlandman like you, not a witch! I'm no cannibal!' He looked to Isbister. 'At least let Jemmy go! She's a woman, for the love of Christ!'

'I told you I'd kill you, Sinclair.' Leaning close, but still favouring his tender groin, Torrie hawked deeply and spat on the tall man. 'Put the boot in to me, eh? Not twice you won't, you big bastard!'

'Jesus! Albert, please! No!'

Terror made Isbister inarticulate but she screamed in an incoherent ululation, staring in horror at the crew who clustered around, slapping at her face, prodding and squeezing her body as they jeered.

'Murder Macks, eh? Kill Sooty and Leerie? We'll show you!' Donaldson was taunting, thrilling at the anguish of his victims just as he had enjoyed killing the seals. Pratt pulled him back, his face pale.

'No. Don't do that, Billy. That's not why we're here; anyway, we don't know what they might do. They're witches; they might raise a spell or something. Kill them quick and be done with it.'

'Maybe we should wait, lads. Maybe…' Thoms stared at me, and back at the terrified victims.

'Doctor!' Isbister found her voice. When she stared directly into my eyes I saw, distinctly but only for an instant, the image of the voluptuous woman. I gasped, recalling my vision of these terrible figures merging, but I could not speak in her defence as Donaldson taunted her with a lighted match and Isbister began to scream again.

'Remember Macks, Tommy? And Sooty? These witches murdered them!' Donaldson held the match high, its flicker dying quickly. 'What do you say now, Tommy? Should we let them go? Or carry on?'

'Over the side with them!' Thoms had taken charge again, veering from doubtfulness to vindictive fear.

'Tommy!' I tried to exploit Thoms' erstwhile hesitation. 'You can't let this happen. It's obscene, man. It's absolute murder!'

Thoms looked at me through glazed eyes, obviously battling his own terror. 'I don't know, Dr Cosgrove. We can't lose any more men. Johnny Pratt and all the rest say ...'

'Don't listen to them, Tommy! We're losing everything by doing this!' Struggling against the lines that held me, I raised my voice. 'You can't do this! These people are innocent!'

'If you don't Tommy, then I will!' Donaldson elbowed the older man aside. 'Into the sea!' Glowering at me, Donaldson gave the fatal order and, cheering, the crew manoeuvred Sinclair's barrel to the rail. It balanced there for a moment, black and pot-bellied, with its human content roaring his fear as tears eased from half closed, unbelieving eyes.

'Over it goes, boys!' Donaldson gave the final push and the barrel tottered and hurtled downward into the dark, smooth sea. Gallons of water splashed on to the deck and for a moment I thought the barrel would capsize and drown Sinclair clean and quick, but it righted itself and floated, bobbing a few yards to port of the ship with Sinclair tied and helpless, still pleading for his life.

'Please, lads, please...'

'And the other one! Over she goes!'

Isbister was still screaming hopelessly as she was dropped overboard, and her barrel pitched and tossed beside Sinclair, spinning in a constant circle so one minute she was facing the crew of *Lady Balgay*, the next she was staring northward to the equally pitiless immensity of the Greenland Sea.

'Now lads, watch this!' Tying a piece of tarry rag to a marlinespike, Donaldson took careful aim and tossed it in a wide arc toward Sinclair.

It missed by a yard and fell among the waves, where it fizzed for only a second before sinking.

'Bad shot, Billy! You're bloody useless, eh?' Torrie jeered, nudging him. 'Me next!'

One by one the crew threw flaming rags tied to spikes and knives, lengths of tarred rope and pieces of discarded wood until one eventually landed within Sinclair's barrel and smoke began to rise. Sinclair struggled, trying desperately to wriggle his body to quench the flames, but tied hand and foot he was helpless, so the fire took slow hold on the greasy blubber and tar that coated the inside of the barrel, gradually spreading all round him.

'Look!' Donaldson yelled excitedly, 'Sinks is coming back!' He laughed, 'stand by to fend him off!'

A waft of wind had caught the burning barrel so it wavered closer to *Lady Balgay*. In an instant flames were licking up the stern, catching hold of the new paint and scorching the taffrail, with sparks spreading to the deck and mizzenmast.

'We're on fire! Put it out, Tommy!'

Men backed off as smoke billowed on board, but Donaldson grabbed a boathook and, leaning over, pushed at the barrel. It moved slightly further away, gyrating as Sinclair pleaded for mercy, but then Torrie lent his strength and pushed the burning horror a safe distance away. Together they put out the flames on the taffrail and stamped out the sparks that had landed on deck.

Sinclair was writhing, but he restrained his groans until the fire scorched through his furs, and then he began to thrash in earnest. Donaldson led the taunting, but it was Torrie who rolled a length of canvas into a tube, dipped it in tar and set it alight. Quite unemotionally he tossed it into Isbister's barrel.

'You should be burning too, witch.'

'No,' I begged, 'please, no,' but my voice was soft among the raucous yells of the crew and they cheered as Isbister's screeches of panic altered to those of pain. When they reached a new pitch of horror, I also began to scream, but nobody heard my personal agony. Unable to help, unwilling to watch, I looked away; until Donaldson grabbed my head and painfully held open my eyes with callous thumbs. 'That's what we do with witches,' Donaldson told me. 'That's how we treat the witches that murdered Macks!'

'They're not witches,' I tried to say, but I no longer pleaded for their lives, for I doubted they would any longer want to survive.

The cheers gradually faded as we watched Isbister and Sinclair die. We saw the flames rise around them, spitting fiercely as the residue of the blubber caught fire and the victims writhed and yelled and squealed. First their clothing caught light, then their hair, and finally, as their eyeballs melted and their skin blistered and turned black, only Donaldson and Torrie could watch. When Torrie also looked away only Donaldson leered over the rail, gloating.

'That's for Macks,' he repeated, again and again. 'That's for Macks.'

The screaming continued long after smoke obscured the barrels, and then there was incoherent high pitched whimpering. When even that faded there was only a crackling and the terrible stench of burned flesh. As the flames died, the barrels still smouldered, and nauseating smoke clung to the clothing and hair of every man in *Lady Balgay* until, sated and subdued, the crew trooped below. Only I was left on deck, and tears blurred my view of the pitiful blackened things that remained in the charred casks until the never ending Arctic day gradually faded with a smirr of mercifully concealing snow.

Chapter Twenty Three

GREENLAND SEA

AUGUST 1914

No ship of one hundred tons burthen can proceed to sea unless at least one officer beside the master possesses a certificate appropriate to grade of mate
  Merchant Shipping Act, 1854

They released me next morning, nearly frozen from a night on the open deck, but the residual heat from the burning bodies had kept me alive and the horror kept me awake. I said nothing to the shamefaced men who helped me down below. I was too cold to move and too sick at heart to even curse them. That night broke me, for I was no longer a man.

Pratt brought me hot coffee but I could not drink it, and when Thoms tried to speak I could not reply. At that moment I did not care if I lived or died. I had expected new experiences in the Arctic, but I had seen spectacles I knew would haunt me for the rest of my life. I no longer felt fit to return to Jennifer. How could I live with her innocence after witnessing what I had witnessed? How could I share her joyous bed after spending a night in a hell that would have caused

Dante to shudder? I was no longer the idealistic young doctor who had signed on to *Lady Balgay*, but a damaged man with ancient eyes and the memories of an executioner.

I wondered, pitifully and uncaring, if I were sane any longer, or if my memories were the tortured dreams of a lunatic, the delirious fantasies of a man driven beyond hope by strain and fear and hardship. What was worse, I no longer cared. As I said, that night had broken me.

'It's done,' Donaldson told me, too calmly to be rational, 'and it can't be undone.'

'The evil is cleansed,' Pratt announced solemnly, 'and we can sail home in safety.'

'We are all murderers,' Thoms at least was affected by what he had done. He sat weeping on his bunk with his face buried in his hands. 'We're damned forever.' He looked up with his face swollen. 'Has anybody told the captain?'

One by one, the crew backed away, looking at me through eyes shadowed with shame and self-revulsion. I knew that I had to pass on the news; perhaps that was my one remaining duty before madness or death finally claimed me.

'What is it?' Captain Milne looked up from the tangled mess of his bunk. He had slept in his day clothes and the place reeked of alcohol, stale urine and the mess that he had spewed up. When I told him what had happened he listened, at first with disbelief and finally with his mouth opening and closing in shock. 'Oh Sweet Jesus have mercy. Show me.'

Staggering unshaven on deck with his jacket stained and flapping open and only one boot on, he sniffed the tainted air and vomited over the side.

'Where are they? Where are the hands?'

They gathered slowly, keeping their distance as Captain Milne rocked on his feet, holding on to the mizzen for support as he stared at his crew.

'Why?' He did not raise his voice, but the hoarse whisper carried throughout the ship. 'Why did you do it?'

'They were witches, Captain,' Donaldson was the only man who could face the captain's eyes. 'They were murdering us, one by one.'

'Witches?' Captain Milne swallowed the word. He seemed unable to speak. 'Good God; there's no such thing. You can't believe in that nonsense.' He looked over the taffrail, where a bobbing barrel displayed its charred and hideous contents, and promptly vomited on to the deck of which he had once been so proud. Then he began to swear. He paused, speaking in a low, broken voice. 'You murdered these people. They were shipwrecked survivors, for God's sake. They came to us for help!'

'They were cannibals, Captain,' Pratt faced Milne's anger with a courage I had not expected. 'The ballast brought them.'

'The ballast brought them?' Milne shook his head. 'The ballast is stones, man. It's pebbles and stones from the beach, nothing else!'

'No,' Pratt stood his ground, although I could see that he was trembling. 'It's cursed, Captain. We have to put the bones back; please, Captain?'

For a long moment, Milne stared at Pratt, and then he dropped his eyes and shuffled past, an old, broken man. 'Why did somebody not tell me?' He stopped in front of me and raised eyes liquid with tears. 'Doctor! You're an intelligent man. Why did you not stop this madness?'

'I tried, Captain,' I did not then meet his eyes, 'I tried.'

'We tied the doctor up,' Donaldson sounded proud of his part in the affair. 'And we made him watch.'

'Sweet God in heaven.' Ignoring Donaldson, Milne raised a hand as though to strike me. I did not flinch. 'I could have stopped it. I would have saved them, Doctor ... Mr Cosgrove, Iain, why did you not fetch me?'

'You were drunk,' I said bluntly and raised my head. I could feel the anger burning within me and this time the captain winced. 'You were lying as drunk as a lord in your cabin. You were incapable of commanding the ship when your crew murdered two innocent people.' I leaned closer as anger replaced my habitual academic reticence. 'You were as much responsible for their deaths as the superstitious fools who set fire to the barrels. You were in a position of responsibility, Captain, and you failed your trust.'

When Captain Milne opened his mouth, I thought he was going to blast me for my insolence, but instead he closed it again and turned away as meek as a child. 'You're right,' Milne said. 'Oh God, Doctor but you're right.' When he looked at me again, there was no fire left in him, he was hollow.

Milne staggered down below, round-shouldered and with his stockinged foot ludicrous and undignified. I heard the opening and closing of doors as he wandered through his final command and them a louder bang as he slammed the door of his own cabin.

Pratt grinned nervously. 'Do you think the captain's very angry, Doctor?'

Unable to reply, I could only walk away. The stench of burned blubber and human flesh clung to me like a skin of guilt.

It was five minutes later that I heard the sharp crack of the pistol shot, and when I rushed to the captain's cabin, Milne was sprawled backward on his chair with my revolver held tight in his right hand and his brains spattered across the far bulkhead. Blood oozed slowly down the varnished teak, forming an obscene puddle on the deck.

'Oh, God no.' I stared numbly at the corpse for a good two minutes before I prized my revolver from the dead man's hand and placed it on the desk. It lay there accusingly; my property left lying carelessly to be used in a suicide. 'Now I am every bit as bad as the rest,' I whispered. 'Oh Jennifer, how can you forgive me?'

The sound of the shot had alerted the remnants of the crew, who crowded in a voiceless knot behind me, staring at the corpse of the man who had once been their captain.

'He's dead,' Pratt said, needlessly, but he helped me bind a rag around the shattered skull and carry the body on to the deck. We laid it there, in the lee of the iceberg and under the uncaring sky.

'And then there were six,' I said with intended viciousness, 'and this time you can't blame Isbister or Sinclair, for you've already murdered them.' My voice rose until I checked it, but with considerable effort. 'Perhaps you'd like to murder me too?'

Pratt shook his shaggy head. 'It's the ballast,' he explained patiently. 'We'll be damned until the bones are returned to Gass Skerry.'

'Aye. So you say.' There was no need to examine Captain Milne to determine the cause of death, but guilt at leaving the unattended revolver ripped at my conscience. 'Well, maybe we'll stop off that way on our return journey; if we have enough men left to handle the ship.'

Pratt rammed his empty pipe between his teeth and fingered the scrimshaw mermaid. 'It's worse than that, Doctor Cosgrove. Six men can handle *Lady Balgay* quite comfortably, but we need somebody to navigate.'

'What?' I looked at him, not understanding this new complication. 'Surely any seaman can navigate?'

'Hardly,' Pratt frowned his contempt at the idea. 'Leery and the Captain were the only two who knew how.' He avoided my eyes. 'You need to be able to do sums and calculations, and I never went to school, eh? But you are clever, Doctor. You'll be able to take us home, won't you?'

I said nothing for a while, but stared around at the grey sky and the waiting sea. How were my navigational skills? I knew enough to aim southeast and hope to strike Scotland, but no more than that. 'Well then, we'll just do our best.' Fighting a desire to either break into hysterical laughter or burst into tears, I glanced aft. Strangely, after so much death and disaster, I no longer felt the same intense fury. I analysed my feelings and found only a numb resignation. There were no emotions left, but I did sense something lurking beneath the calmness. Afraid of what madness I would find if I delved too deep, I concentrated on the matter in hand. 'We'd best bury the captain, Mr Pratt. Go and find Tommy, would you? He's still in charge of things nautical.'

The captain's burial was the most formal so far, with what remained of the crew standing to attention as his body slid into the sea with a Union Flag, dredged from some obscure corner of the ship, draped over the top. There was no sermon and no hymns, for after the murder of the two survivors, nobody considered that anything religious was appropriate. Anyway, as Donaldson kindly pointed out, 'suicides don't get holy burials.'

'He was a hard, hard man,' Ross said, and nudged Pratt who was quietly sobbing as he watched the body sink. 'What the hell's up with you, Johnnie?'

'I liked the captain.'

'Well, more fool you,' Ross told him. 'And that's the only memorial he'll get from me.'

It may have been coincidence that a seal broke surface just as Captain Milne slid under, but we all watched as half a score followed the corpse into the depths as if to ensure that the man who had killed so many of their kind was finally gone.

'Take us south, Tommy,' I said at last. A few days ago the order would have been greeted with cheers, but now there was no reaction at all.

'Aye, Doctor.' Thoms glanced at the featureless sky. 'And which way would that be?'

'Use the binnacle compass,' I had anticipated the question.

'I'd like to, Doctor, but it's buggered. Big Sinclair booted it when he was struggling the other day.'

The binnacle's broken?' I felt as though I would never escape from this nightmare.

'Smashed to pieces.' Thoms stared at me as if expecting an instant solution and I suddenly realised that all the crew had done that with Captain Milne. Some had hated him, all had feared him, but they had expected him to be the oracle of all maritime wisdom. Now, I realised, I was the man to ask, although I had no more nautical knowledge than a babe in arms and less experience than any of them.

'Is there another compass on board?'

A thorough search revealed that there was not, and when I made enquiries, nobody knew how to navigate by the stars. These were before-the-mast seamen, experienced in every practical skill of seamanship, but with no interest in navigation or 'book work' as Donaldson contemptuously dismissed it. The foc'sle was their place, not aft of the mainmast.

Again they transferred responsibility on to me, smiling sycophantically as they waited for a miracle. They stood around in a semi-circle, some staring openly but others more shame-faced as they contemplated the deck, or the glistening iceberg behind the ship.

'What are we going to do, Doctor Cosgrove?'

It was Pratt who put the direct question, and the others nodded, eager that somebody should help them out of the chaos that their actions had created.

'We're going to sit tight just now,' I told them slowly, 'and consider our position. Nobody among us can navigate, and we are not exactly sure where we are, so all we can do is head south.'

They nodded eagerly at that and mumbled agreement, still waiting for orders.

'Excellent.' I waited until they were quiet. 'So as soon as we work out in which direction south lies, we can get moving.'

They looked at each other, and at the sky and the sea. Pratt pointed over the stern. 'That's south, Doctor Cosgrove.'

'No, no,' Thoms pointed toward the iceberg. 'The wind came from the south, and the berg protected us, so it's to the south.'

'It's shifted with the current,' Ross said. 'It's to starboard now.'

As the voices rose, I watched them. When I had come aboard I had felt some fear mixing with these amazingly competent men, an emotion that had altered to respect for their toughness and nautical skill, but now I felt growing contempt, disgust and near hatred. They had performed two of the most brutal murders I had ever heard of, and now came to me like sheepish children, looking for help.

What could I do? If I refused them, I would also be condemned to remain on this forsaken ship attached to an iceberg in the Arctic wastes. I had to help them, but the thought was growing more repugnant by the minute. I closed my eyes, trying to make sense of the situation. They must be brought to justice for their murders, so I had to get them back to Scotland, which meant working with them, as I could not return alone.

It was then that I realised the two images had not entered my mind for two days. My dreams had been troubled by memories of the survivors' deaths and of polar bears, but nothing else. I looked furtively at Pratt, who waited for my words with an expression like a cowed collie dog, and tried to keep the terrible thought from my mind. Perhaps the two images had indeed been linked to Sinclair and Isbister?

No! That was impossible. That was falling into the deepest, rankest superstition, returning to the murderous psychosis of witch-hunts and human sacrifice.

'Will we ever get back, Doctor Cosgrove?' Apparently forgetting the way he had treated me only two days before, Donaldson could hardly have been more respectful.

I wrestled away my clouded thoughts, although I knew the doubt would return later, when I lay alone in the dark. Once more I thought about Mrs Adams, the old Orcadian fortune teller, and drew some comfort from my own superstition.

'We'll get back,' I tried to sound confident, 'as soon as we see the North Star; we can steer in the opposite direction.'

They laughed at this simple solution to our problem, but frowned as another difficulty struck them.

'Doctor,' Thoms had a strained expression on his face. 'You won't tell anybody what happened here, will you?'

The others crowded round; pleading with their smiles, fawning with words that were intended to convince me they had only committed natural justice for the sake of the ship.

I waited for a moment, aware that I was only a whisker of education from accepting their fears, if not their solution. I knew that if my circumstances had been different, I might be as credulous as they were, and if, like them, I had grown up in some festering slum, brawling for survival against screaming poverty, I might have acted similarly. I was judging from a different viewpoint, and social standing was no reason for assuming moral superiority.

And then the memory of Isbister's desperate shrieks returned, and I knew I could not let them walk calmly away. Nothing excused such cruelty.

If I told them my plans, they were as likely as not to kill me too, so it was common sense to lie, despite that being against all my training and moral convictions. 'You think that what you did was right,' I told them truthfully, and they nodded, eager for justification. 'You honestly believed that Sinclair and Isbister were witches.'

They nodded again and all began to speak, loquacious in their desire to justify themselves.

'And cannibals,' Torrie said seriously. 'Remember Rab's arm.'

I sighed, trying to fight the loathing that was directed as much against myself as against the crew; these were not inherently wicked men, just simple, superstitious fools, seeking for some method of controlling a situation they did not understand. It was utterly unfortunate that Sinclair and Isbister were outsiders into their world, and pure bad luck that Pratt had spread his tales about cursed ballast during a voyage dogged by disaster.

'I will have to make a report to the authorities,' I told them. I could see Thoms touching the hilt of the sealing knife, Torrie flexing these massive fireman's muscles and Pratt watching me through eyes dulled by decades of hard work, degradation and suffering. 'And I will say nothing that is not true.'

They nodded at that, unsure quite what I meant but willing to grasp at any straw. I looked over the rail. Sinclair and Isbister were gone; some unknown current had spirited away the charred barrels and the smoke from the burning seal blubber tubs was barely a taste in the air, but the crew were increasingly uneasy at their own actions. With the perceived danger now absent, they had time for introversion.

'Will you write that down?' Like so many illiterate men, Pratt had uncanny faith in the power of the written word. He looked slyly at me, with a greasy grin on his bearded face and a query in his eyes. 'You could write that we only did what was best for the ship.'

The other men pressed closer, nodding their eager agreement. 'You could do that, couldn't you Doctor?'

'You will, won't you?'

'You know that we were right.'

'They'll listen to you, Doctor Cosgrove.'

I saw the mingled hope and fear in the weathered faces and remembered their recent actions. I also saw the glint of light along the blade of Thoms' knife and knew I would do anything they asked of me. Jennifer was waiting in Dundee, I had made a solemn promise and I could not let her down. I must get home; I would get home, no matter what it took in compromising my principles.

'I'll compose something,' I hated myself for my weakness, but desperate fear and honour make ill bed fellows, 'and I'll read it out to you.'

They were waiting outside my cabin when I emerged, five anxious men, from the broken Pratt to volatile young Torrie.

'Read it, Doctor,' Donaldson urged.

'To whom it may concern,' I began, and they nodded approval at such an auspicious start. 'I, Iain Cosgrove, surgeon on board the sealing ketch *Lady Balgay* of Dundee, at present attached to an iceberg in the Greenland Sea, wrote these words on the 3rd August 1914.'

They nodded again, fervent for my acceptance, desperate to be absolved of murder, hopeful of understanding.

I continued. 'After a series of unfortunate misadventures on board *Lady Balgay*, we had lost the crew men Robert Mitchell, Walter Learmonth, James Soutar and Charles Mackie. Believing that the deaths were caused by a combination of evil brought aboard by tainted ballast, and the witchcraft of two people we rescued from the ice, the crew of *Lady Balgay* nearly unanimously decided to remove the two people.'

I looked up as the crew nodded. They agreed with everything I had written so far. Sighing, I continued.

'Accordingly the hands removed the two additions to the crew. Unfortunately, Captain Milne, possibly suffering from nervous exhaustion after the rigours of the voyage, shot himself the following day.'

I lowered my voice. 'I have signed it, Iain Cosgrove, Doctor, and I think you should sign it too.'

'You didn't mention that we killed them,' Pratt said.

'No.' I shook my head. I did not say that there would be an inquiry and all the details would come out in court.

'Thank you, Doctor.' Pratt took hold of the paper, holding it with something like reverence in his huge hands. 'I'll put my cross on this book.'

He was first to sign, with the others adding their signatures underneath so the single sheet was decorated with a variety of semi-legible scrawls plus the neat name of George Ross.

'I'll keep this safe,' I said, 'and hand it in when we reach Dundee.' You poor fools, I looked over them with a mixture of contempt and pity. You have just signed a confession that could result in every one of you swinging from the gallows. I closed my eyes, seeing myself in the dock giving evidence that might, and probably would, condemn these men to death. The murders would rock the country and probably ruin my career before it had begun, and what would Jennifer think of me then?

Maybe, I thought, maybe it would be best if I said nothing, pulled a veil over all that had happened and tried to live a normal life. The prospect was so enticing that I nearly convinced myself it was possible. But I knew it was not.

'Doctor! There's a sail! A ship is coming in!'

Chapter Twenty Four

GREENLAND SEA

AUGUST 1914

The ship proved to be the Brahmoor *of Hanover, which had been among the seals and was now on her way north to the whale fishing. The master immediately agreed to relieve the poor wanderers. These in the boat were taken on board the* Brahmoor, *and the master of the* Felix *getting a crew of Hanoverians, put off for the ice, and picked up the rest of his ship's company, many of whom were now in a very famished and exhausted state.*
Banffshire Journal, 16 May 1854

'A ship!' The cry ran was taken up by the rest of the hands and while Pratt scampered up the masts with that agility that still astonished me, others ran to the side to stare. Only Thoms had the sense to snatch the captain's telescope and scan the newcomer.

'She's a ship, right enough, Three masts, but foreign built. You'll never see anything made that way in a British yard! She's seen some foul weather too, judging by the state of her sails. They're patched to buggery.'

When I lifted a hand to wave, Donaldson nudged Torrie and glanced at him. 'What about the doctor?'

'We've got his book,' Torrie said doubtfully.

'Aye, but can we trust him?'

'I've given my word,' I defended myself. I had no desire to be the next victim of Donaldson's brutality. 'And I won't say anything until we're back in Dundee.'

'All the same,' sliding his skinning knife from its sheath, Torrie glanced at me and then looked sidelong at Donaldson. 'We've killed two; one more won't make much difference.'

'Don't be a fool!' Thoms knocked away the knife. 'These two were witches. Dr Cosgrove helped us. Rather than murdering an innocent man, Albert, run over to the captain's cabin and find the ship's papers. Throw them overboard in case Captain Milne wrote anything before he died and the master of this foreign ship asks any fool questions.'

As Torrie moved, still in a half crouch to obey, Thoms nodded doubtfully to me. 'Albert did have a point, Doctor; I don't want you blowing your mouth off.'

'I won't say a word,' I placed a trembling finger over my lips. 'I promise.'

'Aye, well, promises don't always mean much.' Thoms frowned doubtfully. 'Maybe we can take you on trust, Doctor, but maybe not...'

'It's a foreign ship, right enough.' Pratt raised his voice. 'She's German by the flag.' Returning to the deck, he looked at me. 'She looks like that Prussian that gave us the rum! *Fortuna Gretel*, wasn't she?'

'Aye.' Thoms nodded. 'That'll be her. There can't be too many Prussians in these waters.' He grunted. 'And these two witches told us she had foundered in the ice!'

'So they did!' Pratt nearly shouted. 'That means they were lying!'

'More proof, if we needed any!' Donaldson looked at me in triumph. 'What do you say now, Doctor?'

'The doctor will be leaving us for a while,' Thoms said quietly. 'Doctor, I want you to go into your cabin for a minute. Just for a minute.'

'What? Why?'

Thoms had produced the marlinespike from up his sleeve and the blow on the head took me by surprise. I staggered, yelling, and Thoms hit me again, knocking me to the deck. I lay there, holding the pain in both hands as Thoms roared: 'give a hand here, boys!'

'No! He won't say anything!' I heard Pratt move forward to defend me, but Donaldson blocked his passage easily enough.

'Shut up you old fool! We know what's best!'

With Ross and Donaldson holding me secure, it took Thoms only a moment to tie my hands and feet and gag me with a piece of filthy rag.

'Throw him into the foc'sle,' Thoms ordered, and they bundled me inside, crashing me callously to the unyielding deck. 'Sorry Doctor, but we can't allow you to meet the Prussians. You might say something we would all regret.'

Straining against the gag, I fought my bonds, but the seamen knew their knots and I could do nothing but glare my fury as the foc'sle door slammed shut. I was left in the turgid air, with no company but my dark thoughts and the sound of the ship.

I heard the soft thump as a small boat moored alongside, and the sharp patter of feet on the deck planking. The voice was low and gruff, first in German and then in English.

'Hello again, *Lady Balgay*! Remember us? We spoke with you months ago!'

'We remember you well,' Thoms assured him. 'And we are very glad to see you, my friends.'

There was low laughter and the slight sounds of backslapping before the German spoke again. 'What has happened here? We saw smoke in the distance and came to investigate. Where is your master, please? The jovial Captain Milne? I wish to speak with him.'

'He's dead,' Thoms said truthfully. 'So are half the crew. We have had a bad time.'

There was a moment's silence, presumably as the German looked around the deck. 'So, how can I help?'

I wriggled to the bulkhead and tried to drum my feet, hoping to attract attention to my plight, but the rope was so tight around my ankles that I could hardly move, and the small noise I made was lost within the greater workings of the ship.

'We don't have a navigator left,' Thoms spoke casually, as if he was discussing the weather. 'Can you spare one?'

'Alas not,' the German said. 'We have only the two, and where would we be if one was lost?' His barking laugh was probably intended to reassure the crew of *Lady Balgay*. 'However, I can offer you all passage home in our ship. We have room in *Fortuna Gretel*.'

There was a pause, then grunts of obvious agreement.

'But before I do,' the German said. 'I must ask you a question.'

'Of course,' Thoms said.

'Have you seen, or heard of, a man and a woman? They are countrymen of yours, but they were part of our crew. We were trapped in the ice, you see, and believed all was lost so our captain ordered everybody away in the boats.'

'Oh?' Thoms sounded as though he were genuinely interested in the story.

'But *Fortuna* freed herself and the master picked up everybody except these two. We have searched for them ever since. Maybe you have seen them?'

'Oh Jesus!' I tried to shout my anguish and despair, but the gag was effective and my words were stifled stillborn. I tried to hammer my feet against the deck, but the cords held me tight. All I could do was sob, with the tears oozing from my eyes and my throat constricted with bitter irony. Sinclair and Isbister had indeed sailed in this German ship. Their story had been correct in every detail except that *Fortuna Gretel* had not sunk. The master was still searching for them, all these weeks later.

Sinclair and Isbister were neither cannibals nor witches, but two unfortunate survivors, two people who had got lost in the Arctic, like so many scores of men before. The crew of *Lady Balgay* had murdered them for no reason save the illogical imaginings created by superstition and sheer bad luck. I felt like screaming in frustration, but still, somewhere deep inside me, was an acknowledgement of relief that my scientific side had triumphed over the emergence of buried super-stition.

'A man and a woman?' I heard the disbelief in Thoms' voice. Would he admit his guilt now, throw himself on the mercy of whatever court could judge such matters and accept justice? Or would he deny every-thing knowing that he had been party to one of the foulest murders that Iain could ever conceive?

'Except for the Yakkies, I don't think I've ever seen a woman in the Arctic in my life', Thoms said, with scarcely a second's hesitation. He raised his voice. 'Have any of you lads seen a man and a woman around here? This German fellow says they were on his ship but they got lost.'

There was a murmur of denials as one by one the crew of *Lady Balgay* rejected any knowledge of the people they had murdered.

'A pity; they were a cheerful couple and it was unusual to have a woman on board,' the German accepted their word. 'She was useful when it came to darning socks.'

Thoms gave a small laugh.

'So gentlemen, if you would care to come aboard *Fortuna*, we will sail soon. We will leave your vessel here; she can harm nobody. Please hurry.'

I felt my spirits rise. When the hands entered the foc'sle surely one of the Germans would see me and then I could reveal everything. I wriggled closer to the door, ready to make as much fuss as I possibly could.

'We'll hurry,' Thoms promised, and raised his voice. 'Tell Ross to close down the engines, and just come as you are, lads. You've nothing much to collect in the foc'sle anyway!'

'No! Don't leave me here!' I tried to shout, but the gag kept the words inside my mouth. No sound escaped as I writhed in terrified frustration, sobbing for help.

There was a rush of feet and a gabble of excited voices as the crew of *Lady Balgay* left the ship. Nobody came back for me, nobody opened the door of the foc'sle and within twenty minutes I heard muffled or-ders in German and knew that I was left alone.

Unable to shout, I felt the great veins in my temple straining as I tried to kick my feet and wrestle myself free, but could manage only a few feeble thumps that could not possibly be heard outside the ketch. The tears flowed unbidden as I finally gave up and a sense of absolute abandonment overwhelmed me.

I was alone, tied and gagged, in a deserted ship hundreds of miles from civilisation, and nobody knew where I was. The crew of *Lady Balgay* would certainly not report my whereabouts, so I was doomed to die of thirst and starvation. Thirst? I realised that the ship was very quiet, not just because the crew was gone, but also because Ross had killed the engine, and without the heat from the boiler, the temperature in *Lady Balgay* would plummet. I would die of cold long before I died of thirst.

But I would get home; the fortune teller had promised Jennifer I would come home. Jennifer. The opening lines of her song slipped unbidden into my mind as I lay there, her soft voice soothing my panic so I took a deep breath and considered my position.

In the gloaming, oh my darling,
When the lights are soft and low
And the quiet shadows falling
Softly come and softly go.

Quiet shadows were right, I thought. I was in the land of quiet shadows here, and quickly passing to a land where there were only shadows, and one which Jennifer would not enter for many decades.

The words remained with me, calming me until I could think rationally. I was in the foc'sle of *Lady Balgay*, tied on the floor. The foc'sle was where the seamen berthed, and where their personal kit was stowed. Surely one of them would have a knife? They spent a great deal of their working lives dealing with ropes, so needed sharp tools, and they did not all carry their sea knives with them all the time.

That obvious fact gave me some hope and a little more strength. Rolling to the door, I leaned my back against the wood and used its purchase to struggle upright. The foc'sle was dark, but small, despite the nine bunks that had to crowd inside and the sea chests that acted as seats and tables on the limited floor space. A single hop took me to the first chest with its painted decoration of a splendid clipper ship, so different from the work-stained *Lady Balgay*.

My first attempt to lift the hinged lid failed, so I tried again, crouching down, placing my shoulder under the lid and forcing myself up. This time I managed to hold the lid secure, and it banged open, revealing the contents.

There was not much. A bundle of slop-shop clothes, mostly little more than rags, a pair of shore-going shoes and a few souvenir trinkets gathered from half a lifetime of sweated toil across the globe. If rolling stones gathered no moss, then seagoing labourers collected pathetically few possessions as reward for keeping the world's trading lanes open.

The next chest was no better, with the addition of a half-empty bottle of gin that had obviously been liberated from the Captain's cabin. The third was locked, its painted picture of a grinning skull and crossbones mocking me as I moved on, slowly losing hope as my strength waned and the words of Jennifer's song drained from my mind. I sank down, head on my breast as the cold began to penetrate my limbs, but I struggled up. I knew I had to keep moving or die. I needed to cut myself free and find food and a source of warmth. There were still some chests remaining, still some hope.

Again using my shoulder as a lever, I slammed open the fourth sea chest. This one had no decoration, just the name John Pratt beautifully carved into the surface. As Pratt was illiterate, some kindly shipmate must have worked for hours on that, possibly for a few sippers of rum, or just out of comradeship. I shook my head; did the reason matter? I knew I was drifting away and must concentrate.

There was the usual bundle of clothing, with a collection of letters carefully tied in red ribbon but never opened; perhaps some long-ago sweetheart had sent them in mingled hope and affection, but Pratt had never had the courage to ask somebody to read her letters to him.

There was heartbreak there, and deep sorrow, but this was not the time. Far more significant was the knife that lay, sheathed and oiled, right at the bottom of the chest.

Nearly sobbing in relief, I put all my weight on the edge of the chest, toppling it over so the contents spilled out. The knife slithered on to the deck and lay there like a gift from God. Struggling on to my back, I scrabbled closer. It was the work of a moment to slip off the sheath, and trust Pratt to have the blade sharp enough to slice through the rope around my wrist.

'Thank God!' I prayed my gratitude as I freed my ankles and tore the gag from my mouth. I breathed deeply, finding even the foetid stench of the foc'sle pleasant after gasping through the tarry rag they had stuffed in my mouth.

And then the true horror of my situation returned to me. I was free to roam the ship, and even to clamber on to the iceberg; I could find food and clothes enough for a dozen men, but beyond that I was still trapped. I was stuck on a sealing ketch fastened to an iceberg in the Greenland Sea; I who had sailed north to hunt seals was doomed to die in their home; I who had promised to return home to Jennifer would never see her again. The first burst of laughter caught me by surprise, but I recognised the second as the onset of hysteria and controlled the impulse.

'Oh Jesus, Jennifer, I've let you down in so many ways.' I took a deep breath, knowing that I faced a bitter future. How long would I last, alone in the ice? A month? A year? Two years? Ten? The prospect was appalling, yet I knew I could not let myself die. *Fortuna Gretel* had found us and there might be other ships up here, more sealers in the Arctic. Surely one would find me, this year or maybe next, unless I went mad and died of loneliness and fear.

'I will be a northern Robinson Crusoe,' I told myself, and tried to smile. 'But what can I do? How can I pass the time until I am res- cued?' The answer was obvious. 'I must write my journal,' I told myself severely. 'I promised Jennifer that I would write an account of all that happened, and so far I have not touched pen to paper. I must write it so that I remember everything and when I am found, I can tell Jennifer what happened to me. She will know that I tried to keep my promise and I did not give up hope.'

Round shouldered, I eased into the engine room. The engine was a simple piece of machinery, so it was easy to start, and I shovelled coal from the bunkers into the furnace, keeping the fire low so it would last longer.

'That's better,' I savoured the heat for a long time before walking to my own quarters to retrieve the leather backed notebook I had intended to use for my journal. From there I moved aft, to the larger and more comfortable captain's cabin, and sat behind the captain's desk, on the captain's chair, and opened the box that contained the old wooden handled pens. Lifting one, I began to write, humming the song that Jennifer had sung to me that night, so many months ago.

> *'In the gloaming, oh my darling*
> *When the lights are soft and low*
> *Will you think of me and love me*
> *As you did once long ago?'*

'I'll come home to you, Jennifer,' I promised as he wrote the date: 4th August 1914. Today the German vessel *Fortuna Gretel* rescued all the crew except me. I am the last Greenlandman.

'I'll come home to you.'

Lady Balgay lay still, tied to her iceberg as a slow fall of snow foretold the beginning of the terrible Arctic winter.

Chapter Twenty Five

FIRTH OF TAY
SEPTEMBER

We're captive on the carousel of time
We can't return, we can only look behind from where we came
And go round and round in the circle game
    Joni Mitchell

Closing the journal, Lauren looked over to where Iain sat on the bed, his finger still pointing to the open door and his face as set and tragic as it had been for the past more-than- ninety years.

'So you've come home, Iain Cosgrove,' she said quietly, 'as Mrs Adams promised'.

That tune was back, easing insistently into her head like syrup dripping from a spoon, but now she recognised it for what it was. Jennifer was singing to her husband, her siren song calling him back across a waste of ocean.

It was all so obvious now. Jennifer had looked after Iain when evil had stalked the ship, either in the person of frightened crewmen or in the guise as cannibals from another time. Jennifer had kept him safe, and Jennifer had guided her, and Kenny, to this ketch in which her man remained. Jennifer had brought him home; somewhere she waited for him still.

'So nobody found him?' Kenny was at Lauren's shoulder, his voice somehow intrusive.

'How long have you been there?' Reaching out, she touched his hand. It was cold but dry.

'All the time; I didn't want to leave you alone in here.' He tightened his grip reassuringly. 'Were there no more sealing ships?'

'Look at the date: August 1914.' Lauren shook her head. 'That's when the First World War started. There would be no ships up that way during the war.'

Kenny nodded. 'Poor bugger. But what did it all mean? Were the survivors innocent, or were they cannibals from the past, as Pratt thought?'

Lauren stood up, holding the journal in her hand, feeling the slight rasp as tiny pieces of seashell stuck in her palm. 'I'm not sure. Iain thought they were innocent survivors, and he was there.'

'But the deaths and the things that he saw; what were they?' Kenny seemed much quieter now, as if he had matured while reading the journal.

'God knows.' Lauren shrugged. 'Maybe Iain was right; maybe they were just dragged from his imagination. It must have been hard to have just the one night with his wife and then disappear into the Arctic for months.'

'And the music? He said he heard Jennifer singing to him.'

Lauren smiled. 'Can't you hear that too?'

'What?' Kenny shook his head. 'I can't hear anything.'

It was louder now, the words distinct. Lauren listened for a minute, allowing the song of a long past generation to seep into this cabin and ease around the body of the man to whom it had meant so much.

'In the gloaming, oh my darling
When the lights are soft and low
Will you think of me and love me

As you did once long ago?'

Lifting the journal, Lauren tucked it securely under her arm. 'Come on, Kenny; let's go on deck and see where we are. Somebody must have seen us and come to investigate.'

Leaving the cabin with its lonely surgeon still sitting on the bed, she led Kenny into the passage outside and up the companionway to the deck. The mist remained; a thick barrier that continued to swirl slowly anti-clockwise around *Lady Balgay*.

'So where are we?' Kenny raised his voice. 'Hello! Is there anybody there?'

The echo came back to him, distorted but recognisably his own voice. He tried again, louder, but with the same result.

The mist absorbed the sound; the mist kept them trapped, isolated; the mist was either a barrier or a protection, Lauren was unsure which.

'Let me try.' Carefully avoiding the scorch marks, she reached for the speaking trumpet that sat in a bracket on the mizzen mast and placed it to her lips.

'Hello!' She shouted and the words, strangely metallic, clashed into the circulating mist.

'Hello!' The reply was indistinct but immediate. 'Who's there?'

'Lauren MacPherson and Kenny Brown!' She felt the devil of mischief in her eyes when she winked at Kenny, 'of the whaling ketch *Lady Balgay*!'

There was a long pause before the reply came, but even through the mist Lauren could sense the strain. 'Of what ship? Could you repeat that please?'

'The whaling ketch *Lady Balgay* of Dundee.' As she waited for a response, she felt the temperature rise. The mist began to thin, and then the spiralling motion slowed and stopped completely. *Lady Balgay* sat quiet on a calm sea, her masts no longer skeletal but proud, her bowsprit pointing home and the scars honourable trophies of a long voyage.

We're home. We're back home.

As the last remaining shreds of mist cleared and lifted, Lauren could see the great hump of Dundee Law behind its outrider of multi-storey flats, with the Tay Road Bridge a few hundred yards upstream and the bulk of the city stretching east, west and north, a hive of activity, alive with the hum of traffic.

'Dear God but that's a beautiful sight.' For a moment Lauren just stared at the view, enjoying every inch of this city that had been her home for all her twenty-five years. She had left on the fishing trip only that morning, yet she felt as though she had been gone for years. It was as if she had embodied the memories of Iain Cosgrove and taken his thoughts and perceptions with her, so much that she hummed that poignant little song and allowed her eye to wander along the shore to West Ferry, where Balgay House had once stood.

And she started, remembering Jennifer's words.

'I will leave a candle shining in the window to guide you home. I will light it every night and count every day until we are together again'

The light was there, small enough to be a candle but powerful enough to shine directly into her eyes, clear across the centuries, but when she blinked it had gone.

Don't be stupid, Lauren! Now you're imagining things.

Balgay House was long gone, victim of dry rot and the decline of manufacturing fortunes after the First World War, but now she shared the memories of a man who had seen the jute barons at their most powerful. The thought was sobering and just a little frightening.

'Lauren? Are you all right?' Kenny was beside her, wide eyed and anxious; she wondered how she could have forgotten about him.

'Of course I am. I was just thinking how good it is to be home after so many years.'

'It's only been a few hours.' He looked at her, his head to one side but his eyes more thoughtful than she remembered. His voice was low and considered. 'The man who wrote that journal is long dead, Lauren.'

'Of course,' Lauren forced a smile, wondering what Iain had been like in life, how his voice had sounded, if he had smelled of quality tobacco and the fresh outdoors and how it would have felt to be touched by him.

No! Behave yourself; that was another time and a dead man's journal.

'*Lady Balgay*! Stand by'

The sleekly powerful grey vessel that approached was obviously official, from the flag she proudly wore to the uniformed men on board and the air of neat authority. 'This is the Scottish Government's Fishery Protection vessel *Jura*.' The voice was now familiar but still bemused. 'Stand by to be boarded, *Lady Balgay*!'

'We're standing by but be careful,' Lauren shouted back, 'I'm not sure how secure this deck is.'

'We're safe,' Kenny put an arm around her, looking at the silver glint of the Firth of Tay and the bustling city of Dundee. 'That storm's behind us.'

'The storm?' The capsizing of their fishing boat seemed so long ago that Lauren had almost forgotten it. 'Yes; we survived, didn't we?' She watched as *Jura* drew alongside, all bustle and modernity, bristling with twenty first century technology. It was a different world from Iain Cosgrove and *Lady Balgay*. Her wash creamed along the hull of the ancient ketch, white and frothy and reassuringly real.

Within minutes, a squad of seamen from *Jura* boarded, their boots thundering hollowly on the deck, and the smartly uniformed captain approaching Lauren to ask her a host of questions.

'I'm not sure about the legal ownership of *Lady Balgay*,' he was very tall and dark haired and utterly competent. She knew there would be no mistakes with this man in charge. 'I suspect that you can claim salvage as you found her abandoned, but if we tow her in, the government may have a say.'

'I never thought of salvage,' Lauren admitted. She glanced at Kenny. 'We were just trying to keep alive.'

The captain nodded. 'That's understandable, but 'I'm afraid I'm going to have to take her in, unless you can afford to pay for a tug?' The saturnine face creased into a grin that seemed to wrap itself around Lauren's heart. 'I can't leave her out here as a hazard to shipping, so you had better decide quickly.'

Lauren shrugged. 'There's no help for it,' she watched as tow ropes were fitted and *Lady Balgay* shepherded into the shelter of Dundee. 'You're good at this.'

'I've had many years practise.'

'I'll bet you have.' That tune was still there, insistent, too sentimental for her now she was re- adapting to this twenty-first century, but familiar as an old friend.

The captain glanced sideways at her. 'It will be busy in Dundee,' he warned, 'news of *Lady Balgay* spread quickly. It's something for the media to get its teeth into, something other than wars and celebrities and corrupt politicians.'

He was correct; the press were waiting when they came ashore, a score of photographers and reporters backed by camera crews from half a dozen television stations, all eager to interview the couple who had discovered an ancient vessel trapped within an iceberg. The transformation from the early twentieth century journal with its ancient superstitions to the modern world of brashness and information technology was a culture shock, but Lauren adapted quickly, pushing aside that still insistent tune.

'We're famous,' Kenny posed for yet another photograph as Lauren once more gave details about *Lady Balgay*.

'We are,' Lauren agreed. She smiled across to the female reporter who had stalked her as she tried to escape across the Quay shopping centre.

'Miss MacPherson; Mr Brown: could you spare a few moments of your time?' The woman was confident, blonde and very good looking. 'My name is Lee-Anne Webster and I represent the Independent Scottish Television Network.'

No. Not this one, Lauren; run; run fast and run hard.

But Kenny had stopped, 'I think we have time for one more,' he grinned across to Lauren and she could only shake away the whispering warning and nod acquiescence.

'Excellent: I have arranged a meeting. There are only a few of us, an informal press conference for a select handful of people.'

Before Lauren could voice her protest she was being ushered into a stretch limousine that purred the few hundred yards to the Premier Inn, where a succession of very polite people escorted them to a small room with a splendid view over the Tay. As well as Lee-Anne and a cameraman, there was a tall, worried looking brunette, the master of *Jura* and a woman in a similarly smart uniform that could only have been his first officer.

'This is Jacqueline Cosgrove,' Lee-Anne introduced Lauren to the brunette, who gave a small smile. 'Dr Jacqueline Cosgrove.'

'You found my great-great grandfather's ship,' Doctor Cosgrove said simply, and Lauren stared at her.

'Your great-great grandfather? Iain Cosgrove? But he was barely married …'

Dr Cosgrove looked down her long nose at Lauren, but her smile broadened into something much more friendly. 'He seems to have made the most of the time he had, Ms MacPherson. He spent one night with my great-great grandmother,' she spoke slowly but with great precision. 'And nine months later my great grandfather was born.'

'Well, good for him,' Kenny approved.

'Good for them both,' Dr Cosgrove amended.

'I would like to have got changed before meeting you…' belatedly realising she still wore the baggy orange survival suit she had donned just before the fishing boat capsized, Lauren glanced around the room. Save for Kenny, who seemed quite at home in the company of a tankard of beer, everybody present appeared as smart as if they had just emerged from the window of a fashion shop.

'I think we quite understand,' Dr Cosgrove thawed even more. 'I heard you found something of my great- great grandfather's?' She looked pointedly at the journal that Lauren still carried. 'May I see it? I know so little about him.'

'Of course you may.'

As she handed over the journal, a tiny fragment of shell fell to the ground. Lauren watched as the light reflected from the smooth surface, spinning slowly toward the carpet, but Dr Cosgrove stooped quickly, catching it in her left hand. She was smiling as she examined it.

'My God; it's a piece of bone: human bone I believe.'

'What?' Lauren felt the first shock as the words from Iain's journal returned.

'Human bone?' The first officer of *Jura* was small in stature, but shapely enough to attract Kenny's attention. 'From where could that come?'

It came from Gass Skerry; it came from the cannibals.

'I really do not know,' Lauren lied. She fought the sudden dread that rose from memories not her own.

'No matter,' the lieutenant brushed fleetingly against Kenny, holding her hand out to Lauren. 'We have never been introduced. I am Lieutenant Isbister; Captain Sinclair of course, you already know.'

The music increased in Lauren's head as she stared at the beautiful, indistinct face.

Dear reader,

We hope you enjoyed reading *Dark Voyage*. Please take a moment to leave a review, even if it's a short one. Your opinion is important to us.

Discover more books by Helen Susan Swift at
https://www.nextchapter.pub/authors/helen-susan-swift

Want to know when one of our books is free or discounted for Kindle? Join the newsletter at http://eepurl.com/bqqB3H

Best regards,

Helen Susan Swift and the Next Chapter Team

You might also like:

Dark Mountain by Helen Susan Swift

To read first chapter for free, head to:
https://www.nextchapter.pub/books/dark-mountain

Books by the Author

- Dark Voyage (Tales From The Dark Past Book 1)
- Dark Mountain (Tales From The Dark Past Book 2)
- The Handfasters (Lowland Romance Book 1)
- The Tweedie Passion (Lowland Romance Book 2)
- A Turn of Cards (Lowland Romance Book 3)
- The Name of Love (Lowland Romance Book 4)
- The Malvern Mystery
- Sarah's Story
- Women of Scotland

CPSIA information can be obtained
at www.ICGtesting.com
Printed in the USA
LVHW051234050520
654998LV00016B/3007